THE DEFIANCE

THE BRILLIANT DARKNESS SERIES, BOOK TWO

A. G. HENLEY

Text copyright © 2013 by A.G. Henley

Cover design by Najla Qamber Designs

All rights reserved by A. G. Henley

Visit me at aghenley.com

Summary: A boy and girl are determined to guide their people to safety, but first they must convince them that everything they believe is a lie.

For my children. I love you.

CONTENTS

HEY, READERS!

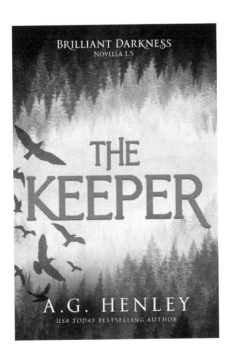

Get a FREE ebook in the Brilliant Darkness series, *The Keeper*, when you join my Reader Tribe. Subscribe and be the first to learn about new releases, giveaways, and book recommendations!

CHAPTER ONE

In the place where a tree meets the earth, roots grow. They twist and twine together through the ground, stabilizing the tree. The soil provides nutrients the tree needs to survive. In return, the tree shelters the land around it, protecting the earth from the erosive power of winds and water. When the tree dies, it sustains the earth and allows it to bring forth new life.

They work together. Cooperate. That's what our teacher, Bream, taught us. It's a beautiful thought.

My people, the Groundlings, live on the earth. Peree's people, the Lofties, live in the trees above us. We have common roots. What we can't seem to find is a way to shelter and sustain each other.

When I decided to come home after finding the protected village of Koolkuna, I hoped I'd be able to persuade our people to cooperate for long enough to get them safely back there. Peree and I discovered that our soil and water was poisoned during war many years ago, causing huge numbers of people and animals every generation to die or become ill. The toxins cause the rest of us to believe the ill people are terrifying, flesh-eating monsters—the Scourge.

I want to believe that when our people drink the pure water in Koolkuna, and they are free of the delusions about the Scourge, they will let our violent past die a quiet death. Like Peree and I have. The Reckoning proved it wouldn't be so easy. Many people on both sides died when our people clashed, including my foster mother, Aloe, and Peree's foster father, Shrike.

I allowed myself to hope again when the Confluence formed to try to work together and solve our problems. But it's been a week, and they haven't even persuaded our people to shake hands, much less make any progress on the issue of leaving for Koolkuna. The Confluence hasn't gone well. Not at all.

The Lofties refused to leave their homes unprotected and come to the ground to meet with us. They only allowed the new, hastily assembled Groundling Council of Three—Fox, Pinion, and Bream—to enter the trees for the Confluence. An entire meeting was wasted negotiating that. At least the Three aren't under armed guard during the meetings anymore. But I'm learning that words can pierce a fragile peace as absolutely as a spear or arrow.

Peree and I have made it clear we intend to partner. Since then, we've endured the disapproving silences and openly hostile barbs about how unnatural it is for a Lofty and a Groundling to want to spend their lives together. Why can't they understand how unnatural it is for our people, related by blood and by place, to live apart?

Peree and I want to spend time together without feeling judged, so we've taken to sneaking around. In the trees, we hide out and talk in a lonely shelter far away along the perimeter of the walkways. On the ground, a dense grove of greenheart trees will do. Today we sought out the thick swathes of maiden grass along the banks of the water hole.

A duck honks irritably as we slip through the stiff stalks of its home. The tops of the late-summer grasses shiver well above our heads, concealing waterfowl and lovers alike. We emerge from them now.

With my lips pressed against Peree's, as they were only moments ago, I can ignore the pain of losing Aloe. I can forget the disappointment in our people. These fleeting moments with him are gifts, like the heady scent of the greenheart trees after a storm, or the feel of a silky, unblemished stone from the water hole. Unremarkable to others, maybe, but precious to me.

We slink through the shadowy forest toward the gardens, our arms snaked around each other. Peree still limps, thanks to our harrowing journey through the caves searching for the mythical Hidden Waters. We found Koolkuna instead. He doesn't complain, but I can hear in his shallow breathing and feel in the tension of his torso how much it cost him to follow me home from Koolkuna before his injured leg was fully healed.

"What are you thinking about?" His voice is a soothing compress for my troubled thoughts.

"Nothing I want to talk about."

He tugs me to a stop. "What kind of nothing?"

"I just wonder how long we can keep this up."

"Keep what up?" He kisses me playfully. "This? Forever, I hope."

I smile half-heartedly. "I mean I wonder how long we can be together. Here. In this place."

"What are you saying? Are you ready to go back to Koolkuna?"

"I don't know. Maybe."

"Say the word and we're gone."

I cock my head. "Really? What about your people? You were so focused on finding a way to help them."

He smoothes my hair. "I have other things to focus on now."

His lips find mine again, and I feel woozy when we finally break apart, as if I've been swimming underwater for too long.

We walk on, my scarred hand in his bow-callused one. Being Sightless, the sudden brightening of the light is the only thing I'm able to "see"; it tells me we've left the forest and entered the large clearing encompassing the gardens.

I pull away from Peree as soon as I hear Groundling voices. He hates my strict no-touching-in-public rule, and I *detest* it. Still, I don't think we should make things harder for ourselves by flaunting our relationship. Deciding to partner has caused trouble enough.

"Fennel . . . Peree!" Eland's feet thump across the ground toward us.

My little brother doesn't take my hand like he might have before. Any childishness about him was stamped out by our mother's death, and the hardship our people faced in the caves while besieged by the Lofties and the Scourge. But there are flashes of it, like his willingness to let me tuck him in at night when no one else can see. That's when he feels Aloe's loss the most. No matter how busy or preoccupied she was she never missed saying goodnight to him. So now, neither will I.

"I strung my bow," Eland says proudly.

"Nice work." Peree helped him choose a suitable tree branch yesterday and they shaped the bow together. "We can tighten it up a bit, and I'll show you how to make arrows next. *Good* arrows, like we use."

"Can we do it now?"

"Sure, if your sister can stand to let me go." Peree's voice is teasing; he nudges me.

I snort. "Eland, you aren't neglecting your work, are you?"

He's helping clear and replant the beds in the garden. He grumbles that it's work for children and elders, arguing that at almost thirteen years old he should be allowed to go out scouting for game with the hunting party now. So far the Three haven't agreed.

"Acacia said I could go. C'mon, Fenn," Eland pleads. Calli's mother took over management of the gardens since the Reckoning.

I purse my lips. "Fine. You boys go have fun playing with your instruments of death and destruction."

Eland tears off toward the archery range, hooting like an owl. I haven't heard him so excited since I returned from Koolkuna. It's a beautiful sound.

Peree leans in very close, pausing a breath away from my face, as if to kiss me again. My cautious, responsible side instantly frets about who might be watching. The rest of me, tingling with anticipation, couldn't care less.

I soak in his summery scent, so much like honeysuckle, trying desperately to prevent my traitorous arms from slipping around him. I'm sure he's smirking, watching me get all flustered. I wish I could touch his mouth to find out for sure, but I don't dare.

He doesn't kiss me. Instead, he touches the pendant at my neck, the bird he carved for me. Technically, it violates my no public touching rule, but I don't care. I love the gesture—an unspoken reminder of his feelings for me, and our commitment to each other. I want to hold on to him and never let go. But I point myself toward home instead, and he follows Eland.

The rhythmic sound of wood being dissected meets me as I approach the clearing. The Lofties must have agreed to let us cut down a few trees, probably in exchange for extra water. My people have pushed hard since the Reckoning to clean up the gardens, fix our neglected shelters, and hunt for small game. The forest reclaimed our homes with astonishing avidity while we hid in the caves. It took Eland and me hours to march the dust and dirt out of our shelter at broom-point.

Bear's husky voice mingles with those of the axmen in the clearing. I tense, tempted to go back the way I came. He hasn't been treating me differently since I told him I would partner with Peree, but something's definitely off in his voice, and he vanishes whenever Peree's around. I understand, but it still hurts. He's one of my best friends. Or he was.

Calli, my other best friend, shouts from the direction of her shelter, a baiting note in her voice. "Oh, *look*, it's Fennel! Where do you think *she's* been?"

My lips flatten into a hard line as she comes toward me. She knows exactly where I've been.

Calli's scent is sharp and spicy from working in the stillroom. The potent smell summons memories of Nerang, the talented healer who saved Peree's life in Koolkuna. I long to be with him, little Kora, and my other friends there again.

"How'd you get all this maiden grass in your hair?" Her voice is light, but it has an edge of cattiness. She plucks something off the top of my head.

"You know I was with Peree."

She lowers her voice. "You were with him, but were you *with* him?"

"None of your business." *Especially if you're going to act like this.* I try to change the subject. "What about you and Cricket? Any progress there?"

She moans. "Fox won't let us go *anywhere* alone now that he knows Cricket wants to partner with me."

I frown. "I'm sorry he's being a stickler."

"He's not being a stickler with you and your Lofty. It's like none of the rules apply to you anymore." Is that what her hostility is about?

"Maybe it's because I'm not his child." I keep my voice quiet, unsure who might be listening. "Listen, I didn't plan for any of this to happen the way it did. It's not like I wanted to fall in love with a Lofty. Far from it." I reach out for her hand. "But I did, and I wish you could be happy for me."

"I'm trying. Really." Her voice is serious now. "It's not easy. It's so strange . . . a Groundling and a Lofty . . . and it's really hard watching Bear's face when he sees you two together."

Ouch. The wonderful—and terrible—thing about knowing someone your whole life is that they know exactly what to say to influence you. I gather up the guilt and regret about hurting Bear and bury it all in a shallow spot inside me. I'll dig it up later to agonize over when I'm alone.

Ignoring the lump in my throat, I tug on her hand. "Let's forget about boys and go in my shelter and . . ." I cast around for a second, trying to come up with something fun we used to do, "and fix each other's hair. Clearly mine's a wreck."

She hesitates, but only for a moment. She loves messing with my hair. Smiling, I open the door of our shelter and pull her in behind me. My nose wrinkles at the unexpected musky smell inside. And is something . . . dripping?

Calli screams.

I freeze. "What? What's wrong?"

She can't answer; she's too busy shrieking. I yank us back outside, bracing myself for whatever might come flying out. All I hear are the sounds of shouting and running feet as her cry subsides.

She whimpers. "The poor things."

"Are you okay? What happened?" Bear grips my arms. His touch is both comforting and uncomfortable at the same time.

"In there," Calli tells him.

He pulls us behind him and steps toward my shelter. People have gathered around us. Some gasp as they apparently see whatever Calli saw inside; others are silent.

"What *is* it?" I ask.

"Animals . . . a bird and a rabbit." Bear sounds disgusted. "Someone gutted them. And nailed them to the wall over your bed."

I stumble back, swallowing hard at his words. "What? Why?"

No one answers at first. Bear finally speaks.

"I think it's a message. A pretty sick one."

CHAPTER TWO

I have trouble grasping what Bear said. Someone killed and flayed open some animals? And hung them in our shelter? I shiver from the ill will of the act. Bear tucks me under his arm, a gesture that should be reassuring.

"*Aww*, isn't that sweet," Moray's horrible drawl breaks the stunned silence around us. "You're a glutton for punishment, aren't you, hero?"

Moray. I wouldn't put it past him to kill defenseless *humans*, much less animals. I'm pleased to hear he still sports a hint of a lisp from the badly bitten tongue I gave him, but it enrages me that he didn't face any other consequences for assaulting me and leaving me to die in a pit in the ground before the Reckoning. Neither did his family— his mother Thistle, brother Cuda, and the other brother whose name I never remember—after they threatened Eland and plotted against Aloe.

They were working with Adder, one of the old Council of Three, who had them convinced that the Lofties wanted to destroy us and take our land. Adder died in the Reckoning, and the new Council didn't have the will to really punish Moray's family after all our losses.

"Shut it, Moray. Fenn's scared," Bear says.

"You might want to think about being scared, too. Here comes the Lofty. You remember him—the one she actually wants? Don't think he's gonna like you pawing all over his woman."

Bear draws himself up like he's about to answer Moray with a quick fist to his face. I step away so Peree won't see Bear draped over me, but I keep a hand on his arm—half apology, half warning not to start anything. And then Peree is there. I forget about that whole no-touching thing and curl into his arms.

"I heard the scream. Are you alright?" He sounds angry. I've decided that usually means he's worried or scared.

"I'm fine. I guess someone wanted to tell me something but wasn't brave enough to do it in person." I try to sound brave myself as I point to the door of our shelter; inside I'm still reeling.

Peree goes to look, and he holds me even tighter than before when he returns.

My head snaps up. "Where's Eland?"

"I'm here." His voice, soft and sad, breaks my heart. I pull him to me with my free arm.

"We'll meet later to discuss this," Fox says, his voice serious. "Right now I need volunteers to take those carcasses down and clean up the mess."

Peree half drags me away again. He doesn't let go of me, and I don't let go of Eland. I have no idea where he's taking us.

"Climb." Peree puts ropes in my hands.

"Why?"

"I don't know who did that to those animals, or why. But I do know the one place I can keep you two safe is in the trees." He sounds like he's speaking through clenched teeth. "Get going."

I'm too rattled to argue. I pick my way up the swinging rope ladder. At the top, I scramble onto the walkway and hang on to the scratchy rope handhold like my life depends on it. Because it might. Eland scampers after me like a natural; Peree follows him.

"Wow. This is so *cool!*" My brother keeps his voice down, but it squeaks with suppressed enthusiasm. I have to smile. I forgot this was his first time in the trees. "The walkways are everywhere! You can't tell that from the ground. And the way they build their shelters is different: round instead of rectangular like ours, and wrapped around tree trunks."

Peree points a few things out to him, pride in his voice, as we walk along the narrow planks. I concentrate on not plunging to my death. My stomach churns with what I've come to accept as my tree-sickness. I still don't have a good sense of the layout of the Lofty community, which is partly what leads me to feel uneasy. At least Eland doesn't seem to have the same reaction to heights.

"Can I see inside a shelter?" he asks Peree.

"Course you can, little man," a familiar voice says. Petrel. I relax a bit. I haven't had the chance to talk to him very much, but Peree assures me his cousin is on our side. "You can come on over to our place. Hey, Fennel, how's it going? You look a little green."

"I'm . . ." I wave my hand around.

"Fenn doesn't like heights," Peree says. From the sound of his voice I'm quite sure he has a huge grin on his face.

"Oh, no, and you two were so well matched in every other way," Petrel says sarcastically.

"How is Moonlight feeling?" I ask. His partner is expecting their first child soon.

"Grumpy as a thrasher and about as puffy. The little one can't get here soon enough. Come meet her; she could use the distraction."

We're only a few paces farther down the walkway when a high male voice confronts us. "Who gave you permission to bring them up here?"

"Back off, Osprey. I don't need permission," Peree says.

"The Covey says you do," the man insists. Peree told me the Covey is what the Lofties call themselves when they gather to make decisions.

Peree snorts. "Nobody told me that. And I don't care."

"Stop," I hiss. I don't want him to fight with anyone, especially his own people. And I definitely don't want Eland in the middle of it. "We'll leave."

"No way. You're staying." Peree is nothing if not stubborn.

Persuading an impending thunderstorm to change course would be easier.

"Cool it, Osprey," Petrel says. "They're just here for a visit."

"They shouldn't be up here!" the man snaps.

"Hey, Fenn's my future cousin," Petrel says. "And Eland's my . . . I don't even know what, but something family-ish. I'm with Peree on this one."

"You're with Peree on *every* one," Osprey growls. "This won't end here." I slide Eland closer to me, but Peree only laughs.

"And that was supposed to be . . . what? A threat? I'm sweating. How about you, Petrel?"

"I'm shaking over here. You're good at that, Osprey. Keep it up. C'mon, Eland, let's give you a tour."

Peree throws his arm around my shoulders and snickers as we follow Petrel and Eland.

"Was that funny?" I ask him.

"Yeah, it kind of was. You'd have to see Osprey. He has this weird thing he does with his tongue. Like a frog catching flies or something. And he's skinnier than Eland."

"What does that have to do with anything? Small people can still be dangerous. Like Shrike." The words pop out unbidden, scalding drops from a pan. I instantly regret them. Peree doesn't need a painful reminder of his father's death.

"Totally different," he says flatly. "When Shrike threatened someone, he could back it up."

I squeeze his waist. "I'm sorry."

"You don't need to be." He kisses the side of my head. "I hate that my people are acting like this."

"It's not like mine are being any better."

We take a walkway to the left, and another to the right, this one going up. The paths sway under my feet, making me clutch the handholds even though I know Peree won't let me fall. The caves might be freezing, and dangerously disorienting, but at least they're stationary.

Petrel calls to Moon ahead of us. A moment later we enter some kind of dwelling. I haven't been to their home before. The couple of times Peree and I have come up in the trees together, we were pretty much by ourselves.

I wish I could see—and not for the first time, either—as we enter their home. I'm as curious as Eland about the Lofties and the way they live, but I can't exactly barge in and start feeling people's furniture. The space feels cooled by a light cross-breeze, and the smell in here is nice: floral, but shot through with a peppery scent. It must be a combination of Moon and Petrel.

"Well, who are you?" a female voice asks.

"I'm . . . Eland. Fenn's brother."

He sounds a little star-struck; Moon must be pretty. She's a Lofty, so she probably has fair hair. And Peree compared the color of her eyes to the Myuna, the untainted water hole in Koolkuna, which is supposed to be an amazing shade of blue. He called my eyes muddy, but he said it like mud was even more beautiful to behold. That's one of Peree's many talents—insulting me in ways that make me feel special.

"Come on in, Eland. Are you hungry? My little brother Thrush is always hungry." Moon sounds like a hovering hummingbird, barely pausing between words. "He's probably a year or two younger than you, but he's almost as tall. You'll have to meet him."

Petrel laughs. "Watch it, little man. Moon'll stuff you till you're sick. And she's in full nesting mode, too. You might be trussed up and tucked into bed next to Thrush before long."

"Speaking of beds, did you finish the cradle yet?" Moon coos, sounding like she already knows the answer. Petrel doesn't answer. "That's what I thought. At least *someone* is getting ready for the changes around here. So! You must be Fennel. You were right, Peree. She's beautiful." I smile awkwardly, embarrassed by the compliment. "We've been waiting to meet you. Where are your manners, Peregrine? You should introduce us!" Her tone skips from scolding to welcoming and back to scolding with dizzying speed.

"You didn't exactly give me a chance, cousin." He puts his hand on my low back. "Moonlight, this is my intended, Fennel. It's strange to say that, you know?"

I chuckle. "It's strange to hear. I'm pleased to meet you, Moonlight." I hold out my hand, and she takes it. Her hand is petite and her skin surprisingly silky, but I can feel the hard bones lying underneath, like grass-covered tree roots.

"Call me Moon. Oh, and feel free to laugh." Her voice turns sly. "Peree already told us you think our names are funny."

I turn on him. "Peree! I can't believe you told them that!"

"Sorry." He sounds totally unapologetic. Like he's trying not to crack up, in fact.

"They're just . . . different," I stammer. "I'm sure our names sound strange to you, too."

"No doubt about that," Petrel says. "Then again, there's nothing that's *not* strange about you and Peree getting together."

"There's someone else for you to meet, Fenn," Peree says. His voice is a little more serious. "This is my grandmother, Breeze."

Someone makes a noise—kind of a rattling breath. I turn toward the sound, smiling at her.

"I'm glad to finally meet you," I say. Breeze doesn't respond. I bite my lip and try again. "I'm so sorry for your loss . . . Shrike was a good man. My foster mother, Aloe, respected him very much."

"Thank you." Her voice is terribly weak. After an awkward silence, she shuffles to the door, muttering something to Moon that I can't make out.

"Don't mind her," Moon says after the door closes. "She's really upset about Shrike."

"I understand."

And I do. I'm familiar with the bleak landscape of loss. Even with Peree and Eland to comfort me, I feel its wintry wind against my own skin.

Peree told me the Lofties often looked to Breeze for leadership. She was strong, opinionated, and fierce with a bow and arrow. But since Shrike, her son, was killed in the Reckoning, she's been almost paralyzed with grief. She sure doesn't sound like the confident woman Peree told me stories about.

"I wish this was only a social visit," Peree says, guiding me to sit with him on a low, planked bench along the wall.

He tells Petrel and Moon about the dead animals in my shelter. My body tenses as he describes how the rabbit and the bird—a dove —were sliced open and nailed to the wall, their bodies splayed out grotesquely. I could've done without the details. Falling asleep tonight with the scent of a blood-splashed wall, no matter how clean they get it, won't be easy.

"Who do you think did it?" Petrel asks.

"Had to be a Groundling," Peree says.

I frown. "It could've been a Lofty."

"Not likely. I stick out like a flesh-eater down there. Someone would have noticed if another Lofty was wandering around."

I don't like to believe the culprit was a Groundling—other than Moray, maybe—but Peree has a point. And yet a small part of me can't help wondering if he might be unconsciously prejudiced against my people, the way I'm trying not to be against his.

"*Why* did they do it?" Eland asks through a mouthful of food. Moon must have made good on her offer.

"I'll bet someone wanted to scare your sister a little," she says. "It was probably just a cruel joke."

"I don't think it was as simple as that," a gentle, familiar voice says from the doorway. It's Kadee—Peree's foster mother and my natural mother. I'm trying to forget that our relationship to her makes Peree and me sort-of siblings. Our tangled history is a not-uncommon consequence of the Exchange.

The Exchange began generations ago, after the Fall of Civilization, as an attempt to divide and preserve the meager resources in the treetops. It insured only light haired, fair skinned babies were allowed to remain safely in the trees with Lofty parents. Lofty babies born with dark hair and dark skin went to Groundling parents to be raised on the forest floor ... with the constant threat of the Scourge.

Peree was a Groundling baby born with a thatch of blond waves; he was given to Kadee and Shrike to foster. Kadee gave birth to me a few years later. When my eyes grew as dark as the bark of greenheart trees, she had to give me up to Aloe. Aloe had Eland several years later, and Eland's father died soon after; I barely remember him.

Peree and I found Kadee living in Koolkuna after disappearing from the trees almost ten years ago. She'd left Shrike and Peree, devastated by the knowledge that the Groundling Council of Three of the time intentionally blinded her child—me—so I could serve as the Water Bearer one day.

The Exchange spun a messy, tangled web between the ground and the trees and wove generations of heartache. I had hoped it would be one of the first issues tackled by the Confluence. I'm not feeling as optimistic now.

"The news spread up here already?" Peree asks in the cool tone he reserves only for Kadee. I guess there's no time limit on bitterness after your mother abandons you.

"I'm sorry, Fennel, Eland," Kadee says. "What a terrible thing for someone to do."

"I'd like to believe it was a joke," I say to Moon. "But it feels like a threat." Peree leans closer, putting a hand on my knee.

"The choice of a bird and a ground animal sure wasn't random," Petrel says. "And the way they mounted them over Fennel's bed . . . you probably shouldn't leave her alone too much, cousin. Not that you leave her alone that much as it is."

"Now I have another excuse," Peree says with grim satisfaction. "But he's right, Fenn. You and Eland shouldn't be by yourselves anymore."

I lay my hand on top of his. "We did manage to keep ourselves alive for years before I met you, you know."

"I can protect her." Eland sounds a little hurt.

"I know you can," Peree tells him. "You're lethal with that spear. And with a little more practice they'll have to watch out for your arrows, too."

I can almost hear Eland's face crack open in a wide smile. If someone could glow with pride, he would probably be burning like the sun. Peree is the only person who has that effect on him these days, and I love him even more for it.

"More bread, Eland? Or squirrel meat?" Moon asks. "How about some water? Petrel, pass the plate around to Fennel and Peree. Maybe what happened today will help. It could give us a common problem to solve." I struggle to keep up with her rapid-fire speech.

"I don't know," Peree says. "Our little thrown-together group here might be the only ones who care."

"I don't think that's true," Kadee says. "We have some allies, even if they aren't as vocal. Fox seems sympathetic, and there's Breeze."

"It would be even better if our ally hadn't kind of lost it," Petrel mutters about their grandmother. There was no love lost between Breeze and her grandsons. Peree said she adored her son Shrike, but Peree and Petrel were born Groundlings, not Lofties, and Breeze never let them forget it.

"Peree, I'd like to talk to you and Fennel," Kadee says.

"Now?" he grumbles. "At least let me eat first. I'm starving."

"When you're ready." She's careful not to stray too far into authority-figure territory with him.

"They grow up," Moon says with an exaggerated sigh, "but there's always a part of them that stays thirteen years old— their stomachs. Leave a little bread for Fennel, cousin. She could do with a few more curves."

My face flares. I lost some weight when we were stuck in the caves, but I didn't think it was that obvious. And I'm not used to people talking about how I look right in front of me. I'm getting the feeling the Lofties are less formal with each other than we are. Or maybe it's only Peree's family.

"She's perfect, curves or no curves," he says around a bite of food. I smile and sample the bread Peree handed me. It smells freshly baked, with a crisp crust that reluctantly gives way to the softer center. The taste is sharp and a bit salty. Lofty bread is *almost* as delicious as ours I have to admit.

"I need to do a repair on the perimeter," Petrel says. "Wanna come, Eland? You've been staring out at the walkways like a caged squirrel."

"Really? I can go with you?"

"Sure thing."

"Find Thrush and take him, too!" Moon urges, as Petrel and Eland head for the door. "He's been *helping* in the storeroom today. Driving everyone batty. Which reminds me. Will you collect more fenugreek and blessed thistle from the herb garden so I can make some teas?" She steps closer to me, half-whispering near my ear, "For after the baby's born. Good to encourage your milk." She continues in a louder voice, "Oh, it was so nice to meet you two. I want you to consider this your home now."

My throat closes unexpectedly at her words of acceptance. I stand and give her a careful hug, startling when the baby moves between us. She places my palm over what must be a tiny hand or foot poking out. It draws back into the safety of its watery cocoon, and I shake my head at the small wonder.

The solid swell of Moon's belly fitted between us feels like a sign of hope for our combined future. At the same time it reminds me of the last pregnant woman I embraced, Rose, who disappeared after encountering the Scourge.

I hang on to the hope instead of the sadness, because I need it. I can't shake the feeling that whoever threatened me won't stop with killing a few animals.

Peree and I follow Kadee out the door. The sun must be about to fall below the tree line; the heat is momentarily intense. Birds call to each other like old friends from different parts of the treetops while the leaves whisper their secret conversations. The sounds of the trees are so much louder here than on the ground. I wonder if the Lofties even notice.

"What did you want to talk to us about?" Peree asks impatiently.

"I'm afraid it's not good news," Kadee says.

"Of course not. What now?"

"The Confluence met again today. They decided that you and

Fennel should ask for permission from the Covey or the Three before you spend time together."

Peree curses and paces away.

"That's what that man Osprey was talking about," I say.

"I'm sorry," Kadee says. "I thought you should know, before someone sees you up here."

I thank her for telling us and hurry to catch up to Peree.

He waits for me, then hustles us along. He's moving so fast we're practically running. The path swings wildly, which doesn't help my upset stomach.

"I need to find Eland and get back to the ground," I tell him.

He doesn't answer. After several twists and turns, he stops and thrusts a thick rope into my hands.

"Hold on tight. It's a firebreak." His voice is toneless; I can't read it. "We have to swing across."

I drop it and step back, clutching my gut. "No swinging. Please. Give me a minute to catch my breath. And to think."

He takes my hands. His are trembling. "There's nothing to think about. I'm taking you to the furthest shelter on the perimeter. I *know* I can protect you there, from your people and from mine. I'll go find Eland; we're leaving tomorrow."

"Wait, Peree. I know you're upset—"

"You bet I am. I'm not going to let them tell us when and where we can meet. You think they'll stop with a few dead animals? I can't let anyone hurt you, Fennel. Don't ask me to do that. I watched you from the trees for years. I couldn't be with you, and I couldn't do anything to protect you. Now I can, and I will."

"I know. I understand. But I'm . . . are you really ready to turn your back on your people without giving them a little more time?"

"Don't you understand where this is going? First they put rules around how we spend time together. What's next? Preventing us from being together at all? I'm not going to risk that." He takes my face between his callused fingers. "I love you, Fennel. You're mine and I'm yours for as long as you want me. We'll go wherever we need to, but I have to be with you."

"That's what I want, too." I stand on my toes to kiss him. I only meant to reassure him, but his mouth meets mine with a ferocity that's different from the passion I've tasted on his lips before.

There's fear in this kiss. Fear and possessiveness. It's as unsettling as it is intoxicating. Maybe he wasn't kidding when he said he would've ended up alone if I hadn't agreed to partner with him, thanks to the fever that decimated their community a few years ago. Moon is the only Lofty woman I've met who sounds anywhere near our age.

I'm sure I would've ended up with Bear, or another Groundling man, if I hadn't fallen in love with Peree. Even if I hadn't partnered, I would've had Eland and my friends. Peree only has Breeze and Petrel. And Petrel has his own family to worry about now. Maybe Peree really was facing a lifetime of loneliness if he hadn't met me.

Just when I think I've learned all there is to know about my intended, something like this makes me realize there's probably much more to him. Like the fear that he keeps well hidden behind all his anger and jokes.

I pull away from him gently and touch his face. "Hey, I'm here. I'm not going anywhere."

He crushes me to his chest. The thumping of his heart reminds me of playing hide-and-seek as a child, pressing my ear to the earth to hear approaching footsteps. I hold him while he lets out a long breath over my head. Insects trill in the greenheart trees around us; darkness has swept away the last of the light.

"Let's go back to Koolkuna. Now. Please." His voice is soft.

"Running away isn't the answer, Peree. What will the Reckoning have meant, and losing Aloe and Shrike, if we do that?"

He doesn't answer right away. "Then stay with me in the trees while we figure this out. You and Eland. Let me keep you safe."

"How long before your people find out you've got us stashed in a shelter up here? A day? Two days? What will that do?"

"Fine. I'll sleep on the ground with you."

I scratch my neck. This isn't the first time we've had this conversation. "The Three and the Covey want us to get permission to *visit* each other. What are they going to say if they catch you in my shelter some morning? And you know how good we are at actually sleeping when we're together." Which is to say not very.

He brushes his lips across mine, making them tingle. "I can be good, I promise."

"You can't even be good while you're promising to be good." I laugh, inching his hands back up from where they were straying. "Anyway, even if *you* can control yourself, *I* can't."

He groans. "I can tell I'm going to hate your plan. Go ahead and spit it out."

I hold his hands in mine. "Nothing that happened today really changes anything. No one was hurt. We already knew pretty much everyone hated the idea of us being together. Now they confirmed it. I think we need to keep trying to show them there's no threat in us being together. In *any* of us being together. How else can we get them to live peacefully in Koolkuna?"

"I think the animals nailed to your wall would disagree that no one was hurt," he points out. "Right now, I could care less if we ever get this bunch of ingrates to Koolkuna. They can't see a good thing when it's right in front of them. Clearly . . . or they would be worshipping the ground you walk on by now."

"You might be a *tiny* bit biased, but thank you." I kiss him again. The scary intensity has been replaced with what feels like surrender —for now. "Can we please go find Eland?"

"He's safe with Petrel. And I'm not ready to let you go yet. Stay with me for a few more minutes."

He leads me to the edge of the walkway. We sit and dangle our legs; the early evening breeze tickles my feet. I lean against Peree, and his fingers weave through my hair.

"I keep thinking about a story Wirrim told us the night after the Feast of Deliverance. The night you left Koolkuna," he says. Kadee learned many of the stories she told Peree, and that he told me, from Wirrim, Koolkuna's aged Memory Keeper. "He said this one came from one of those books you were telling me about. I think it reminded him of you."

"What was the story?"

Peree settles in, like he always does before telling a tale. "It's about a man who gets lost, deep in the mountains. He's lost for days, cold and hungry, until he stumbles on a place where all the people are Sightless. He's the only one who can see. At first he kind of thinks that makes him special, better than them. He thinks he can be their leader. But no matter how much he tries to describe the way things look, or what it's like to see, the Sightless don't believe him. They have no way to understand. In fact, they think he's slow in the head. So he starts to doubt himself."

My mouth twitches with the irony. "I can relate to that."

"The man slowly gets used to living among the Sightless, in their world of brilliant darkness, but he can't quite bring himself to forget that there's a whole sighted world out there. He pines for it. The elders try to convince him to let them take his eyes. If he didn't have them, he'd feel better."

Peree pauses; I can tell he's thinking of what the Three did to me.

"What happens?" I nudge.

"He almost agrees to let the elders have his eyes. Then at the last minute he changes his mind and escapes. He doesn't make it home, but at least he dies able to see the beauty of the mountains around him."

I let that sink in. "Okay . . . that's sort of a horrible story."

"I think Wirrim was warning me, Fenn. About how hard it would be for our people to believe us about Koolkuna and the Scourge. They've been blind all their lives. No way to relate to what we're telling them. I was, too, before we went to Koolkuna and I saw for myself. How can they suddenly believe the truth?"

How indeed.

I shake my head. "I didn't like that one. Next time tell me another animal story. Let's go find Eland. I need to get to the ground so I can stop feeling like I'm going throw up."

Peree helps me stand. "You two sleeping down there alone isn't a good idea, Fenn."

"I thought you said he was lethal with a spear?" I tease.

"Not *that* lethal. And do you realize how dead to the world twelve-year-old boys are when they're sleeping? Shrike had to blast me out of bed when I was that age."

I wince. "Please don't use the word *dead* when you're talking about Eland."

"I won't let anything happen to him, or you, if I can help it. But that's just it. I'm helpless when you're on the ground and I'm up here."

My hands find his shoulders, where his wavy hair ends. "I can't think of any way around it for now. We knew this wasn't going to be easy, but I won't leave without at least *trying* to persuade our people to go with us."

He presses his fingers to the carved bird against my chest. "Stay safe, Fennel. I don't want to go back to living without you."

"You won't have to."

But we both know I can't promise that. None of us can. That's the rub when you love someone.

CHAPTER THREE

R *un.*
I'm being chased through the forest. I stumble through the trees as hands grasp at my back and arms. But these hands are warm, human, unlike the flesh eaters. They close around my throat just as I start to scream.

I wake, gasping for air and clutching my blanket. I listen for Eland. His measured breaths are audible from his pallet across our shelter. My fists start to open, until I realize Eland isn't the only one I can hear breathing. There's a low rumble near the door.

Is that . . . a snore?

I rip my blanket off and tiptoe over until I stumble into something solid. "Peree! What are you doing here? You have to go! If someone catches you—"

"Leave off with the kicking, will you?" a muffled voice says. And it's not Peree's.

"*Bear*?" I crouch, feeling around by my feet. He's sprawled across the floor in front of the door.

"Yeah." He yawns. "Sorry to disappoint."

"Get *out* of here!" It might look bad for Peree to be in my shelter, but at least we're intended. I can only imagine the reaction if Bear is found in here. "What were you thinking?"

"I was *thinking* that I don't want to see you or Eland nailed to the walls next."

I can't decide if I should hug him or throttle him. "When did you come in?"

"I watched until your light went out, then I ducked in a little later."

It took me forever to relax enough to extinguish the torch last night. The metallic odor of animal blood still clung to the wall over my bed. Bear must have been sitting out there in the dark for hours.

"Thank you for looking out for us . . . I mean, I know it's not your responsibility."

"I had to make sure you were safe," he says softly. "I heard they weren't going to let your Lofty Keeper down here. Thought you might stay with him."

"I'm not allowed up there anymore, either. Not without permission. But either way, I'm not going to let whoever did this scare Eland and me out of our home. He's lost enough." I sound more resolved than I feel. "Still, you have to go. If anyone sees you in here at this hour of the morning . . . it would be bad. And Peree wouldn't be too happy, either."

He lies back again. "You know, I think I'm still tired."

"Bear! Go!" I shove him. It's like trying to roll a downed tree.

"Okay, okay. Help me up?" I haul him to his feet. He holds my hand for a long moment. The door creaks open, and he's gone. He can be surprisingly quiet.

I listen, but all I hear is the feverish early morning chatter of birds —no humans. I let out the breath I was holding.

"He loves you," Eland says, startling me. I didn't know he was awake. So much for twelve-year-olds having to be blown out of bed.

I busy myself with tidying my pallet. "He's just being a good friend."

"No. It's more than that."

I stop and frown at him. "How do you know?"

"The look on his face."

"Don't you start, too," I mutter.

Eland trudges off to work after breakfast, complaining all the way. I try not to worry about him. The gardens are well trafficked these days.

People greet me along the way as I follow the opposite path to the caves. Most are as friendly as ever. It's only when Peree is around that we get the pointed silences or angry mumbling. *Ridiculous.*

I've returned to my duty of restocking the caves. I hate feeling like I'm reverting to status quo, but I had to do something productive while the Confluence was being totally *un*productive. I spent the last few mornings pushing armloads of logs into the storage room in the caves, then pulling the resulting splinters out of my hands. Peree wants to help, but so far I've refused. He has his own work to do: patrolling the Lofty perimeter; repairing damage to the walkways with his cousin, Petrel; checking the animal traps. And keeping watch for the sick ones.

I've taken to using the term for the Scourge that the *anuna,* the people of Koolkuna, use. I'm trying to think of the creatures as ill people, like they do. Of course, the *anuna* have the benefit of drinking from the pure water from the Myuna, the underground river we called the Hidden Waters, which protects their minds from the delusions that make the sick ones appear to be terrible flesh-eating monsters.

The Myuna is far away. We have no choice but to drink the poisoned water from our water hole, so we don't know how we'll react when the creatures are near. Will we be able to remember they're mostly harmless? Or will we once again believe them to have the power to overwhelm and consume us? I don't have any answers.

One thing I do know: dealing with another extended internment in the caves and trees would be far more than our communities could deal with right now. I hope the sick ones stay away.

I enter the caves, already breathing more shallowly. The smell is still terrible; my people were stuck in here for weeks.

Footsteps echo close by, and arms trap me from behind. I stiffen as a mouth presses against my neck.

"Morning . . ." Peree says. "Did you sleep okay?"

My heart pounds unevenly, but I can't quite bring myself to tell him not to grab me like that. Instead I twist around and hug him. My fingers get hung up on his bow, which is slung across his back. "Hey, Lofty . . . did you get *permission* to come down here?"

"Moon gave me permission. Well, it wasn't so much permission as an order to get out of the house. She was sick of me pacing the floors. I missed you." His lips search out mine.

"I missed you, too." I consider telling him about Bear and immediately reject the idea. Why make things more difficult for him? Or for myself? This is all hard enough.

"I guess there's no way you'd think about *not* working in the caves today?" he asks.

"The caves are probably the safest place for me. Everyone hates them. Everyone avoids them. I might as well get some work done. And there are so many people in the gardens all the time—Eland should be safe."

"I thought you'd say that. And you're probably right. But I'll come in with you if you want."

My intuition jangles. He folded way too easily; I was expecting a fight. "No, I'll be fine. So . . . what are *you* going to do today?"

He chuckles. "You see through me already."

"Amazing, isn't it? Considering I'm Sightless and everything?"

"Right. Bad choice of words. But . . . now that you mention it . . . a hunting party is forming, and I thought I'd join them."

"Why am I not surprised? Never miss an opportunity to shoot something," I joke. "What are you hunting, though? I thought you Lofties got most of your meat from traps you set in the trees—possums and birds and things?"

He slides his hands slowly down my arms.

"Big Lofty secret," he whispers, his lips brushing my ear. "We hunt on the ground sometimes. *Without* permission."

I gasp in mock horror, but truthfully I am kind of shocked. I'm sure the Three would not be pleased to hear that bit of intelligence. Not that I'd be the one to tell them. My conscience pokes at me like a child with a stick. Inviting a Lofty into my life might require me to keep a lot more secrets than I'm used to.

"Please be careful. Don't let anyone see you down here," I say.

"Oh, we're always careful. And well armed. Don't worry, Groundling, we only do this when our meat supply is depleted, and we don't feel like haggling with your lot for more."

"Did Aloe know about this?"

"Doubtful. Shrike trusted her, but not that far."

"Are you sure *you* trust *me* that far?" I tease.

"I trust you with my life," he says simply.

He shatters me sometimes with how easily he shifts from frivolous banter to absolute, sweet sincerity. My eyes fill with tears.

"What?" He cradles my face in his hands, roughing the moisture away with his thumbs.

"Nothing. I love you. Be careful."

He kisses my cheeks, my eyebrows, where my jaw meets my neck. I'm breathing a lot faster by the time he touches my necklace in farewell.

"*You* be careful," he whispers. "I'll be back this afternoon, in case you want to check out our shelter way out on the perimeter again . . . or spend a little time by the banks of the water hole . . ."

I push him away, laughing. "Go hunt."

The morning passes quickly. There was more wood to move into the storeroom in the caves this morning, new stores of salt meat and dried beans to deliver, and our herbalist, Marjoram, told me she has some poultices and teas she wants me to bring in. Marj was underprepared for the accidents and illnesses resulting from such a long confinement last time. She won't make the same mistake again.

There's plenty of space in the storeroom—it was almost empty by the time we left the caves after the Reckoning. It's an easy job to stow the supplies neatly along the natural stone shelves. My stomach rumbles, anticipating a midday meal, as I cross the cavern to the storeroom carrying the second-to-last load of wood. Even the lingering stench of crampberries doesn't deter my appetite.

"Fennel." The word whispers across the cave.

I freeze. "Who's there?"

"Stay away from the Lofty. Groundlings and Lofties aren't meant to be together. You've been warned."

I can't tell anything about the speaker—man, woman, their age. But quiet as the person's words are, it's hard to miss the implied threat. I drop most of the wood, keeping one thick log as a potential weapon. The person is between the passage out and me.

I hold the log firmly in front of me, trying to tame my wild breathing so I can hear. Fear strangles my thoughts. An indefinable amount of time passes. Finally wrestling the courage to move, I step forward, keeping the log at the ready.

And I cough.

The air is wrong, and not simply human-waste wrong. Something else. There's light where there shouldn't be, and . . . smoke. That's what I'm tasting and smelling.

There's a fire in the passageway, and it's blocking my way out. Terror doesn't steal through me. It rips my head off.

Every instinct spurs me to run, but I resist. Fall and injure myself and I may never escape. I don't even know if the whisperer is still in the caves.

I step closer to the fire, trying to figure out exactly where it is. It spits and hisses at me like a beast straight out of one of Kadee's darker fables. One thing's for sure, I can't go this way.

Smoke creeps into my lungs. I crouch down, seeking clean air, and double back into the cavern. I know the honeycomb of passages that spread off the main cavern as well as I know the paths of the forest.

Thinking quickly, I choose a tunnel that meanders deeper into the cave system, but eventually leads back to the exit Moray pushed me out of not long ago. The fright of that moment shoulders its way through the confusion in my head, making me shudder.

I hurry forward, running my fingers along the chilled walls to stay oriented. The smoke dissipates the farther I go, receding gradually, but the threat replays over and over again in my memory. Plucking identifying characteristics from a whisper is as frustrating as trying to name a flavor I know I've tasted before but can't identify.

I give up, but I commit the words and timbre to memory. If I hear the whisperer again, I'll know.

It was probably easy to start the fire. The final pile of logs and kindling sat inside the cave mouth, waiting for me to store it away. We keep a pile of torches by the entrance, too. Every Groundling—and probably Lofty—learns to start a fire from an early age, although I never really mastered it. Too much potential for turning myself into a smoking pile of ash.

So was the whisperer a Groundling or a Lofty?

If it was a Groundling, I don't think the fire was expected to kill me. We all know there are multiple passages leading out of the main cavern, even if the rest of my people can't find their way around them with a map and all five senses. A Lofty, on the other hand, couldn't possibly know that.

It's hard to believe any Groundling, with the possible exception of Moray, would start a fire only to scare me. Especially when Jackal, Rose, and their unborn child were so recently killed after Jack set a Lofty tree alight. Arson can be destructive in more ways than one.

I stop, coughing deeply. I smell like smoked meat.

Peree was right. The whisperer preyed on my inability to see. I need someone sighted with me. And he'll insist he should be that person. Which isn't going to go over well with anyone.

I start moving again. Whoever set the fire must be the same person responsible for the dead animals. And now there's no doubt at all what they want. I smack my numb palm against the wall. What is so terrible about Peree and I being happy together? How are we hurting anyone?

My thirst grows thanks to my exertions this morning and the acrid smoke that stole down my throat. I long for my water sack, thrown carelessly on a stone shelf in the storeroom. Thankfully I'm close to the exit now. Daylight mingles with the darkness ahead. I pass out of the caves and into the forest, following the rock wall back toward our part of the forest.

Urgent voices slingshot through the air as I draw closer to home. From the sound of it, the fire was already discovered and is being extinguished. I skirt the cave entrance, having no desire to go anywhere near them again today, and step out of the trees. I'm on the path to the clearing, aiming for a drink of water and a change of clothes, when I hear Calli shout my name.

She embraces me, her hair flowing around my shoulders like a blanket. "Fennel's here! She's okay!"

People crowd us, firing questions at me faster than I can answer. How did the fire start? Did I know who might have set it? Was I hurt? How did I escape?

As I struggle to respond, I realize there's another commotion in the opposite direction from the caves. More raised voices and the unmistakable sound . . . of a second fire.

"The trees!" I say. "Are they on—"

"Yes," Calli says. Her voice is grim. "Someone set one there, too."

My heart convulses. "Have you seen Peree?" Surely he'd be with me by now if he were on the ground.

"No. A Lofty wouldn't be welcome down here right now."

I realize she's right. A dark note of violence rumbles beneath the tenor of fear and confusion in the voices around me. I hope Peree is hunting far away in the forest somewhere.

I clutch at Calli's hand. "Eland?"

"With my mother. He's safe."

Someone asks again who set the fire. I shake my head and hunch my shoulders. I don't know who set the fires. All I know is that this could lead to all-out war. Again.

"Give us a few minutes, then she'll answer your questions." Calli puts her arm around me and guides us out of the crowd and toward our shelters. I lean into her. It's comforting to feel like our friendship is intact, at least for the moment.

I can hear the crackling of the Lofty fire more distinctly from the clearing. Luckily it isn't right above us, where I think their homes and important community spaces are mostly located. Instead, it seems to be somewhere further along the perimeter. I hear Lofties shouting and their footsteps pounding along the wooden walkways, an unsettling echo of those I heard just now at the entrance to the caves.

Did the same person set both fires? Or was this some kind of retribution by a Groundling after they discovered the cave fire? It couldn't be a coincidence.

Calli takes me to a bench in the clearing and sits beside me, pressing a water sack into my hands. I drink deeply, easing my raw throat.

People bolt in both directions along the paths in and out of the clearing. We hear that the cave fire is mostly out; there was too little fuel for it to burn for long. The group that had gathered around us dispersed, off to gawk at the Lofty fire, no doubt.

"Fennel, I'm sorry," Calli says.

I offer her the sack. She takes it, but I don't hear her drink. "For what?"

"For how I've been acting since you . . . you know."

I touch the side of my head to hers.

"All of this has been so hard," she continues. "Everything since the Solstice . . . it's like a nightmare that won't end."

I know what she means. Our people have suffered. I've had my fair share of awful experiences, too. But despite everything, I'd never call the past few months a nightmare. They brought me Peree and the hope of living in peace and safety.

"We'll be okay. We just need—" A scream from the other side of the clearing cuts me off. I jump up. "What now?"

Calli grabs my hand and jerks me forward so quickly I almost fall. Her fingers claw my arm. "Not again. Please not again."

Vines of fear slither up my body when I hear them. The moans and shrieks of the Scourge pushing toward us through the forest.

CHAPTER FOUR

O kay, *this* is a nightmare.

Calli and I run hand-in-hand toward the caves, following the same path Eland and I did the night of the Solstice. It's so overwhelmingly familiar that I catch myself listening for another weak plea for help from the bushes. But that cry won't come. Willow, the elder I helped to the caves that night, died before the Reckoning.

That's when it hits me.

This is not that night. The sick ones are not the same as the Scourge. I'm the Water Bearer. And I've survived much worse than this.

I slow. "You go on, Calli."

"What are you doing? Come with me!" She tries to pull me forward again.

"I'm staying to help who I can. Tell Fox I'll collect the water tonight."

My voice is weary, but sure. I realize I sound a little like Aloe did that night after the Scourge came. The thought gives me confidence.

Calli goes on, and I turn back toward the clearing. People part around me, barely slowing down. I listen for shouts of help or the sounds of a struggle. Mostly I hear gasping breath and footfalls on the hard ground as my people run. And I hear the sick ones close behind them, coming toward me.

I tell myself there's nothing to be afraid of. I've done this before. I've spent hours among them. They aren't monsters; they're ill. That's what I tell myself.

But the stench of decaying flesh is as bad as I remember. And as sickening as the smell is, their sounds are worse. I can no longer hear them speak, like I could in Koolkuna when I was drinking the pure water. I only hear their terrifying shrieks and groans. My heart stutters as the space between us closes. I slow to a stop, dry my sweating palms on my dress, and hold my breath.

The wave of creatures breaks over me, screaming in my ears. When I finally breathe, I gag. I cover my face with my shaking hands. The smell of rot makes my eyes water. My mind flashes to the stories of creatures tearing their victims' heads off and bathing in their blood. As they dart in and out at me, hovering so close I can almost feel them, the terror is acute.

It takes every ounce of courage I have to remember who I am and what I've already lived through, so that I don't turn and sprint back to the caves. I remember Aloe. She did this every time the sick ones came. Every time. I must do my duty.

Part of me rejects that thought. Why should I? We could have already mobilized a group to go back to Koolkuna, where we'd be safe and protected. Instead the Confluence has wasted a colossal amount of time worrying about who might be double-crossing whom.

But if I don't collect the water, innocent people—Groundlings *and* Lofties—will suffer. Children. Elders. I can't ignore that.

Water is my first priority, because it's the only thing we can't store for long in the caves. The sick ones swarm around me as I hurry through the forest to the sled track. I follow it to the water hole.

Two empty sacks huddle in the bottom of the sled. I drag the first sack into the water to fill it, ignoring the creatures howling at me, their hot breath on my skin. The fire in the trees still rages as far as I can tell. The shouts of the Lofties occasionally reach me over the cries of the sick ones. I'm worried about Petrel, Moon, and Kadee. And where is Peree?

A sick one moans next to me while I load the full sack into the sled; I shiver with disgust. I step back into the water with the second sack, half-expecting to hear the gruesome but familiar sound of Peree's arrow penetrating the creature's flesh. Would I really want him to kill them, knowing what I know now? The creature presses closer, panting and making a revolting sucking sound. I grimace. Maybe I do.

I push the second sack into the sled, puffing and sweating with exertion. It's mid-afternoon, and the late summer sun is still pumping out heat like a cooking fire. My feet are the only reasonably cool parts of my body, submersed in the water as they are.

At least I seem to be able to remember that the sick ones aren't monsters. No one really knows how the poison works on our minds; I was worried I would succumb to the delusions when the creatures surrounded me again. *And they aren't touching me, thank the stars.* That's what I'm thinking, when one of them grabs my arm.

My scream is loud enough to revivify the dead. And it startles the almost-dead enough to push them back.

"It's me, Fennel!" Kadee says. "I came down to help you."

I hug her, relief ushering the fear out of my body as quickly as it rushed in. I can't believe I didn't think about this possibility. Kadee is one of the rare people unaffected by the poison in the water. She's never seen the sick ones as monsters. She won't go mad being exposed to them.

I have *help*.

Grateful tears mingle with the sweat and dust on my cheeks. "I am *so* glad you're here. What's going on up there? Where's Peree?"

"Fennel, listen. We desperately need more water to fight the fire." Kadee's voice is taut. "The firebreaks are containing it for now, but if the wind picks up, it could reach our homes in a matter of minutes. Can we have these sacks? Petrel can bring them up."

I hesitate. The Three gave me no instructions, but it's hard to forget the last Council's outrage when I allowed the Lofties to take more water than I brought my people.

"The cave fire is under control," she reminds me. "I'll help you bring as much water to your people as they need. I promise. We'll work together, Fennel."

Work together. It's what I've wanted so badly for us all to do. And working together means putting someone else's needs first sometimes. I tip my head up to the night sky and take a deep breath. I guess I have to start somewhere, even if it means infuriating my people all over again.

We get to it. Pushing the sled up the hill, physically the most difficult part of my duty, is almost a breeze with Kadee helping. Having two people—and one set of functional eyes, I have to admit—makes every task so much easier. She ties the rope to the sacks and Petrel hauls them up. We hurry the sled back down to the water hole. The sick ones hover around us like a bilious cloud, but talking to Kadee provides an excellent distractor.

She tells me no one knows how the tree fire started. The Lofties had just heard the Groundling cries of alarm after the cave fire was discovered when they realized a shelter along the perimeter was also ablaze.

"Whose shelter?" I ask.

"That's the odd part," Kadee says as we fill two more water sacks. "It's one of the furthest away from the community, and hardly ever used. Petrel said Peree will be upset when he finds out it was destroyed. Apparently he went there to be alone sometimes."

Sharp nails of apprehension slide through my gut and my cheeks boil. "Lately he hasn't been alone. We've . . . been there a few times." I tell her about the warning I received in the caves. "Your fire was another message for me. And for Peree, too, I guess."

"I'm sorry to hear that." Kadee sounds worried.

"Have you seen him?"

"The hunting party will keep their distance as soon as they realize the sick ones are here." I must have looked worried myself, because she adds, "They're all excellent climbers. They have to be, growing up in the trees."

I hope she's right.

We create a steady rhythm, filling sacks and pushing them up the hill for Petrel to collect and bring to the fire. Fill, push, lift, repeat. Kadee speaks to the creatures pressing in on us, offering them comfort. I wish I could still hear them speak. It would make being around them bearable. Sort of. Slowly the hungry flames devouring the trees abate; Petrel finally sends word the fire is out. Their homes are safe.

We make several more trips to the water hole, and Kadee helps me drag the sacks back to the cave mouth. Petrel follows above, hauling more than his share. I tire with the weight of the water sacks, but I don't stop until we're safe inside the caves.

"Would you like me to come in with you to see if I can help?" Kadee asks.

I imagine my people's reaction to a Lofty entering the caves this soon after the fire. I shake my head. "I don't think that would be a great idea."

She seems to understand. "Then I'll send word as soon as Peree is back."

I reach for her hands. "Thank you."

"Of course. I'm here for you, Fennel."

Her words sound like an apology for all the times she wasn't here for me. I can't afford to think like that, though. Kadee's the only parent I have left.

I shuffle toward the main cavern, dragging one of the heavy sacks of water behind me. The others sit inside the entrance, waiting to be brought in. The fire in the cave is out, but thick smoke chokes the air, and me in turn, as I move through the passageway.

The flicker of torches and echo of muttering voices bring the interminable days in the caves back to me with alarming clarity.

The sick ones can't stay as long this time. They can't. There's no chance my people will survive that. And I have doubts about my own ability to go back to the routine of gathering the water for them every day.

"Look who finally showed up? Our little Fenn."

I stiffen at the sound of Moray's voice, listening for the sounds of others. Anyone. I won't let him get the best of me again. I hear voices nearby, but I don't entirely relax.

"What do *you* want?" I ask.

"Nothing. Nothing at all." His voice is an aggravating concoction of concern and pure taunt. Why does he always have to sound like he's mocking me? It brings out the false bravado in me, which I hate.

I push past him. "There's more water sacks by the entrance to the caves. Make yourself useful and bring them in."

He steps in front of me. "Why don't I take this one for you instead? You look tired; you've got dark circles and everything." His blunt fingers skim under my eyes.

I smack his hand away and step back; almost tripping over the sack I'm dragging. "Don't touch me."

"Aw, c'mon, Fenn. Don't be like that. We're supposed to forgive each other, right? I forgive you for biting the hell out of my tongue. Now it's your turn."

Again he sounds genuine, like he thinks a simple apology will make me forget he tried to kill me. I take another big step away from him, fully aware I'm being driven back toward the dark, empty passageway.

My hands clench the neck of the sack. "Get out of my way, Moray."

"You heard her. Back off." Bear's voice, rumbling from behind Moray, is a welcome sound.

"Don't get all worked up, hero. I'm having a chat with my new friend."

"I'm not your friend," I say. "Go away."

Bear comes to my side. "Here, Fenn, I'll take that water."

"I've got it," Moray says. He takes the sack from my hand.

"What's he up to?" I mutter, after Moray saunters off.

"Who knows?" Bear says. "But I'll give you the advice you gave me once. Stay away from him."

"My pleasure. Hey, there are more sacks where that came from. Can you get some help to bring them in? I need to talk to the Three and find out what else I need to go fetch."

Bear takes my arm. "Fenn, wait. There's something you should know."

I stop cold. "What?"

"Fennel . . . I'm so sorry. I thought he was with me." Acacia, usually difficult to tell apart from Calli because their voices are so similar, sounds distraught. "I was collecting the younger children and I assumed he would follow us back to the caves. But when I turned around . . . he wasn't there."

"Wait . . . who?" I have a bad feeling I already know.

"We were washing up down at the water hole, when we heard the flesh-eaters coming. I had several of the younger children, and I thought Eland was with us. I never would have left him behind, Fennel, you know that . . ." Her voice fades as blood pounds in my head.

"No. Not Eland. *Not. Eland.*" I turn and bolt back through the passage to the cave mouth, my hand bouncing painfully along the wall, panic snapping at my heels.

Bear follows, calling my name. As the cave opens up to the outside, I hear the sick ones. Their groans and shrieks fill the air. It's impossible to think of Eland among them. Or as one of them.

Maybe he found somewhere to hide. Maybe knowing I thought the sick ones weren't harmful was enough to protect him. I have to believe something, anything, other than that he's gone. Bear grabs my hand, yanking me backward.

"Fenn, wait . . . I want to help," he pants. But what can he do?

"Let me go. I have to find him. It might not be too late."

"I'm sorry, Fenn. So sorry."

"Don't say that to me. Not yet." I try to jerk my arm away from him, but he hangs on. "If you think he's already gone, then you don't believe me about the Scourge. If you did believe me, you'd know there's hope."

Some logical part of me, buried under a rockslide of fear, knows that isn't fair. I'm terrified Eland is in danger myself. But I want to lash out at someone, and Bear is the only one here. "I have to go."

"I'm coming with you." His voice is equal parts determined and petrified.

"Bear, no. You can't." I put my hand over his on my arm. "I'm sorry, I shouldn't have said what I did. Don't put yourself in danger to prove you believe me."

"I won't be in danger. As we believe they can't harm us, then they can't . . . Right?"

I pace toward the open air impatiently. The sick ones pace and howl at us a few steps away. "In theory. I'm not willing to let you test it, though. Go back inside. Bring the water."

"I'm going with you." His tone tells me he's done arguing. I try anyway.

"I don't know where Peree is, and now Eland is out there with them." I motion to the creatures. "If you set foot outside this cave, then every male I care about could be in danger. Please stay here. Please. I can't risk losing you, too." I hope he won't read more into that than I mean.

"So you do care what happens to me."

I step away again, moving outside of the shelter of the cave mouth. The sick ones shriek at my back; I raise my voice to be heard. "Of course I care, you stupid boy. You're one of my best friends."

"I'll hold your hand. If I can feel your hand in mine, I think I can do this."

"No! Don't—"

It's too late. He lunges out next to me, grabbing my arm. I can only stand there, too stunned to react. It even seems to surprise the sick ones. But not for long. They surround us.

Bear pulverizes the bones of my hand, but unbelievably he also manages to stand his ground . . . for a few seconds. His grip weakens, and he moans. He sounds like he might pass out from the fear.

"They're going to . . . no, don't . . . Fenn! Help me—"

I dash back into the cave mouth, hauling him with me while he's still upright. He crashes to the ground a few steps inside. Other voices approach from the main cavern, probably coming for the water.

"Bear! Are you okay?"

There's no answer. I grab his scruffy cheeks and put my ear to his mouth. He's breathing, thank the stars.

So I leave him to the others and run out into the night, hoping against hope that I can still save my brother. Hoping he had as much courage as Bear did. But not believing for a moment that it would be enough.

CHAPTER FIVE

I run through the clearing, calling for Eland. I trip and fall over, scraping my knees and palms. Ignoring the pain, I pick myself up and listen. The sick ones roam around our shelters, probably searching for food. I push into each structure thinking Eland could have barricaded himself in somehow. But he's not here.

Where would he have gone? Kadee and I worked down by the water hole for some time. If he'd been there, and still . . . human, I would have heard him. Where else could he be?

I search the gardens, listening to the sounds of the sick ones, hoping to make out a word. Rose talked to me after she became one of them. Maybe Eland would, too. *Eland help me. Help me find you.*

I wander, moving slower and slower, and end up by the water hole again. He wouldn't have left the area, not with the sick ones here. Not unless he no longer had the use of his reason.

Grief whispers malevolently in my ear, threatening to dissolve the last of my self-control. I can't lose Eland. How would I survive that? Losing Aloe was hard enough.

"Fennel." A man calls to me from the trees. His voice is quiet, but I still recognize it.

"Petrel! Eland's out here somewhere. I can't find him. I . . . can't hear him. Kadee and I were so busy with the water—" My words dip and weave. I'm dangerously close to losing it.

"It's okay, Fennel. He's with us."

I shy away from a few of the sick ones groaning for me and automatically lower my voice to match Petrel's, although I could sing with relief. "How did he get up there?"

"I found him hanging on a tree. Said he climbed up when the fleshies came. Sounds like he had to hold on for a long time, but he's fine."

I'm torn between crying and laughing, so I settle for inane chatter. "He is a pretty good climber, although he hasn't had much chance to practice." The Lofties don't allow us to climb their trees. "And I guess he was desperate to get away from the sick ones." But what I'm thinking is: *Eland's alive.*

"I came looking for you—figured you'd be crazy worried about him. I can bring you up, but we have to be quick and quiet. Step toward the tree to your left. Here comes a rope."

I do as he says, searching the air over my head with my hands, and tie the rope quickly under my arms when I find it. Petrel pulls me up. Despite his warning, the ascent seems agonizingly slow. As soon as my feet touch the walkway, he hurries me forward without speaking.

Muffled voices carry from other parts of the treetops as we move, and smoke poisons the air. The tree-sickness strikes hard and fast. My stomach flip-flops like I'm somersaulting underwater. I grit my teeth and follow Petrel.

We make a few turns and stop briefly. There's a scraping sound— a door. We walk through, and he shuts it quickly behind us. I rejoice at the familiar scent—the reek of adolescent boy. Eland.

We cling to each other.

"You found her," Moon says. "Good."

"What happened?" I ask Eland, my voice shaking like the hand of an elder.

"I got cut off from Acacia and the others. We were by the water hole and heard the fleshies—I mean the sick ones." He's working on calling the Scourge something different, like Peree and I do. "We started running toward the caves, but a few of them were getting close to the little kids, so I sort of distracted them and took off in another direction. I had to climb a tree to get away, but I only got far enough up so I couldn't be dragged down."

I hug him to me, thinking about what might have happened if he had been forced to let go.

Petrel thumps Eland on the back. I feel it right through my brother's thin chest. "Little man's a hero. Although now that I think about it, he didn't look so heroic hanging onto that tree trunk like an overgrown spider."

I laugh. Thinking of him clinging to a tree, while frightening, is suddenly also funny. Far better than the other, much more horrible scenarios that have haunted me since I heard he didn't make it to the caves.

"Would you like to sit down, Fenn?" Moon asks. She seats Eland and me on the same bench Peree and I shared before. I wish he was here now. "Are you hungry? Eland's already eaten."

She brings me a wooden board, perfectly smooth to the touch, and a small oilskin sack of water. I drink, eat some tart berries I don't think I've tasted before—maybe they only grow in the trees—and take a few bites of bread.

"I'm sorry there's not more," Moon says. "We have to ration ourselves when the fleshies are here, in case they make themselves at home. Petrel, you better go back. They'll be needing you as soon as it's safe to work on the walkway." Moon's voice accelerates as she speaks, like a bird beating its wings faster and faster.

I hear Petrel kiss her. "You okay?"

"We're fine. Go on, now. It'll look suspicious if you aren't out there helping."

Petrel leaves, closing the door firmly behind him. Abruptly, I realize the danger we may be putting Peree's family in by being up here.

"I'm sorry," I say to Moon. "I know this isn't exactly a great time to be harboring a couple of Groundlings. We don't want to cause you any trouble."

"Nothing we can do about it now," she replies, not unkindly. "And we should be okay; everyone was so focused on the fires . . . But what happened, Fennel? Of course people are claiming the fires were started by a Groundling, but how would one of your people even get up here? And why would a Groundling set a fire in the *caves*, the only place you can go when the fleshies come? That doesn't make much sense, does it?"

I tell them about the whisperer's threats. Eland slides closer to me, while Moon makes a disgusted sound.

"We finally have a chance to figure out how to work together, and someone has to go and do something stupid like this. I can't understand it."

"Where's Peree?" Eland asks.

"I'll leave that one for you to explain," Moons says to me, chuckling. She struggles to her feet, groaning a little. Eland and I hop up to help her. "I'm going to go see if I'm needed in the kitchens, and make sure Thrush isn't underfoot. People are going to be tired and hungry after fighting the fire all evening."

"What about the hunting party?" I ask her.

"Oh, we won't start worrying about them for a few days, at least. They always carry enough supplies to hole up in the trees for a while in case something like this happens. Don't worry, Fennel. Peree can take care of himself." She's bustling around the shelter now. Even heavily pregnant, she's full of energy. I imagine she's a force of nature when she's not carrying a child.

"Now, you two stay in here," she says. "Petrel will come for you when it's safe to go back down. Okay?"

"Thank you, again, Moon. I hope we haven't caused you any trouble."

I embrace her for the second time in two days, molding myself around her belly. They took a big chance, rescuing Eland and bringing me up here to be with him. And I just felt exactly how much they have to lose.

~

When Moon leaves, I take my chance to explore how their home is laid out. It's circular in shape, with the thick, supporting tree occupying the center of the space.

The sitting area is near the door while the sleeping area is around the back of the tree, allowing the family a little privacy. There are two beds—one must belong to Moon's brother, Thrush—and several windows, which we avoid. Fading light filters in from outside. Evening can't come soon enough for me. I need to get Eland back to the relative safety of the caves, but we should wait until it's dark.

The furniture in the shelter is solid and well built, and there's more of it than I'm used to. I keep knocking my shins and already-sore knees on things like chairs and extra tables. The hazards of visiting the home of a woodworker, I guess. Carved into the tree trunk are small niches, places to store extra clothing, dishes, and a pitcher and basin for washing up.

Our shelter is about half the size of this one, although we had the same number of people living in it until Aloe was killed. Now that I think about it, the shelters in Koolkuna were larger than ours too. Maybe bigger, permanent homes are somehow a result of enjoying more safety and security. I wouldn't know. We haven't had that luxury.

Eland and I plunk down on the floor in the back, by the bed, to wait for Petrel to return. I wonder what's happening on the ground. The people will be distraught to be back in the caves again. At least I was able to deliver some water before I disappeared to find Eland. I hope Fox, Pinion, and Bream can get everyone organized and keep them calm. This is the first real test of the new Council's authority. Not that it's been exactly easy for them so far.

"Fenn?" Eland says.

"Hmm?" I put my arm around him.

"I tried. To think of them as human. To believe what you told us, that they wouldn't consume me, or turn me into one of them." He pauses. "I stood there while they got closer to me . . . but it was really,

really hard. They look so scary, Fenn. Their faces . . . the blood and stuff . . . and all that screaming. I tried, but I couldn't do it."

I nod. "You don't need to feel bad. Even after Peree and I drank the pure water from the Myuna, and I could hear them talk, it was still hard to believe."

"Where *is* Peree?" he asks. I can feel him studying my face as I fill him in on Peree's illegal activities.

"He'll be okay," Eland says. "They only have to hold out until the Scour—, I mean the sick ones, go away."

I give him a half smile. "And when will that be, O Wise One?"

"Everyone says they won't stay as long as last time. Not even the elders remember hearing about them staying that long. It was a fluke."

I sit back against the wall, pulling him against me. "Hope you're right."

"Wow. If Adder had known the Lofties sneak off to hunt like that, he would've gone bat shit sooner."

I nudge him. "Watch your language. And don't tell anyone about it. Things are too tense right now to risk the Three finding out." I smooth my dress over my legs. "I wish Aloe were here."

I miss her more in this moment than I have since I first learned she was dead. I'd felt stronger grief and sorrow, but I really *miss* her calm strength right now.

"How are you doing?" I ask. "I mean about . . . her."

He shrugs. "I'm okay."

We haven't talked much about losing Aloe. But I want him to know he can. So I tell him how *I* feel. "It hurts. Every day it hurts. I miss her."

"Yeah."

I wait, but he doesn't say anything else. "Don't want to talk about it, huh?"

"Not really." His voice is thick.

I hesitate. I don't want to make things more difficult for him, but I don't want to lose an opportunity to draw him out, either. It's hard enough for *me* to talk about her. I try a different approach.

"You know what I miss? The way she smelled."

"Rosemary," he says after a pause.

"And something else, too. Something sort of sharp smelling. And I miss her hugs. When she hugged me, it was like she gave me some of her strength. It kind of oozed out of her and into me. Know what I mean?"

His hair whispers against the wall as he nods. I tuck him in closer to me. Voices and footsteps pass by outside. It's been surprisingly quiet. Maybe these shelters are built sturdier than ours, like their furniture.

"Remember our midnight swims?" Eland asks.

I laugh. Who could forget? We weren't supposed to swim after dark—too dangerous—but Aloe said her mother used to take her and she was going to take us—rules or no rules. She didn't swim; she stayed on the shore to listen for trouble.

Eland and I loved those rare nights slipping through the cool water, staying far enough away from land to almost feel like we were the only people on earth. It was as peaceful as it got as a Groundling.

"I think I saw him once. While we were swimming," Eland says.

"Who?" I ask.

"Peree. I didn't know who he was then, but I think it was him. There was a really bright moon that night, and he was standing on the platform that looks out over the water. He was just leaning on his bow, watching us swim. He looked kind of sad. I wondered what a Lofty would be sad about."

"You'd be surprised," I say gently.

Someone pounds on something nearby. It must be a door, because wood scrapes together, and a voice answers. I can't hear the exchange.

"Nothing amiss there," a woman says. Her voice is clear now . . . because she's right outside our door.

"Moving on, then," a man replies. Chill bumps press up all over my body and my pulse quickens. It's Osprey—the man who told Peree that Eland and I shouldn't be in the trees. The door to our shelter shakes as the people bang on it.

Eland and I huddle together. The huge tree trunk should hide us from sight if they open the door. But not if they come all the way in and look around. My stomach knots like the roots of a plant with nowhere else to grow.

The door creaks open, and footfalls cross the sitting area on the other side of the tree.

"Look what we have here. A couple of Groundling fire bugs."

CHAPTER SIX

Darkness falls like a heavy, black cloak as Osprey and the Lofty woman push Eland and me down the walkway. Osprey has some kind of weapon he prods me with every time I slow down a little. It threatens to slice through the back of my dress and pierce my skin. He must be using it on Eland, too, because I feel him twitch uncomfortably.

I hang on to my brother's arm, fighting the queasiness prompted by rushing through the dark night sky, moving up and down walkways at a near run. I'm still sweating, partly from fear and partly because the air is warmer and more humid than it usually is this time of day. Rain is coming.

I tried to ask the Lofties what they intended to do with us, but neither one spoke after they found us. They seem to be trying to make as little noise as possible. All I can hear are our hurried footsteps and the groans of the sick ones below. Even the night insects are hushed. I wonder if it might be worth shouting or making some other noise to draw attention to us. But I'm frozen in place by the weapon at my back and the hostility I feel boiling out of Osprey and the woman.

Before I can formulate any other kind of plan, we're back inside a shelter. This one feels smaller and more cramped than the other two

Lofty shelters I've been in. My nose wrinkles. It smells like the place holds some kind of compost pile. I immediately start breathing through my mouth as Eland and I are shoved on to the dirt-covered floor. I try not to think about what kinds of creepy crawlies might be under us.

"What are you going to do with us?" I ask the Lofties again.

"You'll be disposed of," the woman answers curtly. The absolute lack of emotion in her voice sucks the last of the warmth from my body, the way rolling into the freezing Hidden Waters did. She clearly means what she said.

"Why? What did we do?" Eland asks. His voice is shaky, but he also manages to sound a little defiant. It makes me proud.

"Don't act like you don't know. You deliberately set a fire. That's an act of war," Osprey says. "And once *you're* gone,"—I have the feeling he's speaking to me—"we can go back to some semblance of normal."

"Normal? Is it normal for your people to *dispose* of twelve-year-old boys?" I ask.

"The boy was in the wrong place at the wrong time and definitely keeping the wrong company," the woman says.

"Then let him go," I argue. "He won't say a word about this—right, Eland? Let him go, and you can do whatever you want with me."

"Too late, I'm afraid," Osprey says.

Without another word, the Lofties step back outside, bolting the door as they leave. The wind has picked up; it carries off the sound of their footsteps and anything else they might have said.

"Are you okay?" I whisper to Eland after a minute.

He exhales in a small *whoosh* of pent-up tension. "I guess. Except for the smell. It's pretty bad in here." He's not wrong about that.

He stands and tries the door, but it doesn't give at all.

"Let's both try pushing on it," I suggest.

"I don't think it will help."

He sounds half-apprehensive, half-mutinous—like he used to when he knew Aloe was going to be angry with him for some mischief he'd made—but less frightened than I might expect. I'm reminded again of how much more mature he seems than a few short months ago. Everything has happened so quickly since I got home; there hasn't been time to process all the changes. Now we really may be out of time.

I wish Peree would come home right about now. This is his territory. I'm lost in the trees. Those thoughts scatter the next moment like leaves across the forest floor. I've never relied on anyone to save me before, and I'm not going to start now.

"How do you think they knew we were up here?" Eland asks, sitting again.

"Maybe someone saw one of us with Petrel."

A grasping, choking thought sprouts in my head. What if Petrel or Moon told Osprey where to find us? Did they falsely accuse us of having set the fires? Maybe Petrel believed Eland really *had* set the fire when he saw him clinging to that tree.

I try to pinch off the poisonous shoot in my mind, but it's not easy. Why do I think I can trust Peree's family? *My* friends don't trust *him*. Why would Moon and Petrel feel any different about me? If they got rid of me, they'd have Peree back and all would be right in their sunny, leafy little world again. But how could they involve Eland?

I want to believe that family means the same thing in the trees that it does on the ground. We take care of each other; we don't betray one another. But family has never included Lofties when you're a Groundling. Or vice versa.

The wind dashes and dodges through cracks in the shelter around us. Fingers of rain begin to drum against the roof. I hold Eland's hand, ignoring the filth.

"I think she knew she was going to die. Mother." He stops. From his choked tone it sounds like he's wanted to let go of this for a while. When he speaks again, his voice is halting, and haunted. "She looked bad at the end, Fenn. Really bad. Kind of shriveled, like a thirsty plant in the garden. She didn't smile anymore, not even for me. I was scared, because Moray's brother and his knife were always hanging around me, but I was just as scared about what was happening to her." I squeeze his hand, letting him know I'm listening.

"She came to me a few days before the Reckoning. She told me she thought there was a good chance you'd still come back. That she trusted you and knew you would do whatever you could to help our people. She said if you came back, you would take care of me, and I should take care of you. I didn't know why she was telling me all that stuff. She sounded . . . like she'd given up. Mother never sounded like that." He swipes at his face and sniffs.

"And she said something else. Something I haven't told you, because I didn't know why she said it. It didn't make any sense. But it makes more sense now, after you told me what the Three did to you." He hesitates. "You know, to your eyes."

A foreboding feeling slithers through me—one I've learned the hard way to pay attention to. The rain beats on the wood over our heads now, and thunder snarls in the distance. The storm sounds louder and feels closer being in the trees.

"What did she say?" I have to raise my voice over the noise.

"She told me, 'Don't trust the Three. Not now. Not ever.'"

I only have a moment to wonder at Aloe's message before lightning explodes over our heads, and the door creaks open.

"Groundlings, listen to me. We don't have much time."

I try to place the voice, but I don't think I've heard it before. She sounds younger than me, and her tone is soft and rushed. "I'll help you get out of here, but I need you to promise me something first. Promise you'll take a message to someone. One of your people."

"Who are you?" I ask, totally confused.

"It doesn't matter."

"Who's the message for?" Eland asks.

"Moray," she says.

I almost snort. "*Moray?* You want us to give *him* a message? About what?"

"We'll give him the message, whatever it is," Eland says quickly. "Please help us."

The eagerness and relief in his voice brings me to my senses. Of course he's more frightened than he was letting on before. He's twelve. And he's right. Whatever the message is and whomever it's for, we need to deliver it so we can get out of here. So much for not relying on other people to rescue me.

"I want your word, too, Water Bearer," the girl says.

I can't imagine what a Lofty would want to tell Moray, but I say, "We'll bring him your message. I promise."

She's quiet for a moment, probably deciding if she can trust a couple of dirty Groundling hostages. "Then follow me. *Quietly*. Osprey and the others are sheltering from the storm, but the moment it stops they'll be coming for you."

Her words focus me. We have to get out of the trees. Now. Eland helps me up and wraps my hand around his arm. Goosebumps rise on his skin like spirits called forth by the howling storm. The branches scrape and groan around us, whipped into a frenzied dance by the wind, and the rain soaks us in a matter of moments.

We move forward, the sound of our footsteps thankfully drowned out by the storm. I have to rely on Eland's sight because I can't hear anything. After a minute or so we stop, and he speaks into my ear.

"I think we're going a different way than the other Lofties took us. We have to use one of those ropes to swing." He can't hide the thrill in his voice. I, on the other hand, grimace.

We situate ourselves around the rope swing. I give it a strong pull to be sure it's tied securely, then I wrap my arms around Eland's thin torso.

We take a few steps and push off. It's only when we're mid-swing, my feet dangling and my stomach trailing somewhere behind me, that I wonder if we can even trust this Lofty.

Too late now.

The storm rages over us as we walk on, following the Lofty girl. Instead of being frightened, I'm grateful for the cover it provides. I don't think anyone could possibly hear us. But *seeing* us is another problem entirely.

The girl mutters to hurry up in a tone so low it's almost lost in the wind. We pass a few homes. Narrow pools of light spill out in the darkness, probably from small fires lit inside as people wait out the surging storm.

"We're going through the main area now. Lots of shelters here," Eland whispers. "Be extra quiet."

I squeeze his arm to let him know I understand. I have to remind myself to ease up; I'm probably leaving bruises.

My shoulders brush the wet, wooden walls of the shelters as we creep along, hesitating at every squeak of the boards under our feet. At first I don't understand why we're staying close to the structures containing an untold number of hostile Lofties, rather than as far away from them as we can get.

Until I hear a door open in front of us. A new Lofty woman speaks, so close it sounds like I could reach out and touch her. I don't know where our guide is, but Eland and I go rigid against the wall of the shelter next to us.

"I wonder what they'll do with the Groundlings," the woman is saying.

"Don't know," a man answers.

I guess that the couple is standing inside their open door, looking out at the storm. The one we're standing a mere few feet from. I clutch Eland's arm, willing him not to move. From the tense set of his muscle, I needn't have worried. The scent of cooking food makes my stomach protest loudly. I hope they can't hear it.

"I suppose we have to do something," the woman says. "First there was the raid on the trees, then this fire. But it doesn't seem right. They're children. Even if they are Groundling children. What kind of people sends their young to do something like that?"

"Nothing happens down there without the approval of their Council. They had to know someone was about to set the fire. Or it was their idea." His voice is grim.

"I don't understand it."

The man grunts. "I don't understand half of what the bottom-feeders do."

"I feel badly for Peree, though. First his father, now the girl."

"He never should've gotten involved with her. This is what happens when we let young people have too much freedom. They make poor choices. Peree's old enough to learn that lesson. Don't think he'll forget it now—"

The man continues, but the door creaks shut, muffling his voice. I release the lungful of air I'd been holding on to.

"Did you hear all that?" Eland whispers, sounding younger than he has all night.

"We'll talk about it later . . . when we get back to our bottom-feeding friends," I say bitterly. Peree never told me about that lovely nickname. Or about their illegal hunting parties. Not that I really blame him, but what else isn't he telling me? "Where's the girl?"

Apparently our guide had barely gotten out of sight when the couple opened their door. Eland leads us to her, and we continue across what seems like a very wide platform. It must have been built between multiple trees because there are lots of shelters here. We beetle from home to home, sticking to their wooden sides as much as possible.

I wish I could get a better fix on how close we are to the platform that overlooks the cave mouth. The rumble and clatter of the storm isolates me completely. I listen . . . and a long groan ghosts through the trees.

My heart sinks into my stomach. Why didn't I think of this before? Even if our mysterious Lofty girl-guide can get us out of the trees, how will Eland reach the caves safely?

He pushes me back against some kind of structure, interrupting my thoughts. He doesn't have to tell me to be quiet.

"You shouldn't be out here," our guide says. "Your sister will worry."

"I was tired of being inside." The other voice belongs to a boy. He sounds younger than Eland, but maybe only by a few years. My stomach churns when I hear his next words. "Who're they? They look like Groundlings."

My brother steps forward. "It's me, Thrush. Eland." I'm surprised, until I remember Petrel took the boys with him to do his repairs. Could that only have been yesterday?

"What're you doing, Eland?" Thrush asks.

"We're on our way home."

"What are you doing up here, I mean?"

"Visiting."

"Did you start the fire?"

I cringe.

"Of course not," Eland says, sounding admirably relaxed. "We would never do something like that. But if anyone knows we were up here, they may think we did. Hey, remember I didn't tell Petrel about how you accidentally dropped your quiver off the platform? Do me a favor and don't tell anyone about seeing us in the trees. Deal?"

"I got it back," Thrush says. "I snuck out last night and climbed down to the branch it was hanging on."

"Nice work," Eland says, which makes me smile. He picked up that expression from Peree. "How about if I make some new arrows for it?"

"Groundlings arrows don't fly straight. Everyone says so."

"Peree's been helping me make mine. His arrows are good, right?"

"Yeah . . . *his* are."

"So what do you say? I kept your secret. Keep mine? That's what friends do."

"Okay," the boy says reluctantly.

"You better get home before Moon makes you scrape the bird poop off your shelter again," Eland says. And I thought Aloe was hard on Eland sometimes.

"Don't forget about my arrows," Thrush says. We listen to him run off down the walkway.

"He won't keep his mouth shut," the Lofty girl says darkly. "Not that one. It isn't possible."

"It was all I could think of," Eland whispers defensively.

"You did great," I say. "And if he tells anyone, hopefully it will be Moon or Petrel. They won't give us away." *I think.*

"Let's keep moving," the girl says. "We're almost there."

We start walking again.

"What about you?" I ask her. "What if he says he saw you with us?"

"Let's hope he doesn't." Her voice is sharp. It makes me worry a little about Thrush's safety.

"What will you do?" I ask warily.

"I'm not going to hurt an eight-year-old boy, if that's what you're thinking." She scoffs. "If I was capable of that, I would've let them get rid of you and your brother here."

"Why *did* you help us? What's the message you want us to give to Moray?"

She doesn't answer for a minute. She must have stopped walking, because Eland tugs me to a halt, too.

"It's okay," he says, his voice gentle. "Whatever it is. You can tell us."

I don't know what he's seeing that made him say that, but his words seem to have an impact.

She draws a shaky breath. "Tell Moray . . . that he's going to be a father."

My mouth drops open. "A father? You . . . you're expecting his—? How? When?" I'm so astonished I can't form a cohesive question.

"It's none of your business," the girl says, her voice abruptly turning fierce. "I'm only telling you because I have no other way to reach him. Especially now, after the fires. And I think he'll want to know."

"You sure about that?" Eland mutters.

"What do you mean?" the girl says.

I elbow him in the ribs. "It's only that Moray and his family . . . they aren't fond of Lofties."

"Well he seemed fond of me."

I'll bet. As obnoxious as Moray is, he can also be charming when he wants to be. That is, when he wants something.

"What would you like us to tell him?" I ask.

Whatever it is, I'm sure he won't respond the way she wants him to. I'm not sure anything matters much to Moray—except for Moray, of course.

"That I need to see him. We need to talk. Tell him I'll try to collect the water again as soon as the fleshies leave. Tell him to come to the water hole at the usual time."

Wow, there's a lot more action going on by the water hole than I thought.

"We're grateful for your help," I say. "And we'll give him your message."

"Thank you."

She sounds so worried and miserable I can't leave it at that. I step to her and search for her hand. I wish I could tell her Moray will support her, stand by her side. But I can't lie.

"It's okay. You'll figure something out."

She squeezes my fingers for a moment before drawing back. I can hear the sick ones roaming around below.

"So—any ideas how I can get my brother inside the caves with the sick ones down there?" I ask.

"You could try to wait them out, but now that Thrush saw you there may not be time. Maybe you could run for it? I've got my bow. I might be able to take a few of the fleshies out. Then again, I'm not a very good shot."

Of course. Just our luck to be rescued by the one Lofty that can't shoot straight.

"You better go," I tell her. "I don't want you to get in trouble. We'll have to take our chances with your people and wait."

"No, I can do it. I can run for it." Eland says.

I remember Bear's reaction to being surrounded by the sick ones. Eland's much smaller, but I'm not sure I can carry him if he passes out. "No, Eland. We can't risk it."

"I only see a few fleshies down there," the girl says. "He just has to control his fear, right?" She says it like a challenge.

"Not exactly." Irritation leaks out of my voice. "And however it works, I don't want to test it on my brother."

Eland touches my arm. "I think I can do this, Fenn. I almost did before, when I was alone. With you there, maybe I can make it this time. I'm pretty fast."

I cup his cheek with my grubby fingers and palm. "And you're fearless. But it's not about courage." If it was, Bear should've been able to withstand the sick ones. He's one of the bravest men I know.

"Then what is it about? Trust? I trust you, Fenn. I believe in you."

And I love him for that. But I still don't think it's enough. "You have to have drunk the pure water, Eland. You know that." I turn to the Lofty. "Go. You shouldn't be seen with us. We'll wait. Maybe we'll get lucky and the sick ones will leave soon."

"I don't think you're going to get lucky."

The platform under our feet begins to vibrate. Someone's coming.

"Go now!" I say.

"Good luck." She slips off into the night.

"C'mon, Fenn! I have the ladder. We have to get to the ground."

"No, Eland." But we have to do something. We're trapped. Panic carves a path through me.

"I don't think we have a choice," he says. "We know what they'll do if we stay up here."

"Maybe Peree's family would help us . . ."

"Fenn, we have to choose. Quick."

He's right. We can stay here and wait for the Lofties to catch and possibly execute us. Or we can take our chances with the sick ones. Which amounts to the same thing for Eland.

I grit my teeth and ignore the voice screaming at me not to risk Eland's life, telling me there must be another way. I shore up my resolve. I have to, because soft and vulnerable things don't survive in our world. They never have.

CHAPTER SEVEN

I climb down, my breath coming hard and fast. Eland's feet find the rungs above my head as soon as my hands let go of them. I can hear the creatures out there in the rain, their howls whipped around by the wind. How will they react when we reach the ground?

"Run. Flat out. Don't wait for me," I say to him for the fifth time.

He doesn't answer. I can only imagine what he's feeling. It has to be ten times worse than the first time I left the caves to collect the water.

At least he doesn't have to do this alone. I'll draw as many of them to me, and away from him, as I can. The rope ladder will still be hanging down, but there's nothing we can do about that. I'm sure the Lofties won't let the sick ones get far if they try to climb up.

"You're almost to the ground." If a voice could curl up on itself, Eland's would be in the fetal position.

"You can do it. Run, Eland. Don't look at them and don't think. Run. I'll meet you in the caves." I reach up and find his ankle on the rung above my hand, passing as much love and protection through my touch as I can. Then I let go.

I land with a squelch on the soggy earth and immediately race away from the caves, waving my arms and shouting. My feet twizzle under me and I almost lose my balance, but the distraction seems to work. The few creatures I can hear follow me, their feet sliding across the ground toward me.

After a moment, I hear Eland scrambling in the other direction. I listen for sounds of the creatures nearing him, but hear only the rain spattering the ground. A creature shrieks from the direction of the caves. Too close to Eland.

"Over here!" I pinwheel my arms toward where I heard the sick one. "I'm here! This way—I have food!"

I don't have food. I don't have anything, except a desperate desire to buy my brother time. The sick ones surround me, gnashing their teeth and moaning. Did they understand me?

"Eland, are you okay? Are you in the caves?" I shout.

The sick one by the caves screams again . . . and so does Eland. I cry out, too. I want to run to him, but I don't dare draw more of the creatures there.

My eyes water with dread and the hideous stench of the sick ones as I again wait to find out if my brother is alive or dead.

A noise drifts through the rain; it sounds like a body hitting the ground.

I slip and slide in that direction, hoping the creatures stay out of my way. I don't know if he's safely inside the caves, or outside of them. I lose my footing and fall in my hurry to get to Eland, barely noticing the mud that cover me.

"Eland!" I shout. There's no answer. I creep through the muck, arms outstretched, searching for his body. My knees scrape against the hard rock, dirt, and gravel inside the cave mouth.

I flail around, feeling only unforgiving stone. And then I find him, slumped like a forgotten water sack. He made it inside. I pull him into my arms.

"Eland! Are you okay?"

Nothing.

"Eland?" I feel his face. His eyelids are closed, lips slack, breathing shallow. "What's wrong? Are you hurt?"

He turns his head and retches. I dodge out of the way just in time.

Then I hold him, making soothing sounds like Aloe used to when we were ill. I smooth his shaggy, soaked hair back from his face. His forehead is clammy.

What's wrong with him? Is it shock, or exposure to the sick ones? Anxiety gnaws at me with sharp, needling teeth.

I can't leave him alone to go fetch help. What if he came to with the creatures right outside? I'm more grateful than usual that the sick ones seem to hate the dark and cold of the caves enough to never come in.

I have to get Eland inside by myself. I would have said I didn't have the strength to lift and carry him, but when I have to, I do. I totter with him in my arms through the tunnel that leads to the main cave, shivering as our wet clothes stiffen in the increasingly frigid air. My thoughts flutter in all directions while we walk.

I wonder what such close contact with the sick ones will do to Eland and how long it will take him to recover. I catalog the medical supplies I brought in for Marjoram, hoping she has what she needs to help him.

And how will Moray take the news that he's going to be a father? What will he do?

I think about Peree, praying he's safe. What will we do now that the fragile peace between our people seems to be shattered?

And I consider Aloe's warning about the Three.

Fox was like a foster father to Eland and me as we grew up, thanks to my close friendship with Calli. He and Acacia fed me, bandaged bloody knees and palms from my frequent falls, and scolded me when necessary, while Aloe was busy doing her duty as the Water Bearer. In other words, they treated me like their own child. If I can't trust Fox, whom *can* I trust?

"Fancy meeting you here again, sweetheart."

I'm not surprised the Three posted a guard after the cave fire, but why, *why* does it have to be *Moray*? From the acrid smell in the air, I'd say he's standing next to the ashy remnants of the fire. The fire I wouldn't put past him to have set.

I clutch Eland tighter to me and stop in front of him, swaying on my feet.

"I need to talk to you, Moray. Later." I'm not sure I could sound any less enthusiastic if I tried. I owe our Lofty guide the courtesy of keeping my word after what she did for Eland and me. But I don't owe Moray a thing.

"Thought you'd come around eventually. That Lofty not man enough for you, then?"

If I could cut out the smugness dangling in his voice with a knife, I would. I hitch Eland up a bit as he slumps in my arms. What kind of boar's ass tries to assault a woman, acts like it wasn't a big deal, and then taunts her, all with a half-drowned, semi-conscious boy in her arms? I can't let it pass.

"Save it for someone else, Moray. You might have gotten away with almost-murder and rape, but you and I both know that's exactly what happened that day." I lower my voice in case anyone else is standing around. "I have a message from your Lofty friend. If you're interested in what she told us, come find me. And keep your hands and your thoughts to yourself when you do."

"You're pretty hot when you're all worked up, know that Water Bearer? Even if you have been out there wallowing in mud with the fleshies. Looks like they got the best of little brother, too."

He still manages to sound arrogant, but also like he has to work harder for it.

"How's your tongue, by the way?" I can't help smirking as I carry Eland on past him.

Calli intercepts us before we get too far into the main cavern, crying tears of relief that I found Eland. Acacia joins us a moment later, her own tears flowing. I push aside my doubts about Fox as I embrace them. Calli is my *best friend*. Her father would never betray me. Then I think about how the Three blinded me as a child and the doubts steal right back in. They make themselves at home when Acacia tells me the Three want to speak with me.

It's like deja vu. They wanted to talk to me the day I gave the Lofties more water than I brought to our people. Tonight, I gave the first water to the Lofties to fight their fire. How is it that doing the right thing can seem so wrong, depending on how you look at it?

Calli helps me deliver Eland to Marj's makeshift clinic off to the side of the main cave. It's empty, apart from the four of us. Calli says they only had a few patients overnight: one or two with minor injuries after the mad dash to the caves the night before, and one distraught woman, agitated over how long we'd have to be in the caves this time. I totally understand her concern.

"What happened?" Marj asks as we lay Eland on a pallet on the ground. He moans, but otherwise doesn't seem conscious.

"He was *outside*," Calli answers in a low tone.

"How long was he exposed to them?" Marj asks.

"A few seconds," I say. "He made it to the caves quickly, but I think maybe one of the sick ones got pretty close to him at the end. He hasn't really come to since then."

Marj snaps into action, bustling around her small workspace. "I'll make him a tea with valerian and hops to help him sleep."

"Will he be okay?" I ask. *Please, please say yes.*

"He should be fine. Leave him here with me. I'll look after him." She sounds confident, so I try to relax and believe her. She adds, "You look like you could use a bit of a rest yourself, Fennel. You're welcome to sleep in here with your brother."

"Thanks, Marj. I'll be back in a few minutes. I need to speak to the Three first."

People stir around the main cave. Small fires dot the area, adding to the already thick canopy of smoke in the air. My eyes sting from it. Calli takes my arm, drawing me closer so she can whisper near my ear.

"Where were you two all this time? Were you in the trees?"

I don't want to lie to Calli. I really don't. But the doubts created by

Aloe's warning haven't gone away. In fact, they've burrowed even deeper into my brain. *Who can I trust?*

"No, the Lofties wouldn't allow us up there after the fire and everything." I think fast. Might as well keep it as close to the truth as I can. "I found Eland halfway up a tree, sitting on a little branch. I waited there with him, until we decided to make a break for it. That's when he was exposed."

My explanation is flimsy, but not entirely unbelievable. The Lofties usually clear the branches off all the trees in and around our communities to discourage climbing. But occasionally they miss a few. In fact, some kids make a game of finding branches the Lofties overlooked and climbing up to them before a Lofty lookout, like Peree, spots them.

Now Peree really *is* up a tree somewhere, hopefully avoiding the sick ones. If the sick ones haven't left after I get some sleep, I'll go out and look for him. Maybe Kadee would come with me. We can at least bring food and water to him and the rest of the hunting party.

Calli hugs me. The anxiety I feel must be obvious. "Marj knows what she's doing. This isn't the first time she's helped someone exposed to the fleshies."

But we both know that it doesn't happen all that often, either.

"Eland was trying so hard to be brave, Calli. He was trying to believe what I said: that the sick ones aren't really dangerous. If anything happens to him—" I swallow hard as my throat tries its best to close shut—"it will be my fault."

She doesn't respond. A second later I understand why. Fox claps me on the shoulder.

"Fennel. Acacia said you and Eland made it back. Thank the stars." His warm, kindly voice evokes conflicting feelings in me. If it had been anyone but Aloe that warned us not to trust the Three, I would probably tell him the truth about what happened. I glue my lips shut. He says, "Calli, see if you can locate some sort of warm meal for Fennel."

She squeezes my hand before she goes, and Fox steers me away to a quieter corner. "The Council is here. What news from the outside?"

"Have the Scourge left?" Pinion's never had a problem tearing away the husk to get to the fleshy heart of the matter.

"No, not yet," I tell them. When they ask, I feed them the same tale I told Calli, feeling guilty the whole time for lying. The more lies I tell, the more I'm trapped by them, weaving myself into a web I don't know if I can escape from.

"And all that time on the outside, gathering the water and looking for Eland, you didn't meet any Lofties?" asks Bream. He sounds a little suspicious. Or maybe not. It was hard to read my old teacher's voice. I was usually too busy trying to stay awake while he spoke.

"I spoke to Peree's mother." I figure it can't hurt to admit that. "She helped me collect the water I brought back."

"Really?" Bream says. "What a fascinating development. A Lofty helping to actually collect the water."

Time for more honesty. "I helped them get water to fight their fire, too." I tilt my chin up, waiting for them to object. They don't. "The Lofties think a Groundling set them."

"Is their fire still burning?" Fox asks.

"It's out," I answer. "It's been raining for a while now."

"Now that *is* excellent news. As we've seen in the past, the flesh-eaters often move on in inclement weather conditions," Bream says.

"Probably because they're wet. And cold. And hungry. They're human remember? Who likes to stand around getting soaked in a thunderstorm?" Fatigue catches up to me, prodding me to speak more sharply than I meant to.

"Yes, well—" Bream begins, but Pinion interrupts him.

"What about your intended? You had no contact with him?" Leave it to her to find the probable hole in my story. Adder didn't have a thing on Pinion when it came to interrogation, although the anger that always blazed out of him was thankfully absent.

"No," I answer honestly. Before lying all over again. "He was . . . injured fighting the fire. But he'll be fine." Not that they would care.

"Glad to hear it," Fox says. He actually sounds sincere.

"Who do you think set the fires, Fennel?" Fox asks. "Calli told us the arsonist spoke to you. Could you tell anything from the person's voice?"

"No, I could barely hear them." Not to mention I was scared stiff. "I couldn't even tell if it was a man or a woman. But if I hear the person again, I'll know," I promise.

"If you remember anything, or have any ideas about who set the fires given your . . . closeness to certain members of the Lofty community, we certainly would like to know," Bream says. "There is little precedent for this situation. There was the fire that Jackal set, which of course we all remember, and there was the forest fire set by lightning during our parent's generation . . . You remember that, surely, Fox, Pinion? It happened during the storm that also blew down the—"

"I think Fennel could use a meal, a wash-up, and some sleep. She's had a difficult night." Fox pats my back, steering me toward the center of the cave. "We may have other questions for you—and for Eland—after you're rested and fed."

Which means I'll have to get my story straight with Eland when he wakes up. *If* he wakes up, a voice in my head whispers.

"And unfortunately we may also need more water at that point, too," Pinion says. "We're already running quite low."

"But we'll manage for now," Fox says. "Go on, and try not to worry about Eland. We'll keep an eye on him as well."

Somehow his words are a lot less comforting than they might once have been.

CHAPTER EIGHT

I wake with a moan, my hand jerking back from the cold, moist flesh of a sick one. I'd been trying to help it . . . or maybe it was helping me?

The dream fades; the dread remains.

I sit up and rub my face; flakes of mud rain into my lap. It reminds me that I didn't have the energy to wash up after eating last night. *Last night* . . . I call out for Eland.

"He's still sleeping," Bear says from close by. He sounds a little sheepish. I wonder if the hand of the sick one in my dream was really a very large, very human hand holding mine while I slept.

"Has he woken up? What's going on?" A small fire snickers nearby, but otherwise it's silent in Marj's corner of the cavern, assuming I'm still where I was when I fell asleep. It's never this hushed in the caves except when I'm here working by myself.

"Take it easy. It's morning . . . or maybe early afternoon now. The fleshies moved on a few hours ago. Everyone took off outside as soon as the Three reckoned it was safe to go home. Eland isn't up yet, but he's been thrashing around like he might come to soon."

I can hear my brother breathing now. I swing my legs over the edge of my pallet, but they're numb and won't take my weight. I shake them impatiently. "Shouldn't he be awake by now? Where's Marj?"

"She's been coming in to check on him. He'll be fine, Fenn. He just needs to sleep it off. Calli was here for most of the night, too, but Cricket came to see her a little while ago . . . and you know how that goes. I said I'd stay with you and Eland." Bear stifles a deep yawn, and I hear joints pop as he stretches.

"Did you get any sleep? Go on out, I'll wait with Eland until he wakes up."

"I'd rather stay." His tone is dark. "The fires, remember?"

I grimace, and more mud sprinkles down my face. "I'm not likely to forget. But you sound like you could use some rest."

"I could . . . but Moray's been hanging around, too."

I snort. "I'll bet he is."

"Why? What happened?"

I wish I hadn't said that out loud. "I saw him on the way in with Eland last night. We had words again."

Bear shifts his weight like he's settling in. "All the more reason for me to stay."

I tuck my blanket up under my chin and over my shoulders, covering my frozen torso and arms. I feel disgusting, covered in caked mud like this, but there's no way I'm leaving Eland in here while I go wash, even with Bear to watch him. *Bear.* How can he still be such a loyal friend?

"We haven't had much of a chance to talk since I got back," I say.

"Well, that's cause I've been avoiding you."

I can't help grinning at his honesty. "Yeah, I know. And I know why. But I hope we can start spending time together again like we used to—as friends."

"What a coincidence. That's my new plan, too. I figured I knew you first, and we were friends first. The Lofty is going to have to get used to me being around."

"His name is Peree. If we're all going to try to be friends, you might start with calling him that."

"Let's not get ahead of ourselves. I said I still want to be friends with *you*, not necessarily *him*."

I can tell he's half-serious, but I laugh anyway. "I guess that's a start. In fact, that's why I came back. I hoped, probably stupidly, that we could all be friends. Groundlings and Lofties."

"One big happy family, huh? You always have been stupid. That's why I—," he stops himself quickly, "tolerate you. You're sort of your own hopeful, stupid force of nature."

"Peree says I'm stubborn and you call me stupid. I'm glad you guys enjoy insulting me." Moray has called me some choice things, too, although the worst is when he calls me *sweetheart*. It makes my whole arm itch with the desire to punch him.

Bear snickers. "What can I say? It's so easy to do."

I choose to ignore that. "Is it still raining?"

"Drenching. Everyone's laying low."

That's probably a good thing. We need the water, and it might give people a chance to cool off, literally, after the fires. Thinking of moisture of any kind is torture. My tongue feels like a handful of berries left out in the sun.

"Is there any water left around here?" I ask.

"Heads up." A small sack sloshes into my lap. "Marj left some for you two. She said Eland might have a headache, like I did. He needs to eat and drink as soon as he wakes up."

I take a few small sips, saving the rest for Eland. I hadn't even thought to ask about how Bear was feeling last night when I came back to the caves. "I'm really sorry about . . . everything . . . yesterday. How are you feeling?"

"My head's pounding, but I'll live. My memories of it are sort of fuzzy. Like I had a nightmare, but I can't remember it now. Marj says that's pretty normal, though."

"Eland was out of it, too."

"If he's like me, he'll feel like he hit the spiced wine way too hard."

Bear sounds frustrated, like he's mad he couldn't wrestle his nightmare to the ground and declare victory. I know how he feels. I have a few I'd like to conquer myself. I hope this doesn't add one more bad dream to Eland's list, but it probably will.

As if on cue, my brother stirs and tries to speak. His voice still sounds slurred, but whether it's from sleep or disorientation, I can't be sure. I hurry to his side. He stiffens when I touch him, so I run my hand gently up and down his arm and murmur, trying not to alarm him.

"You're okay. You're safe. You made it to the caves."

"I did?" He sounds weak, but gratified.

I hug him. "You did. How do you feel?"

"Hungry and thirsty." I help him sit up. "*Ow*, and my head hurts."

"Tell me about it." Bear comes over. "Here, drink some water. Heard you had quite the adventure out there."

My hand tightens on Eland's arm, and I shake my head slightly, trying to give him a silent warning not to tell Bear too much. We need to talk first, given the lies I smeared around the caves like crampberries last night.

"Yeah, it was," Eland says. He must have gotten the message, but when did he learn to lie so smoothly? "Where is everyone? How long have I been out?"

Bear fills Eland in as he eats and drinks. I make sure he finishes the water before I allow him to try to stand up.

"My head still hurts, but it's okay," Eland says, shaking me off. "Let's go home. It's creepy in here when no one's around. And freezing." Like most Groundlings, the caves are probably his least favorite place. Bad memories are etched into the rock walls like the ancient drawings of humans and animals we've occasionally found.

"Good call," Bear agrees.

I scoff. "Wimps."

We move across the main cavern, our footsteps bouncing through the space. Bear repositions himself to walk between Eland and I, probably so he can support him if he has any lingering weakness. Or maybe in case I do. Eland seems okay despite the headache, joking about how the caves smell better. It's true; the smoke from the fire drove out the foul human-waste scents.

We reach the cave mouth. The rain is still pelting, so we make a break for it to our shelter. I hang on to Bear's arm as my feet squish through the mud on the path. We're all panting and laughing by the time we get there. We crash inside, landing in a heap on the floor. Bear hauls us up.

I catch a familiar scent in the air and my heart springs into my mouth.

"Peree!" Eland chirps.

"Hey there, little brother." His voice is warm but cautious.

I reach out for him. I probably resemble some kind of half-drowned ground animal recently ejected from its muddy home, but he doesn't seem to care.

"Hey, you," he whispers, his lips brushing my ear.

I turn my face up to him for a kiss before remembering that Bear must be watching us. He'll have to get used to this, if we're going to be friends, but the chance of us all *becoming* friends might be greater if I don't push him too far, too fast. I pull back a hand's length, which is as far away from him as I can stand.

"Hello, *Peree*." Bear emphasizes the name a little, as if to prove he was listening to me earlier. His voice is surprisingly pleasant.

"Bear," Peree responds. His tone is a lot more horizontal. Then again, he's probably been really worried. He wasn't expecting us to come tumbling in, laughing madly, with Bear in tow.

"When did you . . ." I stop, not wanting to mention the illegal hunting trip in front of Bear. "How long have you been here?"

"I was watching after the sick ones left, but I didn't see you or Eland come out of the caves with the others. I snuck down after everyone went inside." He runs his hand through my dripping hair. "I would've checked the caves, but the guards were keeping a close eye on the entrance."

"Guards?" I ask.

"In the trees and on the ground. I was told by pretty much everyone—my people and yours . . . in no uncertain terms—that I wasn't welcome down here." I can tell from his tone that he took that as a challenge rather than a directive to be obeyed. "Petrel's covering for me at home. I had to create a bit of a distraction to get past the guard down here. It helped that she kept ducking back inside her shelter to get out of the rain."

"What if they catch you?" I say, anxiety sparring with pleasure that he's here. "You shouldn't have come."

"Yeah, I should have." His voice flattens again. "I told you, Fenn. I'm not going to let them keep us apart."

His words pulse with all the frightening intensity I've heard in his voice before. I rest my hand on his chest and nod.

"I guess I'll head home now." Bear sounds like he'd rather be anywhere else than watching this.

I turn to face him. If I could stitch a permanent apology to my lips, I might have done it. "Thank you for everything, Bear. And please don't mention that you saw Per—"

"C'mon, Fenn. Give me some credit." The door doesn't exactly slam behind him, but it's not far off. I sigh. Peree sits on my bed, pulling me into his lap.

I struggle to stand again. "Wait, I'll get you all wet."

"I couldn't care less," he says. I put my head on his shoulder, savoring the closeness, but I'm shivering with cold within seconds. "Okay, maybe you should change first."

Eland's way ahead of me. I guess he's not shy about stripping down in front of Peree, because he's into a dry set of clothes in no time. But I'm not so bold. As usual, Peree notices my problem. He sets me on my feet and moves away.

"Take a look at these, Eland. I made them for you. Had some time on my hands." They must be arrows, given Eland's enthusiasm and the stream of technical questions about shaft lengths and fletchings.

Assuming they've turned their backs by now, I grab my extra set of clothes out of the basket in the corner that Acacia wove for us years ago. Aloe's extra clothes are still in here, too. I wish they fit me.

I'm sure another woman would be very happy to have them; I just can't bring myself to part with them yet. I know it's silly to be so senti-mental about clothes, but hanging on to the bits and pieces of Aloe helps me feel like she's not quite so lost. Or maybe that I'm not.

I quickly scrub as much of the mud off my face and body as I can with my sopping clothes, and let them fall in a pile around my feet. I'm wiggling into my blessedly dry underclothes when the unthinkable happens, at least to a fairly-modest, mostly-naked girl—the door opens.

CHAPTER NINE

I almost scream, but I stop myself at the last second. I don't want to draw attention to our shelter with Peree here.

"Well, *this* is interesting," a male voice says.

"Moray! Get *out* of here!" I hiss.

I scuttle behind the washstand and spread my dry clothes against me, trying—and failing—to cover all of me at once. My whole body burns like a spicy pepper from the garden. *Doesn't anyone knock anymore?*

Peree steps between Moray and me. "You heard her. Go. Now." His voice is so menacing, it's unrecognizable.

"Take your own advice, Lofty. Rain's stopping, and I doubt you want to be seen down here right now. Sorry to interrupt whatever you three were up to," he says suggestively, "but I have business with Fennel."

"Don't be disgusting, Moray!" I say. "Go outside, or at least turn around, and let me get dressed. Then we can talk."

"Wait—you *want* to talk to this low life?" Peree asks.

"Not really, but I promised I would."

"I'm not talking with him here," Moray says.

"I'm not talking at all until I can get dressed without an audience," I huff. "So all of you out! Except you, Peree. He's right; you can't risk being seen."

"I'm going, I'm going," Eland says, chortling. "But I'll be right back. I'm not missing this."

"I'll count to thirty, sweetheart," Moray says, "then I'm coming back in. Looking good, by the way."

"Get out!" Peree and I bark together. "And stop calling me that!" I add.

The door finally closes.

I can't tell who's fuming more, Peree or me, as I hurry into my clothes.

"What does he want?" he asks, as I, finally fully covered, try to locate my lost dignity. I know it was around here somewhere.

"You'll find out in about ten seconds," I grumble.

This was not how I imagined this conversation with Moray starting out. But having Peree here is better than talking to him alone. I don't trust him any farther than I can budge him.

"Ready or not, here I come." Moray pushes his way back in.

"He only counted to twenty." Eland follows him.

Peree must have been lying in wait, because I hear a short scuffle.

"Listen, Groundling." If Peree's voice drops any lower, he'll be picking it up off the floor. "Fennel told me what you did to her. Nothing like that will ever happen again. Got it? Keep your hands off her and a respectful tongue in your mouth."

"Or what?" Moray asks.

"Or next time, she'll bite it all the way off," Peree says smoothly. Eland snickers, but I know I'll face his questions later about what exactly happened with Moray.

"Enough," I say. "Everyone take a seat, and we can have a civil discussion like the adults most of us are supposed to be now."

I sit on my pallet, primly covering my knees with my dress. Peree hovers beside me.

Eland jumps onto his pallet.

Moray doesn't move. "I don't want the Lofty here."

"You don't have a choice, Groundling," Peree says.

"Apparently you two haven't been introduced," I say. "Moray, Peree. Peree, Moray. Now you can call each other by your proper names."

Moray thumps into a chair in the corner. "Give me the message."

"Congratulations," Eland says quickly. "You're going to be a father."

Silence. "What did you say?"

I so wish I could see Moray's face at that moment, but hearing his voice is pretty good, too. He sounds strangled, like he's been kicked between the legs.

"We met your Lofty friend," I say. "Nice girl."

"Wonder what she saw in you," Eland mutters.

"When was this? Who was it?" Peree sounds stunned and sort of amused, probably reacting to whatever he sees on Moray's face.

I shrug. "She wouldn't tell us her name."

"What else did she say?" Moray's voice is already almost nonchalant. Can't shock this one for long.

"She said to meet her by the water hole as soon as the sick ones leave."

"At the *usual* time," Eland says.

Moray jumps out of his chair. "Don't tell anyone else."

"*Please,*" Peree says.

"What?" Moray asks, a little irritably.

"*Please* don't tell anyone else."

"*Please* don't tell anyone or I might have to let it slip to the Three that you were down here today without their permission. How's that sound, Lofty?" Moray asks.

I stand. "Listen, your friend saved our lives, and we promised to deliver her message to you. I don't want to get any more involved in your business than I have to. We'll keep your secret if you keep ours. Don't tell anyone you saw Peree here."

"*Please,*" Eland adds. I frown at him.

"Okay . . . you got a deal," Moray drawls. "Looks like we're in bed together after all, sweetheart, one way or another."

He chuckles as he leaves. Peree drags the chair in front of the door, mumbling about keeping out other unwelcome visitors. I flop onto my pallet, the stress of the last ten minutes catching up to me.

He sits down beside me. "What happened? All I know is Petrel plucked Eland off a tree and brought you up, then you both disappeared."

I tell him the whole story from the whispered threat and the fire, to our frightening dash into the caves. Eland chimes in from time to time, telling him Aloe's message about the Three, and describing how our Lofty girl-guide looked. When he says her hair is so blond it's almost white, Peree thinks he might know who it is. A young girl named Frost. Too young to be partnered with another Lofty, much less to be sneaking off with much older Groundlings.

Moray should be in more trouble than he knows what to do with if the Covey and the Three find out, but based on my own experience, he'll find a way to weasel out of any serious consequences.

"Petrel and Moon didn't know any of that," Peree says. "Moon had a bit of a scare, and you two were gone by the time they got back home. They felt terrible."

"A scare?" I ask.

"Apparently she couldn't feel the hatchling move during all the excitement with the fire in the trees. They're fine now."

I can't help giggling. Eland snickers, too. "*Hatchling?*"

"That's what we call them before they, well, hatch." He sounds defensive. "What do you call 'em?"

"Babies." I laugh.

"Totally uninspired."

"And yet accurate. Anyway, I'm glad they're okay." I lie back. He slides my head into his lap. "So what do we do now? We're getting further away from our goals every day. The Confluence is falling apart."

"You know what we have to do, Fenn. Go to Koolkuna. It's not safe here for you anymore. Or for Eland," Peree says pointedly.

"I know. You're right. But our people . . ."

"Our people are showing us daily that they weren't worth coming back for." His voice is rock hard.

"I can't believe that. Not all of them. There *are* good people here, they're just scared and confused."

"Fennel—at the Feast of Deliverance, I told you you're my whole world now. My past, present, and future, remember? The rest was your agenda."

I snap upright. "My *agenda*? What's that supposed to mean?"

"I mean it was what you wanted. Not me."

Eland shifts on his bed. "Um, should I leave?"

"No, Eland. I want you to hear this," Peree says. "Your sister's everything to me. And you're everything to her. Which makes you pretty important to me, too. I need to know you're both safe, and I want to be with you. That's *my* agenda. If I can't accomplish it in this place, then I want us to go to Koolkuna. It's as simple as that."

I'm flustered Peree is saying all this in front of Eland, but I'm touched by his words.

"Is it as simple as that, though?" I ask him gently. "What about Moon and Petrel, and their, er, hatchling? And Breeze?"

"You two are my family now," Peree says. "And my family is most important."

How can I argue with that? I cup his face in my hands and kiss him, maybe a little too enthusiastically.

"Wow, you guys are gross. I feel a little sick," Eland says. He pretends to retch.

Peree laughs. "Watch and learn, brother. You'll need these skills before long."

I take Peree's hand in a chaste handshake. "Compromise?"

"I'm listening," he says.

"We'll go. But we need a few days to get organized. To collect the food and supplies we need? We'll tell a few people we're leaving—a *few*, Eland—and find out who might want to go. I'll bet it'll be more than you think."

"And what if the Three find out?" Eland asks.

"Or the Covey," Peree adds.

"That's a risk we'll have to take."

I know what Aloe said, but I can't believe Fox would allow Eland or me to be harmed. It doesn't fit with what I know to be true about him: that he's a good man who treated us well all our lives. Maybe I'm naïve to still believe that.

"I doubt they'll be happy about it if they find out, but what can they do to stop us, if enough people really want to go?" I ask .

"Seriously, Fenn," Peree says, concern strong in his voice. "You both need to be careful."

He doesn't need to remind me of that. I know I may be making a huge mistake. But I have a dream of delivering on my promise of a peaceful home for our people to share, and I've fought too hard to give up on it now.

The trees exhale as I crouch in the forest after the rain. Their moist, scented breath covers my skin like an herbal poultice. I'm gathering dry kindling with Calli to make a bonfire. It's not an easy job after so much rain. We would've had more firewood stored up if the Lofties had allowed us to cut down more trees.

Calli's nearby, chattering about spending the afternoon with Cricket and his family. Calli and Cricket still have both their parents. It's unusual among Groundlings. Lofties, too, from what Peree has told me. Between the sick ones, accidents, illness, and occasional violence, the forest has never been an easy place to live.

The Lofties are on the move above us. I hear their footsteps and the sounds of sawing on the walkways. It's too muffled to make out much else.

I wonder what Peree's doing now. He managed to get back into the trees without being spotted by the guards, although Eland said it was close. Peree's distinctive honeysuckle taste lingers on my lips from when he kissed me goodbye. I hate that he had to go.

I stand up and stretch, then balance on one foot, gently rotating the ankle I sprained when Moray pushed me into the pit. My body feels closer to normal, but I still bear the aches and pains of our search for the Waters.

"Fenn. You're not listening," Calli says.

"Sorry, what were you saying?"

"I asked if you'd met up with Peree since the fires. I know he's not supposed to come down now," her voice turns teasing, "but I didn't think that would stop you two for long."

I try not to be suspicious. Is Calli asking as my best friend? Or as an informant for her father and the Three?

"No, I haven't." My voice is even. I need to lie convincingly.

"Can't be too bad. You're still wearing his bird thingy around your neck."

I touch my necklace, recalling the feeling of his hand covering it in farewell. "I hate this. I miss being with him, Calli." I might have to lie about other things, but I can tell her the truth about my feelings.

"Why?"

My laugh is incredulous. "What do you mean, why? I *love* him."

"No, I mean what is it about him that you miss?" She sounds serious now. "I told you I'm trying to understand your choice, but it's . . . hard. How is being with him better than it would have been if you'd chosen Bear? You still could, you know. He would partner with you in a heartbeat."

I lean against a tree, and Calli moves closer. Water drips from the branches in a staccato rhythm around us; I'm almost as wet as I would be if it actually was raining.

The *anuna* sing when it rains in Koolkuna, offering thanks for the life-giving water. All *our* water seems to give us is blindness. It's like the story Peree told me about the sighted man who wanders into the valley of the blind. It's our story, only in reverse. Everyone here might be able to see, except me, but they can't seem to understand anything outside the realm of their own experience. At least Calli is trying to understand.

"I love Bear as a friend," I say. "I always have. But how I feel about Peree is different. Of course I think he's wonderful—thoughtful, kind, strong . . . and sort of sulky sometimes—but there's more to it than the things I love about him." I struggle to put my feelings into words without sounding supercilious.

"Choosing him represents something bigger. Something I want more than only a partner. I'm choosing a new way of life with Peree. If I partnered with Bear, it would feel like accepting the way things were before I found Koolkuna: fearing the Scourge, tolerating the Exchange, hating the Lofties without question. I can't do that now, Calli."

"You wouldn't have to go back to the way things were. Things *are* changing. I've heard Father and Mother talking. Before the fires the Confluence was already discussing getting rid of the Exchange. The Three aren't going to let things go back to the way they were, not exactly. But partnering with a Lofty . . . ." She stops, as if she might be going too far.

"Tell me, Calli. I want to know how you feel; you're my oldest and best friend. It's been too long since we really talked. Nothing you say can make me not care about you. "

"It's only that . . . you partnering with a Lofty . . . it's like saying that everything they've done to us over the years, the way they looked down on us—that it doesn't matter to you." She talks fast, stumbling over her words. "It's like Peree is more important to you than us. I mean, I'm not saying that's what *I* think, but that's kind of how it looks."

Her words sting. After everything I've tried to do to help my people, they don't think they're *important* to me? I try to stay calm.

"I can't help how it looks. I have to do what I think is right and be true to my feelings. I love Peree, and I'm going to partner with him. I want our people to believe that the Lofties aren't all heartless and cruel like we've always thought—and our people aren't always blameless. I mean, look at Adder. Human life didn't mean a whole lot to him—at least the lives of those he saw as different from him."

"Adder was crazy. The Council is different now. Fox, Pinion, and Bream will handle this crisis with the Lofties and find a way to work with them."

I'm not so sure about that, but her confidence in her father is understandable. "Fox is a good man. I know he wants what he thinks is best for us."

"That's what I want for you, too," she says. "I worry you're making a mistake."

I go to her then and wrap my arms around her. "Peree and I are supposed to be together. If I'm sure about anything, it's that."

"I hope you're right." She turns me around and quickly whips my damp, stringy hair into a loose knot. "At least he's not hard on the eyes. Except for all that blond hair and the feathers and everything."

"That doesn't mean anything to me. Sometimes I wish he *wasn't* good looking. He attracted a little too much female attention in Koolkuna."

"You aren't the jealous type, are you?" Calli teases.

"I didn't think I was until I met him. Now I'm not so sure." I pick up my basket and reach for her hand. "Sit with me at the meeting?"

"Of course. We've got to stick together. Plus I'm still playing hard to get with Cricket. I already spent the morning with him; I can't spend all evening with him, too."

"Poor guy. He has no clue what he's in for."

She swings our hands between us as we walk back toward the clearing. "I have to keep him on his toes."

I snicker. "At least he'll be taller then, right?"

She sighs dramatically. "If only." A moment later she stops us. I feel her bend down next to me as she lets go of my hand. "Huh."

"What is it?"

"A feather."

That's not so strange. Animals may be scarce on the forest floor, but birds flourish in the trees. They're a mainstay of the Lofties' diet. "What kind of feather?"

"That's just it. I've never seen one like it. It's colorful . . . I mean, *really* colorful, like red and orange and green. I'd like to see the bird this came from. It probably poops rainbows." She puts it in my hand. "Give it to your Lofty. It'll look so pretty in his hair." She's joking, but for the first time I don't feel like her humor is a thin cover for her anger.

I hope our talk brought us back a little closer to normal. Best friends. Partners in crime.

But I don't know if it's really possible now after everything that's happened, after all of my choices and hers, and all that could still happen before I leave, maybe forever, for Koolkuna.

CHAPTER TEN

I bounce my legs in front of me. They're stiff from sitting through the meal, and now the meeting, in the brisk evening air. At least I have a relatively full stomach, and the fire is warm and comforting.

I watch the firelight frisk against my perpetual darkness. I asked Marj why the contrast of light and dark is the only thing I can sort of see. She speculated it's because I was sighted, for however short a time, before the Three took my vision. The perception of light was all they left. Thinking about it makes me bitter, but then I remember Nerang's gentle reminder that being Sightless has also forced me to be strong. I need that strength now.

Bream is doing his best to make a quick meeting long, drawn out, and skull-crushingly boring. He's going on about the progress made by the Confluence. Or lack of it.

"The Council will get to the bottom of who set the fire in the cave and threatened one of our young people," Bream is saying. "Lofty aggression, while certainly having roots in our shared history of mistrust . . ." he stops to clear his voice and blow his nose, prompting a low, "Oh, for the love of—" from Calli, who's sitting beside me, " . . . is a clear indication of their blatant disregard for our rules and mutual agreements to honor the boundaries of our respective territories. It cannot be tolerated. Of course, this is not the first time the Lofties—"

"Yes, yes, Bream," Vole says. "We know all about the Lofties and their aggression. The question is what the Council plans to do about it?" The crowd murmurs its agreement.

"And what about the fires?" someone else calls out. "Who set them?"

"These are certainly serious questions," Pinion says. " I'm assuming no one wants to admit to setting one or both of the fires?" Silence. "Then I suggest we start with a discussion of how to proceed with the Lofties. The Confluence is indeed in jeopardy. There's no use pretending otherwise. The Lofties will be at least as suspicious of us as we are of them. We don't know yet how they will respond. But do we want to continue our talks with them? What is the will of the people?"

There are sounds of confusion around me. The Three never ask what to do, they tell. This is encouraging, at least to me.

"I've said from the beginning they can't be trusted." It's Thistle, Moray's horrible, meddling mother. I want to stick my fingers in my ears to shut out her piercing voice. "And those who befriend them can't be trusted either." I bristle, but stay silent. "This talk of negotiations and Convergences hasn't gotten us anywhere. The only thing the Lofties pay attention to is action. Words do no good with them. It's like talking to a young child. In one ear and out the other."

"Maybe they're mentally deficient," a woman jokes.

"We already knew that," Moray says. Others laugh.

"Please stay on task," Fox interrupts. "The Council has decided to try a new approach by asking for your thoughts and opinions . . . don't make us regret it." He says the last with his usual humor, getting a few more chuckles.

My first thought is to speak up and encourage cooperation with the Lofties, but I don't. I'd be dismissed as only interested in defending my partner and his people. I need to lay low, find out where this will go.

"I have every reason to hate the Lofties." It's a woman called Ivy.

Her voice is normally high and breezy. Tonight it sinks under all the suffering of the last few weeks. Her partner was killed in the Reckoning, leaving her with a young daughter, Dahlia, to raise. "But isn't this an opportunity? If we work with them, maybe their lookouts would give us more warning when the Scourge comes, or we might get permission to cut down more trees for wood. Or maybe," she pauses, "maybe we could do away with the Exchange."

Her words garner a smattering of claps.

"But will they even consider working with us now? What's your sense, Fox?" someone asks.

"Weren't the fires answer enough?" Thistle says sharply. "They don't want to have anything to do with us, any more than we do."

"Speak for yourself, Thistle," Vole says. "Ivy has a point. We could benefit from developing better relations with the Lofties. And what about the other goal of the Confluence, to talk about what Fennel told us about the water, what the Scourge really is, and this Kookoony place she found?"

Thistle's dismissive laughter is more of a bark. "Are we going to blindly accept what Fennel tells us? We have no proof that this magical place exists."

"Why would Fenn lie, Thistle?" Bear sounds annoyed.

"She's a *Lofty* lover. Bear, you of all people should know she's capable of betrayal."

"She didn't betray me," he mutters. I close my eyes, tamping down my anger and embarrassment.

Fox clears his throat. "Yes, well, perhaps the water and Koolkuna are subjects best left for another time."

I wait for someone to press them to talk about it. From the uncomfortable shifting and muttering around me, the subject of the poisoned water and the possibility that we all might be delusional about the Scourge are even more difficult topics than how to handle the Lofties.

It reminds me of something Aloe used to say: *Better the devil you know than the devil you don't.* The Lofties and the Scourge might be devils, but at least they're familiar devils. Giving up a belief you've held close all your life, a belief that shapes how you live in your world, and embracing something new, is even more frightening.

"Why not discuss it now?" I ask. I can't help it. I have to try one more time before Peree and I pick up and leave. "If we went to Koolkuna, we'd be leaving the problems with the Lofties behind." I hope Peree and Kadee will convince at least some of the Lofties to go, too, but pointing that out now wouldn't be terribly helpful. "When I was sent to the Hidden Waters, I thought the idea was to find somewhere we could go that would be safe from the Scourge. I accomplished that. What's stopping us from leaving, other than our fears? Why are we wasting all this time? We could already be there."

"Spoken like a true heroine," Fox says. "Your journey to the Waters clearly gave you a taste for adventure." His voice is warm, almost paternal, but also condescending. It grates on me.

"Not to mention a taste for Lofty men," Moray says.

"Leave my intended out of this." I face the people and raise my hand, palm up, in a pleading gesture. "Just reacting to this latest crisis isn't our only option. If the Three want our opinions, then let's discuss going to Koolkuna."

"Fennel, we need time to process all that you told us about the Hidden Waters, the Scourge, and this village you found," Pinion says. "And with the recent events—"

"How much time?" I snap. "I mean, I'm just asking. A day? A moon? Until the next Exchange? Ask your questions. I'll tell you anything you want to know."

"Here's one," someone says. "Why do you want to have a relationship with a Lofty after everything that's happened? You lost your mother in the Reckoning, after all."

I'm about to angrily remind them that a Groundling spear, not a Lofty arrow, killed Aloe, but I'm distracted by a new voice.

"Fenn asked us to leave her intended out of it," Calli says, sounding nervous, but determined. I'm surprised she's publicly taking my side. "I think we should respect her wishes. Her relationship with him isn't what we're meeting to talk about, right?"

"Here, here," says Bear from around the other side of the fire. "I want to know more about Koolkuna and how it's protected."

I throw them both a grateful smile. My friends' support means more to me than I can tell them with words. I grab the opportunity they created for me with both hands.

I explain again about how the pure waters of the Myuna protect the *anuna*, the people of Koolkuna. I talk about the easy wonders of life there. With my words, I try to paint a graceful portrait of how our lives could be there. Not perfect, but better than here. Patiently, I answer my people's questions.

Thistle, Moray, and a few others heckle me once or twice, but the majority seems honestly curious about what I have to say. I can tell they aren't quite able to bring themselves to believe me, but they listen. And that was all I asked.

"So we can just pick up and go live there?" Vole asks. He sounds cautious, but optimistic.

"Yes," I respond. "The *anuna* are a generous people."

Thistle cackles. "No one is that generous. Anyone who thinks otherwise is just as mad as Fennel."

I don't respond. Arguing with Thistle won't get me anywhere. And I have no desire to persuade her to come to Koolkuna, anyway.

"Well," Pinion says. "You've given us a lot to think about." Her tone tells me my time is up.

I sit, wondering if there was something more I could have said, one more argument I could have made in favor of the whole group going to Koolkuna. I'm not sure what it would be. I guess it's up to them to decide now.

The meeting ends soon after. People begin moving toward their shelters, and bed. Bream speaks to me as I get to my feet.

"It turned out to be a nice evening after the rain, didn't it?" His voice is unusually wheezy, like he's sickening. He pauses, waiting while others around us move off. "With the weather changing, the Council requests that you to continue to prepare the caves. It may not be long before the Scourge returns."

I'm not surprised at their order. The cooler evening breezes whisper of the approach of autumn. The scent of the greenheart trees has intensified, too, as if they're gathering themselves up, bundling in preparation for the coming of winter. The sick ones do come more often in the colder weather, probably because of the scarcity of food. It must add to their misery even more than it adds to ours.

"While we require and appreciate your efforts in the caves," he continues, "we also feel it is too dangerous for you to work alone now. There was the fire. And the threats, of course, and—"

"I remember." I cut him off before he wanders off topic.

"Yes, well. The Council feels it would be prudent to assign someone to accompany you to the caves. We asked for a volunteer. He will help you with your work, and he has agreed to provide protection."

It must be Bear. That's not going to work. I already begged him to keep a close eye on Eland. It was a lot to ask given all that's unresolved between us, but he agreed without hesitation. He can't watch Eland if he's in the caves with me.

"I'll be fine, Bream. Thanks anyway. Tell Bear he's off the hook."

Bream coughs. "Bear is not the volunteer. Moray will accompany you."

My hands clench into fists at my sides. He can't be serious.

"We understand there was trouble between you and Moray before the Reckoning. However, he has assured us that he has only your best interests at heart now. He would like to make amends for his past mistakes, and he certainly has the physical ability protect you."

Moray herded me through the caves, my hands tied behind my back. He forced himself on me, punched me after I bit his tongue, and threw me into the pit fully expecting I would die there. His family threatened my brother, and they may have been behind Aloe's murder.

I explode.

"My *best interests*? Are you kidding? Are the Three actively trying to get rid of me?"

"Please calm yourself, Fennel. We have no such intentions. As you know, putting differences behind us is essential for the well-being of our community. Our hope is that with this arrangement you and Moray will be able to work things out between you. He understands there will be consequences for any future ill-considered behavior—"

"*Ill-considered behavior*?" They act like he was being a naughty little boy when he attacked me.

Bream ignores my outburst. "If any Lofties are found on the ground, Moray has the authority to do what he must to protect you, our people, and our homes. He will restrain the person and bring him to us for questioning . . . and appropriate punishment. We will not tolerate a Lofty being in our territory without permission. Is that understood?"

I nod stiffly. So that was the real message the Three wanted to give me: stay away from Peree or we'll punish *him*.

I understand all right. And I don't like it one bit.

I wend my way stiffly toward our shelter, leaving Bream and the waning flicker of firelight behind me.

I understand why the Three feel they need someone who will tell them what I'm up to, someone who isn't aligned with me. I haven't exactly followed orders lately. But I can't believe they assigned *Moray* to watch me. They must not care about me or my safety at all. Even Fox, the closest thing I've had to a father. Sadness soaks me to the core.

Someone slips up to me—Eland. I keep walking, too distracted to reach out my hand to him like I usually would. He falls a step behind.

"Do you want to be alone?" he asks.

I take a long, conscious breath to slow the throbbing in my chest and head. "Of course not."

I hook my arm through his and we cross the spongy ground together.

I pull the chair in front of the door as we go in. I really don't want to speak to anyone else tonight. I climb onto my pallet, exhausted, and lie huddled up, as far away from the wall as I can get. The mingling scents of damp wood tinged with mold and animal blood depresses me more.

I give up. I'm ready to leave for Koolkuna. Now. Tonight.

Why wasn't I ready after I found out the Three blinded me as a child? Or when I was thrown into a pit? Or when Aloe and Shrike were killed? Or after the fires? Why weren't dead animals spiked to my wall enough of a hint for me? Why has it taken me this long to give up on my people?

Eland shifts on his pallet.

"Tell me something, E. Do you want to go to Koolkuna? Or do you want to stay here?"

He doesn't hesitate. "I want to be where you are."

His simple devotion brings tears to my eyes. "That's it then. As soon as I can talk to Peree, we'll leave. Just the three of us. Are you okay with that?"

"Yeah." He sounds . . . resigned.

"I'm sorry things are turning out this way. It isn't what I wanted."

Eland doesn't say anything for a minute. "I wonder what Mother would have done. Do you think she would've gone? Or stayed here?"

"I don't know."

But I do know. I just don't want to think about it, because it forces me to compare my choices to hers. Aloe would've thought it was her duty to stay and serve on the Council as long as the majority of the people wanted to stay. Even if it wasn't what she wanted.

Eland says, "If she didn't go, I would've had to choose between staying here with her or going with you. I'm glad I don't have to do that."

"We never would have made you do that. If Aloe was still here . . . everything would be different."

I don't really believe that. I doubt Eland believes it, either. It was never going to be easy, with or without Aloe.

Eland's breath slows and deepens, but I can't fall asleep.

He didn't say he wanted to go to Koolkuna. What he said was he wanted to be with *me*. That's not the same thing. I'm tearing my brother away from his home and his people, everyone and everything he's ever known, right after he lost his mother. All so I can be with Peree. I punch my lumpy pallet.

No, that's not true. This isn't only about being with Peree. I wouldn't make Eland go if I didn't believe he would have a better life in Koolkuna. I want him to grow up in a safe place with people who support—even encourage—differences of opinion. I have to believe I'm taking him away for the right reasons, really believe it, or I can't go through with this.

In the meantime, I steel myself for the task of severing the threads that bind me to my home and my people. I lie there well into the night, listening to the mournful calls of the doves, as one by one the stitches pull free. And I bleed and bleed and bleed.

CHAPTER ELEVEN

Before he went back up to the trees, Peree told me he'd come to the caves to see me while I'm working. It's too dangerous now, but I don't have any way to warn him off. Plus I need to speak to him. We need to plan when and how we're leaving.

I feel stiff and crumpled, like a rag left to dry in the sun after my sleepless night. But I'm prepared to tell him that Eland and I are ready to go now.

People flit in and out of the clearing around me as I eat breakfast. I barely acknowledge their occasional greetings, continuing the painful task of distancing myself that I began the night before.

I hear Moray sitting near by, whistling off-key. The sound sets my teeth on edge.

The obvious response is for me to refuse to work. I should go home and lock myself in. Or stay all day in the clearing where Moray can't possibly touch me. But the caves are the best chance I have to talk with Peree.

I head that direction, struggling with what to do. I can't go in the caves with Moray. That would be insane. Maybe if we were outside, Peree would see us and guess what's happening. I stop outside the entrance and, hands on hips, turn to face Moray. My fingers twitch, wanting to dip into my pocket where Peree's knife lurks. I'm feeling pretty happy he insisted I keep it with me after the Reckoning.

"The Three want you to keep an eye on me. Fine. But let's get one thing straight: if you put anything *else* on me, I'll tell everyone about your Lofty friend. I mean it. If even one finger strays where it doesn't belong, I'll spill my guts." I wince at my own choice of words. Yeah, I'm real scary.

"Ouch, Fennel. That hurts," he says with no trace of emotion in his voice. Unless you count sarcasm. "How will I ever live it down if you tell everyone my little secret?"

My lips form a thin smile, as thin as the blade of my hidden knife. "Look at how people are treating Peree and me—and *we're* trying to do things the right way. People won't take it well that you messed around with a Lofty girl. Especially your mother, with all her talk about Lofty lovers. Gives that term a new meaning doesn't it?"

Moray comes so close I can feel the warmth of his overly muscled body. This is stupid; he's much stronger than me. Fighting Moray would be like a mouse taking on a hawk. Sweat trickles down my back.

"You're hot when you're threatening me. Know that, sweetheart?"

My hand dives into my pocket, tugging out the knife. I step back and hold it between us. "Back off, Moray. I mean it."

"Okay, now you're *trying* to turn me on." He plucks the knife out of my hand. "Sorry, but I can't let you keep this. Might have an accident and cut off one of your pretty little body parts. Don't play the tough girl, Fenn; it's not your style."

I'm dismayed that he disarmed me so easily. At the same time I realize his voice has changed a little. It's warmer than usual, and he actually used my real name. Maybe I disarmed him a little, too. I hold up my hands.

"Convince me I don't need to worry about being alone with you."

He snorts. "Get over yourself. I'm not going to touch you. Look— what happened before with us . . . I saw an opportunity. Simple as that." He doesn't sound contrite. He sounds horribly matter-of-fact. "What can I say, sweetheart? We're not all heroes. Deal with it."

Unbelievable. "How can I be sure you won't see another *opportunity*?"

"I told you before. I don't want to come second to Bear. That goes double for a Lofty. And, frankly, you aren't really my type."

"I'm glad to hear it." I pause. "I want my knife back."

"Nope."

"I'm only going in there with you if you give it back." Wait, am I really thinking about going in there with him? Have I lost my mind?

"So demanding. Here you go, then." He slaps it hilt-first into my hand. "It's not like I have anything to worry about. You don't have a clue how to handle a blade. You're more likely to cut your own throat than mine."

I hate to admit it, but he's probably right. I wave the knife at him anyway. "I'm trusting you."

He steps in until the solid bulk of his torso meets the sharp tip of the knife. Then he leans even closer, so close that I hear the cloth of his shirt give way with a soft pop.

He chortles loudly, startling me. "C'mon, sweetheart. Time for you to work and for me to watch you."

I take a settling breath. There are few things I can trust anymore. My instincts have to be one of them. I pocket the knife and enter the cave behind Moray, hoping I'm not making the worst mistake of my life.

He's doubly true to his word. He doesn't touch me . . . and he sits and watches me do all the work.

I move around the storeroom, cleaning up and preparing the shelves for more supplies after the community's short-but-messy stay. Moray lies around, whistling again. He manages to make the act of blowing air through his lips irritating. I start up a conversation just to get him to stop.

"So—did you ever talk to your Lofty friend?" I ask. "What did you two decide to do?"

"None of your business."

Funny, that's what she said, too. "Fair enough." At least he's not whistling now.

I cast around for another topic of conversation. I really don't know much about him except that he and Bear hate each other's guts. I never had much to do with Thistle or her family until the last few months.

"What's your brother's name, Moray? Not Cuda. The other one. I can never remember it."

"We're being all chummy now? Okay, I'll play. It's Conda."

"Aren't they doubles?" I teeter on my toes, lifting an unwieldy basket onto a shelf over my head. A little help would be nice, not that I'm expecting to get it.

"Yep, look exactly the same. Two identical lumps of rock. Almost killed Thistle to push 'em out. She was bleeding and screaming like a fleshie."

Dust trails from the shelf into my upturned eyes. I stop to rub them. "You remember that? How old were you?"

"About five."

"You must have been scared. Where was your father?"

"Inside a bottle, probably. That's where he usually was."

I vaguely remember Thistle's partner. His voice was husky and loud; it frightened me. Come to think of it, he did smell like alcohol a lot. He died a few years ago. "Do you miss him?"

"What's to miss?"

I wish I could say I hear a pause, or a note of vulnerability, or sadness, or *something* in his voice, but there's nothing. It's flat, emotionless.

"Enough questions about me," he says. "I want to hear more about that Koolkuna place." He sounds like he has a mouthful of food.

"Hey, those are supplies, not snacks!"

"I'm hungry. Don't tell me you never sat in here and helped yourself to the food. No one would have even known."

"No, I didn't. Because then someone else might have gone hungry when the sick ones came. Not that it matters to you." I grab a basket and slide it toward him. "If you're going to eat, then you're going to help. Here, put this on that shelf." I point to the one I mean.

"Damn, you're bossy." But he does what I asked. I decide to find out how far I can take it.

"And these can go up there, too." I gesture at a few other bundles I carried in from the main cavern. I hide my astonishment when he does what I said. "Listen, I'll make you a deal. If you help me carry some stuff in and put it away, I'll tell you about Koolkuna."

"Don't push your luck. I didn't sign up for manual labor. This is guard duty only."

I blow warm air on my hands. They're slowly freezing from the fingertips down, like ten mini icicles. "C'mon, Mr. Helpful."

We go back to the cave entrance and gather a new load of supplies. I get the feeling Moray could carry a lot more if he wanted to, but at least he's working. So I keep my side of the bargain. I talk to him about Koolkuna. I'm afraid of making it sound too good. The last thing our friends there need is Moray showing up. Talk about ruining a good thing. He doesn't say much as I talk. I don't even know if he's listening. At least he doesn't whistle.

I'm describing the Hidden Waters, the underground river that almost killed Peree and me, as we enter the storeroom with the last load. I'm so wrapped up in the memory of the powerful rush of water; it almost doesn't surprise me when Moray shoves me against the wall. He traps my body with his bulk, his hand over my mouth. It's like being crushed by a living, breathing rockslide.

My heart backflips into my throat. *Not again.* I yank my knife out again, but it catches on my pocket. I struggle to free it.

When it comes right down to it, using a deadly weapon on someone—even when that someone is Moray—isn't easy. Cringing, I sort of poke it into his side.

I'm almost positive I puncture his skin, but he doesn't even flinch. Or let up. He whispers near my ear.

"Cut it out. Someone's here . . . a Lofty. I can see his girly hair."

I jerk my head, trying to free my mouth. He pushes a warning finger against my lips, then slowly lets go.

"It's probably Peree, you moron," I hiss. "Let me go! If he sees you holding me like this, he'll kill you."

He doesn't budge. "He can try."

I struggle to get away from him before Peree spots us, but it's too late. Footsteps fly toward us across the storeroom floor. Moray releases me, and I hear a series of punches. Fists meet flesh with noises that sound like the cooks when they're pounding meat, preparing it for curing and drying. Only this particular meat has a familiar honeysuckle scent.

I hop up and down in agitation, knife in hand. "Moray, if you hurt him, I swear I'll tell everyone about your baby. And . . . and you can forget hearing anything else about Koolkuna!" My threats really are pathetic. "Peree, he wasn't hurting me . . . both of you, quit it!"

I'm amazed when the ruckus stops. I don't waste any time jumping between them, hands outstretched.

"You okay?" Peree's voice sounds thin, like he's talking into a cup. A moment later I detect an unmistakable rusty smell.

"Where are you bleeding?" I drop the knife in my pocket and feel around for his face.

"Nose." It sounds like he says *noz*.

I snag one of the baskets off the top shelf, scrambling out of the way as it tumbles down. When my groping hand meets something sufficiently cloth-like, I grab it, pressing it gently to his face.

"Thanks," he says, but it comes out like *tanks*.

"What, no love for me?" Moray's voice isn't exactly normal, either.

"Don't start," I growl.

"You did cut me with that knife. The least you can do is throw me a cloth, too."

I toss one in his direction.

"You cut him?" Peree says, laughter warming his voice. "Good work. I warned you not to touch her again, Moray. What's he doing here, anyway?"

"He's here to *protect* me and to watch out for you. The Three's orders. He only grabbed me because he saw you out there. Believe it or not, he was kind of doing his job."

"Why'd you stab me then?" Moray complains.

"Try telling me what's going on next time before you crush me into the nearest wall," I snap.

"She's a mouthy one, isn't she?" he says.

Peree ignores that. "So what now? What are you supposed to do if you see me, Moray?"

"Bring you to the Three so they can decide on an *appropriate punishment* for you." He imitates Bream.

"You're not going to do that." The knife's back in my hand. I raise it up, and step in front of Peree.

I must look ridiculous, because they both kind of chuckle. At least Peree tries to smother his laughter.

"Relax, sweetheart. I'm not gonna turn your Lofty in," Moray says.

I don't let the knife drop an inch. "Why not?"

"Because it wouldn't get me what I want."

"And what's that?" Now Peree sounds suspicious.

"Koolkuna. I want to go."

CHAPTER TWELVE

I f Moray had said it was his heart's desire to clean the toilet area in the caves every day for the rest of his life, I wouldn't have been more surprised.

"Sorry, what was that?" I ask.

"I want to go to Koolkuna." Moray speaks very slow and loud, like I'm hard of hearing.

"*Why*?" I ask.

"Why not? It sounds better than here. Anywhere sounds better than here."

"But you can't . . . I mean, I'm not sure that's such a—"

Peree interrupts me. "We might consider it. With two conditions."

My mouth drops open. Why would Peree even think about agreeing?

"Like?" Moray asks.

"One: you keep watching out for Fenn until we leave. Protect her when I'm not around. And that means not touching her unless absolutely necessary. Two: if you see me on the ground, that's our secret. Fenn and I need to be able to meet at least one more time to plan."

"Deal," Moray says.

I throw my hands up. "Hold on, no deal. Moray, please give us a minute to talk. Privately." I grab Peree's arm and drag him out of the storeroom. "And put that basket back up, will you?"

"No," Moray says, like I asked him to extract his own tooth for me.

I pull Peree into the main cavern far enough that we can't be over-heard. "What are you doing? We can't trust him!"

"I think we can." His voice still sounds nasally.

"You're pretty confident for someone who got his nose bashed in by the Groundling you think is so trustworthy." I touch his face gingerly to soften my words. Sure enough, he's still holding the cloth up to stanch the flow. "Why did you agree to take him with us?"

"Because I talked to Frost. I know what Moray *really* wants."

I wince. "Do I even want to hear this?"

"It's not quite what you think," Peree says, pushing my hair back from my face with his free hand.

"What then?"

"He told Frost he wants her to go to Koolkuna, and he'd find a way to get there, too."

"Wow. That's . . . unexpected. So he wants to partner with her, then?"

"I wouldn't go that far. But he really wants the hatchling. Going to Koolkuna is the only way Moray knows for certain he'll get to see his child. Frost hopes the rest will come in time."

"Tell her not to hold her breath," I mutter.

"I already did."

"They aren't the only ones that want to go with us, either," Peree says. "People keep cornering me and Kadee, asking us about Koolkuna. I think we might have gotten through to a few people after all." He sounds enthusiastic.

I stretch my neck back and forth; an afternoon headache is brew-ing. "I was all set to tell you Eland and I are ready to leave—the three of us."

He slides a hand along my shoulder to my neck, massaging it. "Bringing a few people with us . . . that's what you said you wanted, right?"

I don't know anymore. I'm confused. "But Moray? Really?"

"If I can bribe him to protect you while I can't be with you, then it's worth it. If Moray's around all the time, maybe whoever it is that threatened you will think twice before trying it again."

"You don't know him, Peree. The *anuna* won't thank us for bringing him."

"I heard that," Moray says from nearby, sounding amused.

"We can't even trust him to mind his own business for a few minutes," I say.

Moray ignores me. "Like I said, you have a deal, Lofty. I keep your girl safe for you and you take me to Koolkuna. And my brothers."

"*What*?" I squeak. "No. Absolutely not. We'll be hand-delivering an entire generation of trouble to the *anuna*."

"It'll be okay. Trust me," Peree says.

"You, I trust. *Them*, not at all."

"This is your chance to earn Fenn's trust, Moray," Peree says.

"It's what I've been living for," he drawls.

I push my hands through my hair, frustrated with Peree for making a deal with Moray literally over my head, even if he did it because he thinks he's ensuring my safety.

"For the record, I think this is a really, really bad idea," I say.

"For the record, no one cares," Moray responds. "And hurry it up, sweetheart. You've got more work to do. Gotta keep up appearances for the Three until it's time to leave for Koolkuna."

"Don't call me that," I say automatically. "And go away."

"Don't take too long," Moray says as he strolls away.

"Peree—"

He stops me with a firm kiss. I'm kind of ashamed to admit it, but I instantly forget whatever I was going to say, forget I'm angry, and ignore that he smells like fresh blood. Instead I hold him to me, hungry for more.

"I miss you," I breathe.

"I miss you, too. That's why I'm doing this. So I won't have to miss you anymore. I'll agree to whatever I have to, to keep you safe and get us to Koolkuna. Together."

I frown. "I hope you're right about Moray."

"We need to organize supplies and decide how and when we'll move everyone there."

"How many people are we talking about?"

"So far I have Frost, Petrel, Moon, and Thrush. A few others are interested, too."

"I'm so glad Petrel and Moon want to go! I was worried they might not. We'll have to leave soon, unless we want to deliver a baby on the way. Will she be able to walk all that way?"

"She's strong. She'll manage."

"All I have is Eland—and now Moray and his brothers." I groan. "They're going to kick me right back out of Koolkuna when we get there."

Peree puts his fingers against my mouth. Then he kisses my neck, my jaw, my ear, my hairline, meandering slowly around to my mouth. By the time he lets up, my thoughts are as jumbled as a pile of unlaundered clothes.

"I have to go," he whispers.

"Not yet," I snuggle into his arms.

"I don't want to, believe me. But Petrel can only make excuses for me for so long. Osprey's paranoid. He would probably have someone spying on me all the time, if he had anyone to spare. Takes everything I have not to knock him out for what he did to you and Eland."

"No more violence. Please. We'll go, and this will all be over." There's a painful tearing in my gut as a few more stitches pull free. I might say I'm ready to go, but I can tell it's not going to be so easy to do.

"Meet me by the water hole tonight when the moon is highest. I'll bring Petrel, and we'll make a plan."

I frown. "Okay, but this has to be the last time. I think the Three—well, probably everyone—know we've been meeting. I don't want them to escalate their threats against you." Our mouths meet one more time. The kiss is sweet, lingering, full of promise. He touches my necklace and leaves.

A little dazed, I wander back into the storeroom.

"Back to work, sweetheart."

"Shut up, Moray."

It was one thing when only Peree, Eland, and I were going to Koolkuna. A lot more people are involved now. And I'm not positive I can trust any of them.

～

A glorious glow fills the sky as I exit the cave mouth after finishing my work. I inhale a fusion of sunlight, soil, and greenheart sap. If the late summer forest had a flavor, this would be it.

If would be a perfect afternoon . . . if Moray wasn't still trailing along behind me.

"Can you at least walk next to me instead of behind me?" I say. "You're making me nervous."

Bear and Calli are in the clearing playing a heated game of Sink. The goal is to toss a small rock into a hole dug in the ground. If you make it, you take a step away from the hole. Whoever is farthest away after ten throws wins. I'm terrible compared to most; it's actually surprising how often I *can* hit the hole.

"Come play, Fenn," Bear says as I walk up. He sounds guarded, probably because Moray is there. "Calli's killing me. I need someone to make me look good."

"Thanks a lot." I turn to my unwanted shadow. "*Goodbye*, Moray."

"I won't be far." He laughs as he walks away.

"What happened? Did you go in the caves with him?" Calli asks anxiously. "We heard Moray was assigned to protect you."

Bear spits on the ground. "What a joke."

"It's okay. He and I have come to an understanding," I say.

"What do you mean?" Bear asks.

I pull the knife out and show them what I imagine to be its blood-soaked surface from where I stuck Moray. "He won't bother me again."

"Did you cut yourself?" Bear sounds concerned.

"Not myself, him! I stabbed him. Don't you see the blood?"

"Um—" Calli says. She takes a step closer. "Oh wait, there's a little on the end."

I skim my fingers along the blade. She's right. The dried blood barely covers the tip. I sigh. "I should give this thing back to Peree, for all the good it's done me."

"He gave you a knife without showing you how to use it?" Bear asks, a hint of scorn in his voice. "I can teach you a few defensive moves if you want."

"Ooh, lets. I need the refresher," Calli says. "I'll be the attacker!"

Most Groundlings are taught to throw a spear and wield a knife. I always got the idea it was meant to be a show of force for the Lofties, like the competitions during the Summer Solstice celebration. Don't mess with us; we know how to defend ourselves. I wasn't ever included in the lessons.

"Okay," I say. "But watch yourselves. You know how skilled I am with weapons." They both snort in answer.

Bear shows me the proper way to hold the knife and different ways to strike. He's adamant that I should aim to wound rather than kill, giving me time to escape.

"Killing something is harder than you'd think," he says, "even when you can *see* where you're aiming."

My lesson doesn't start out well. I can't get the hang of gripping the "knife," a blunt, wooden facsimile used for training purposes. I try to do what Bear tells me, slashing and striking at Calli, but we keep ending up in a fit of giggles on the ground, thanks to her ticklishness and my sad lack of skill. Bear laughs with us at first, but he quickly loses patience. He hauls me up off the ground.

"You have to take this seriously, Fenn. I'll be the attacker now. I'm going to grab you from behind. You twist like this." He takes my shoulders and whips me around, then jerks my knife hand up and into his gut. "Remember—an opponent isn't going to be standing around waiting to see where you'll strike next. He'll be flailing if you cut him, or making his next move if you don't."

I try it, but I accidentally drop the knife before I even get turned around to face Bear. I mop the sweat off my face. "I'm hopeless. It's too easy for someone to get out of my way." I think of Moray. "Or take my weapon away."

"There's always a swift knee to the groin," Calli says cheerfully.

"I'm not even sure I can manage that."

"You'll manage it if you're desperate enough," Bear says. "Now come on. Try again—and this time with the real knife. Maybe that'll make it more real. Start slow, with the moves I showed you."

We've drawn a crowd now, and people can't resist giving advice and encouragement. I'm frightened to be aiming for Bear using the real thing, but he was right. It sobers me up. Even Calli quits laughing when I accidentally nick his arm. Of course Moray cheers me from the sidelines.

I'm exhausted by the time Bear lets me quit. I'm not sure I could stab my dinner, much less a person bent on hurting me. But it feels good to know I won't be utterly helpless the next time someone— Moray or anyone else—puts unwanted hands on me.

We collapse against Bear's shelter with cups of water. "Thanks, you two. For the lessons . . . and for last night. I appreciate that you stood up for Peree and me."

"Doesn't seem right not to let you two meet," Bear says. "The Three are making some pretty poor decisions when it comes to you."

"They're doing the best they can," Calli says. "I think they should let you see each other, too, but . . . there might be stuff we don't know."

I tilt my head. I know her well enough to know when she's trying to decide if she'll spill a secret. "Like what?"

"Oh, nothing. I mean, I'm not sure it's nothing, but . . . I didn't really understand."

"Tell us what you heard," Bear says.

She clears her throat a few times. "I . . . I overheard Mother and Father talking when we were in the caves. They were kind of far away, but you know how there's that weird echo thing sometimes. Anyway, they said something that sounded like . . . maybe like they knew about the Hidden Waters and Koolkuna before you even left to find them."

I sit bolt upright, spilling water into my lap. "How?"

Calli starts to stutter. "I don't know. They . . . they were talking about when Father was told he'd be the old Council's choice to join the Three."

"Wait," I say. "I thought we all chose new Council members."

"Well, we have a say, but the Three have the final decision, don't they? That's why the Council goes to each family individually to ask who they would pick, instead of doing it in a big public meeting. So they could hear the people's choice, then decide if they'll go along with it or not."

I frown. I had always assumed the Three weren't involved in that process, other than tallying votes. I should know by now not to give them so much credit.

"Father told Mother the Three warned him you really might find the Waters, and there might be other people there. He said it like it was a bad thing."

"What did they say might happen?"

"I don't know. They saw me listening and changed the subject."

I hold up my hands. "I don't understand. If the old Council of Three didn't want me to find the Waters, why did they even let me try?"

"Maybe it was Adder's plan all along not to allow you to come back," Bear says. "It's not like he would have told Aloe that before you left. And you did cause a lot of trouble right from the start. At least for Adder."

"But who would've gathered the water if I was permanently gone?" I ask. "Surely he would've considered that?"

Bear thinks about it. "Aloe. She'd have to go back to collecting the water instead of being on the Council. Getting rid of you would've solved two of Adder's problems. Two birds, one stone."

"Then I guess they would have chosen a new Lofty child to . . . to make Sightless. In the next Exchange," Calli says in a low voice.

With growing dismay I realize they could be right. Shrike knew about Koolkuna because Kadee tried to persuade him to go there after she first found it. He could have told Aloe. And knowing Aloe, she would have done her duty and told the Three, either at that time, or when she joined the Council.

I pull on my hair, smoothing it, trying to get it to stick together. It fights me. "I don't understand any of this. Why don't the Three want us to go to Koolkuna?"

"They're afraid. Hell, *I'm* afraid when you talk about it. "I can tell it's hard for Bear to admit that. "The whole thing scares me. But I'd go. I want to see this place for myself."

"I'd like to see it," Calli says slowly, "but my family would never go now that Father's on the Council, and I can't go without them." She pauses. "Fennel, what if a lot of people want to go, but some of us want to stay here? What will happen to us? How will we defend ourselves against the Lofties or the flesh-eaters?"

I open my mouth . . . and close it again. I honestly don't know. It wouldn't be easy, not at all, for any who choose to stay behind.

"How would we survive?" Calli asks. "And how can the Three allow that to happen?"

I can't answer her questions. I don't think anyone can.

CHAPTER THIRTEEN

I'm lying on my bed brooding after dinner. Eland keeps asking me what's wrong, but I don't tell him.

What if Calli is right? Right now my community has plenty of people to do the many tasks that ensure our survival. If enough leave with us for Koolkuna, that won't be true. And that goes double for the Lofties, because there are fewer of them to begin with. We would seal the fate of the people who stay.

But I can't remain here, either. Not the way things are now.

There's a knock. At least someone still has some manners. Eland opens the door.

"Come on in, Marj," he says.

I sit up and greet our herbalist.

"I've come to check on my patient," she says briskly. "How are you feeling, Eland?"

"Better. That stuff you gave me helped."

"Any headaches? Lingering confusion?"

"Not really since the first night," he says. "When I was out there . . . with them."

My forehead bunches. "What stuff? Marj gave you something to take?"

"Some powder to mix in my water," he says. "Tastes awful, like when I ate the rabbit food on a dare that time."

"I've been tinkering," Marj says. "Trying to find something to help with the disorientation after exposure to the sick ones."

"What's in it?" I ask.

"Mostly herbs. Bit of this and that from my workroom." She's moving around the shelter, probably picking up. Eland and I aren't great about keeping things neat and tidy. I can't see the mess, and he doesn't care. Not exactly a recipe for cleanliness.

"How are you two doing without your mother?" Marj asks.

Her question surprises me, but I appreciate her bluntness. Most people either tiptoe around the subject. Which kind of forces me to do the same.

"Okay," Eland and I both say out of habit.

I try again. She asked, after all. "It's hard, you know. I really miss her. I don't know what I'd do without Eland." I smile at him.

"I'm sure that does help. You'll come see me, if either of you begins to feel low, or if you have problems sleeping or with your appetite?" I tell her we will. "Right then, I'll be off. Eland, you don't need to use any more of the powder now that you're feeling better. Do you have any left?"

"Only a pinch. I used most of it," he says.

"Then you overdid it. I gave you much more than enough . . . but that is interesting. Perhaps taking more will shorten the effects of exposure." Marj sounds contemplative as she takes her leave.

"Why didn't you tell me she gave you something to take?" I ask Eland after she goes.

"Sorry, I forgot."

"I'm glad it worked, whatever it was." I lie back down.

Eland settles into his bed as well. "I lied, by the way. I still have more of the powder. I thought it might come in handy in case we run into the Sc—the sick ones—on our way to Koolkuna."

I nod. "Smart thinking. Especially if it actually works. What do you remember about that night? I mean, when you were outside with them?"

"Not very much. I was really scared and pretty convinced I was becoming one of them. Even the next day, I . . . never mind."

"What? Tell me."

"I felt like . . . like my face looked like theirs. I kept touching my eyes and nose and stuff, and licking my lips to be sure they were, you know, still there." He hurries on, like he doesn't want to remember how the creatures looked or how he felt.

"You were really brave, Eland. I was proud of you."

"I don't know," he says. "Brave is when you *choose* to do something dangerous or scary for a good reason. I *had* to do it. That's not all that brave."

I hop onto his bed and muss his hair. "It was brave to me. And when did you get to be so all-knowing?"

"You and Mother were out there with them for days at a time," he mutters, sounding embarrassed. "I didn't do anything like that."

"But it's different for us, being Sightless. You know that." I chuck him under the chin.

"Yeah, I know. How could I not know that?" His tone is bitter, even angry.

I touch his shoulder. "Eland?"

"Forget it."

"Tell me."

He turns his back to me. "Sometimes I felt . . . I don't know. Left out. It was . . . it was like you guys could talk without really talking. Maybe it sounds stupid, but I was sort of jealous of that."

Aloe and I did have our own way of communicating with each other. I knew instantly how she felt, not by what she said or didn't say, but through our small touches. We didn't mean to leave him out. We *doted* on him. Didn't he know that?

I squirm closer to him. "Close your eyes and keep them closed."

My hands pass over his eyelids to make sure they're shut, then I brush his forearm gently with my fingers.

"This meant, 'I'm here with you. I'm listening.'"

I grip his wrist firmly. "This was how she said, 'Be careful.' I got that a lot when I was a little girl, stumbling into one tree trunk after another."

I push his hair back and away from his face. "She did this when I was upset. It was how she showed me she understood, and she cared."

"And this," I take his hands and squeeze them, "meant I love you."

I hug him to me. He sniffs, and I chase away his tears with my fingertips. "She loved you so much, Eland. You meant everything to her. And you do to me, too."

I hold his head in my lap, singing lullabies, until he finally slips into sleep.

I sit awake, missing my mother. When the muted conversations and rustlings from the clearing finally fade, I ease his head onto his pillow and prepare to meet Peree and Petrel. I still think this is a bad idea—how many times do the Three and the Covey have to threaten us? But we need a solid plan for how to move the people we have to Koolkuna.

Only the odd snore rumbles from the other shelters as I crack the door open and slide out. The forest isn't so quiet. Crickets hum hypnotically, leaves shift and sigh in the breeze, and frogs and bats keep the time with their cries. If the greenheart trees offer the forest its scent and flavor, then its animal inhabitants provide the tune.

I creep like prey from dark spot to dark spot, minding the sound of my steps. There's probably a Groundling guard somewhere. The moon illuminates the path, so I walk under the shade of the tree branches. There's a luster ahead.

For a long time I thought the water hole glowed at night. Calli finally told me the moon—which I've heard can be as slim as a curled-up leaf or as spherical as a stone—reflects in the water hole below. It seems unfair, somehow. The sighted see not only the fickle moon, they see two.

The water sweeps softly onto the shore, then recedes, dancing with itself, careless who hears it. I hold under the cover of the forest, soaking in the sounds and scents of the night.

After a few minutes, I hear more deliberate movements in the treetops: the low thump of quiet footsteps along the walkway overhead. They stop above my head. A soft birdcall greets me. I wave, letting them know it's safe.

The rope ladder dives toward me, bumping against the tree trunk as it falls, and I steady it as Peree descends. My heart pulses in my chest as he draws near. I feel like I've stolen these moments with him, moments we'll have to eventually give back. I don't want to steal time with him. I want it to be ours to keep.

We embrace, and I find his ever-present bow and quiver lying in wait across his back. There are new feathers in his hair. Peree's bow and feathers: the things that mark him as a Lofty. One feather drops out of my fingers to the ground. I'm glad I brought the colorful one Calli found to replace it.

"C'mon, you two, quit pawing all over each other," Petrel whispers, hopping off the ladder a minute after Peree. We huddle into the shadows cast by the trees. "You're embarrassing your mother."

"Is Kadee here?" A third person is coming down the ladder.

"They aren't embarrassing me, Petrel," Kadee says as she steps down beside us. "I love seeing them happy together."

I hug her, glad to hear her voice, especially after thinking about Aloe so much tonight. My raw heart is soothed a little to know there's another woman I can turn to for the sort of motherly advice I always thought Aloe would be here to give.

Petrel drops an arm around me, squeezing my shoulders after Kadee releases me. "I'm sorry about how things turned out the last time you and Eland were in the trees. If I'd known what Osprey was up to, I never would've left you two there alone."

"Please don't apologize. If it wasn't for you, Eland might have been hanging on that tree for days," I remind him. "Things worked out in the end. How's Moon?"

"Like a rabid chipmunk. Don't tell her I said that. But seriously. Half the time she's in a frenzy of activity—eating, nesting, and running around—the other half she's crashed out, sleeping. It's exhausting to watch." He chuckles. "She said to tell you to eat. And that she's looking forward to spending more time with you. Actually, she told me to tell you about four other things, but there's no way I could keep it all straight. Anyway, she's good. Ready to pop."

"We'd better find somewhere else to talk," Peree says. "The water hole is too exposed." He shifts his bow and curls my hand around his arm.

We steal through the forest until we reach a thick stand of brush and trees where Peree and I went to be alone the first few days after the Reckoning. Before our people decided we couldn't be together at all.

We push through the wall of undergrowth. Or maybe overgrowth —it feels like the vegetation is clawing at me from every direction.

I don't usually go running through thick bushes and tree branches if I can help it. I usually end up with something hairy with multiple legs attached to me that I don't know about until I'm bitten. I decide I'm safe this time with Peree, Petrel, and Kadee along.

Kadee joins me in the small area concealed behind all the foliage. "What is this place?"

"A pretty good hiding spot." Peree chuckles. "Not that we've ever used it for that, right, Petrel?"

"No, never," Petrel says. "Not even when we were hungry and shot a few rabbits on the ground . . . then climbed down to get them . . . and were stuck in here for hours while two Groundlings sat on the other side gossiping." He laughs. "Being quiet for that long was an extreme test of our newfound manhood. Anyway, eventually we fell asleep. Didn't wake up until after dark. Shrike was furious when we finally got back home—remember, Peree? He made us eat meals with our hands tied behind our backs for days."

"I had no idea you Lofties snuck around on the ground so much." I say it like I'm kidding, but it astonishes me that they got away with it. "And is that an effective punishment? Tying your hands behind your backs?"

"It is when you're a starving teenage boy," Peree says. "There's only so much meat you can get off the bone without holding it in your fingers. We had to live on nuts and berries."

"Almost killed us," Petrel adds.

"You never told me you already knew about this place," I say to Peree.

"Can't tell you all my secrets at once, can I? No mystery in that." There's a smile in his voice.

"We'd better get started," Kadee says. "We can't afford to be caught meeting like this."

That focuses us. I settle onto the mostly dry ground, and Peree sinks down next to me, setting his bow aside. His honeysuckle scent is a bit trampled right now. It's not his fault; we aren't allowing the Lofties frequent access to the water hole for bathing.

"How are things going in the trees?" I ask. The question is met with silence.

"What?" I ask.

"We aren't too popular right now," Peree says. I can tell there's something he's not saying.

"What happened?"

"I was jumped by Osprey and his group. They know I'm talking to people about leaving."

I touch his face. His cheek is puffy, and one of his eyes is swollen completely shut. "Oh, Peree . . ."

"We'll be fine . . . as long as I stay away from you from now on and pretend the plan's off."

"Then you definitely shouldn't be down here! And Kadee, Petrel, you shouldn't be, either."

"I kept telling them that, but they wouldn't listen," Peree says.

"I have to get your back, cousin," Petrel says. His voice is unusually serious. "Moon and I don't want to hatch our baby here anymore, now that we know there's another place to raise her. Not after everything's that happened. And don't even get Moon started on the Exchange. Her family tends to have fair-haired and light-eyed children, but you never know."

"What about Breeze? Have you asked her to come with us?"

Peree answers. "Not yet. She's really not doing well with Shrike and everything. I'll work on her."

"I hope she will." I squeeze his hand. "Okay, the plan. Should we go through the caves to Koolkuna?"

"I think we have to," Peree says. "Although our people won't be too happy about it. You can still follow the crampberries, right?"

I consider the frequent whiffs of the disgusting berries I've caught in the caves. "Oh, yeah. No problem. But we should bring a fresh supply just in case. I'll ask Eland to gather some."

"We're already stockpiling supplies." Peree skims his hand up and down my back. "Food, extra clothing, medicine. I can probably get them into the caves before we leave, if the guards are as sleepy as they were tonight. Your job is to move them into that first passageway we took when we went to find the Waters. Your people don't use that area very much, right?"

"Water's going to be an issue, though," I say.

"Maybe we can leave that up to each person. Spread the word that if they're coming, they have to save and bring a few days worth of drinking water," Petrel says. "How long will the trip take?"

I consider that. "Maybe a day, now that we have the trail of crampberries to follow through the caves." Peree agrees. "When will we go?"

"In five nights," Kadee says. "The moon will be new, which should make it easier for you to get people from the trees to the caves with the least risk of being seen. It could still be dangerous, though. We don't know what the Covey or the Council of Three will do. No one wants a repeat of the Reckoning."

The night air wriggles down the collar of my dress, making me shiver. Five nights. Five more days to spend with my people in the only home I've ever known. I want to go to Koolkuna, but sneaking out in the middle of the night with a group of rebels wasn't how I envisioned doing it.

"Wait, you said it would be easier for *us* to get to the caves. Aren't you coming?" I ask Kadee.

"I'm leaving tomorrow night to prepare the *anuna* for your arrival. I will meet you at the cave mouth where you saw the big cat. That entrance to the caves, if I have the right one in mind, is not terribly far from Koolkuna. If we're fortunate, the sick ones will stay away so we can move the people to the village from there."

I can think of about a million things that could go wrong with that plan, and a million more that could go wrong in the meantime, but I also don't have a better idea. We discuss the potential pitfalls while the moon skates across the sky.

I'm still worried about Peree and his family being caught, but it's wonderful to spend time with them. If Eland and Moon were here, it would be perfect. Hopefully we'll all be together soon. And maybe this isn't the last chance for others to go to Koolkuna, like Calli, or even Fox and Acacia. We can always return and try to convince them to come. I tell myself that, anyway.

Kadee takes me aside when the time comes to say goodbye. Her voice is kind. "You're doing the right thing, you know."

"What do you mean?"

"I see you struggling. You came back to try to persuade your people to go to Koolkuna, and now they won't go. You're worried you're abandoning them. But you're not. Has Peree told you the story about the thirsty horse that was led to water, but wouldn't take a drink? I used to tell him that one when he was being stubborn."

"Peree? Stubborn? Can't imagine that." I laugh. "No, I haven't heard it. What's a horse?" I assume it's some kind of large animal, but I wouldn't know. There are few big animals left in the world; the teeming poison in the water and the soil killed most of them off.

"Never mind. My point is this: the wonderful thing about being human is that we're able to make our own choices. Even if they're the wrong ones."

"But what if *I'm* making the wrong one?"

"At least you will have had the chance to choose. And that's what you're offering your people: a choice."

A memory tugs at me—holding out my hand to Peree at the Summer Solstice the night we met. *At least I'll have made my own choice*, I thought, as I asked him to dance before the sick ones descended. I hold my hand out to him now. He tucks it into his, and I smile.

Peree is my choice. I choose him. And like Petrel and Moon, I want a chance at a peaceful future for my little brother and my future family. Kadee is right. We offered our people two paths, and we have to accept that some may walk a different one than we do. That's the beauty, and the price, of free will.

Kadee and Petrel leave soon after. Peree insists we stay, that we've earned a few minutes alone together. I argue with him that he should go, but he wins by threatening to tickle me until I give away our hiding place. So we sit pressed together in the small clearing with night creatures screeching and croaking in the trees around us.

"I have something for you." I pull out the feather and hand it to him. "Calli found it. She said it would look nice in your hair." He doesn't need to know she said it sarcastically.

"Tell her thanks." After a moment, he ties it in. "I don't think I've ever seen a bird this could have come from."

"That's what she said, too."

"It actually reminds me of a story. Do you want to hear it?"

"Yes . . . but is it a quick one? Guards and rules and punishments and . . ." I gesture around us.

He leans close and kisses my neck, then whispers in my ear, "Don't rush a story-teller. It cramps our creativity."

Lightning races through my veins. It originates at his lips and crackles through the tips of my toes.

"Please, take all the time you want, then." My voice hitches. "If we're caught, I'll say I couldn't possibly ask you to hurry up and finish the story. It would cramp your creativity."

He chuckles. "Okay, here it is. Many years ago, a village existed, perched on the top of a great hill. The people there were safe, living against the blue sky. They had enough food and water, but they were not content. The men and the women of the village were not partners. The men used their strength to overpower the women, they set up rules that kept the women from making decisions, and they favored their boy children over their girls. The women were unhappy, but could not see a way to change their situation. They would gather every day to care for the children, cook the meals, and mend clothing. And they would talk about what it would be like to be as free as the hawks and eagles they saw gliding over their homes each day."

Peree's voice changes as he speaks, caressing and curling around his words like a lover. His voice envelops me, too, until I almost forget about the guards and rules and punishments myself. Almost.

"One day, a colorful bird flew among the gathering of women. It had a small hooked beak of bright orange, like a tiger, with feathers in every hue that shimmered as the bird flew. The women sat still, watching. They were astonished. They did not know such a beautiful bird existed. The bird landed on a nearby tree stump and spoke to them, its voice high and clear. It said, 'Women, I have been watching you. Why do you allow your men to treat you and your children this way? Why do you not rise up against them?' The women hung their heads, pain and anger in their hooded eyes. Finally, one of them spoke. 'We are not strong enough. We have no weapons. We cannot rise up against them.' And the bird said, 'If it is a weapon you need, take one of my feathers. It will slay any man you use it against.'"

I finger the soft feathers in his wavy hair and laugh. "A feather as a weapon?"

"The women scoffed at the little bird, too, who looked as offended as it is possible for a bird to look. 'You reject my gift?' it asked. And the women said, 'A feather, however beautiful, is no weapon.' The bird said, 'I tell you now; you will have what you want. But beware. It will not be as you expected.' And with that it flew away. The women all looked at each other. They did not know what to think.

"A small girl climbed out of her mother's lap and approached the tree stump. 'Look,' she said, 'The pretty bird left a feather.' She picked it up. It was beautiful—bright green, yellow, and red, with touches of blue. 'Put that down,' the girl's mother said sternly. But she held it a moment longer. And sure enough, the feather began to grow in the girl's hand. It grew longer, and thinner, and harder. The tip of the feather sharpened into a point. Before the girl knew what was happening, she was holding a wicked-looking spear. Her mother snatched it from her. 'A weapon! We must hide it from the men.'"

"The bird was right, then," I say.

"In more ways than one. The woman hid the spear in her home. But that night, when her partner beat her in front of her daughter as he did most nights, she snatched up the weapon. The woman brandished it in front of her. The old, familiar pain and anger rose up in her until it became all she could feel, and before she knew what she was doing, she plunged the spear into him. As the woman stood over her partner's body, the bloody spear became a harmless feather in her hand."

I wrap my arms around myself, disturbed by the violent turn the story has taken. Peree moves closer, warming me.

"The next day, the woman passed the bird's gift on to her sister, and one by one, the women of the village used it on their menfolk, slaying them with the feather that became a spear. When there were no more men, the spear became a feather once more. The women took turns wearing it on their bodies, to remind themselves that they would never again be subject to the cruelties of men."

I grimace as he finishes. "What happened to the women?"

"I don't know. That's where the story ended, as I heard it."

"Well, I think we're safe," I joke weakly. "I had the feather for a while. No spear in sight. Who told you that one?"

He hesitates, playing with wisps of my hair. "Kaiya did."

My lips flatten. I have mixed feelings about Peree's friend from Koolkuna. On the one hand I'm grateful to her. She rescued me from the pit Moray threw me into. Without her, I'd be dead. I also feel sorry for her. Kadee said people avoid Kai because she was exposed to the sick ones at length as a child when she was lost in the forest. She was one of the few Nerang was able to nurse back to being fully human. At least I think she's fully human. She seems to be missing a few of the niceties, like any hint of friendliness or manners, and she's testy and churlish.

Except with Peree.

"Oh. When was this?"

"When she brought me back from Koolkuna." His hands wrap gently around my face. "Which I asked her to do, you know, because I was so worried about you."

"I know." I kiss his unshaven cheek. "Your stories have been a little dark lately, Peree. I'm not sure I liked that one, either."

"It was about an animal, as requested."

"Yes, and a bunch of cruel men and murderous women. I'm glad I don't live there. Then I'd have to spear you." I poke him in the ribs. He falls onto his back, groaning like he's been stabbed, and pulls me down with him.

"I'd beg for my life and offer to be your slave," he murmurs.

I kiss him again, this time on his scuffed lips. "Hmm. I'll think about it."

Kissing Peree gets better every time, especially now that we haven't been able to be together as often. It's like finding a late cache of berries when you thought they were done for the season. You savor them all the more for not knowing when you'd taste them again.

We don't speak for a while, not above a whisper at least. But I feel the night wearing on. He has to go home soon.

We slink back to the rope ladder by the water hole, hand in hand, listening for any human sounds. We shouldn't have spent so long together. Morning hovers nearby, waiting for its cue to vanquish the night with bright spears of sunlight.

Peree presses my necklace in silent farewell and climbs the ladder, dragging it up behind him. I wait and listen until I can't hear his footsteps overhead anymore. Then I stay a minute longer, enjoying the harmonious sounds of the water hole. I'm making the right choice to leave with Peree. I know I am.

I start for home, but I'm startled to a stop by the sound of someone moving along the path right in front of me.

CHAPTER FOURTEEN

"Trouble sleeping, Fennel?"

I freeze at the sound of Fox's voice, agonizingly aware that Peree's footsteps faded away only moments before. I pray Fox didn't notice him.

"Yes," I say, keeping my voice relaxed. "I like being near the water when I can't sleep. It's soothing." We both listen for a moment, but I'm anything but soothed now.

"Sleep can be so elusive to a troubled mind," he says. "And it's been a difficult few months for you."

I narrow my eyes. The Three were responsible for much of my *difficult* few months.

"I'm on guard duty," he says. "I usually take the opportunity to think. The water hole is as good a place as any to find peace of mind."

He strolls a few paces farther down the path toward the water. I stay put, hoping against hope there's nothing amiss. If he was really listening or watching me closely, he would hear the guilt in my voice and see the tense set of my shoulders. I give silent thanks that the sighted can be so oblivious sometimes. The breeze blows toward us from the water. I tremble, but not because of the temperature.

"Cold?" he asks.

"I think I'll go home now. Will you walk with me? There's something I've been meaning to ask you."

"Of course." He falls into step beside me.

My arms curl around me. For a moment, I consider telling Fox our plan. Maybe the Three would support us. I know I can't do that. But I *can* ask him the question I've had since Calli put it in my head.

"Did the Three already know about Koolkuna? Before I came back from trying to find the Hidden Waters, I mean?"

If he tells me the truth, then maybe Aloe was wrong. Maybe there's hope that I can be honest with Fox, as I would have been with Aloe, and we can work this out. But if he lies to me, then there's no hope. I won't be able to trust him. The pause seems to stretch and grow like a great, black shadow, gradually overtaking the sky above our heads.

"No. No, of course not," he finally says. "We didn't know it existed until you told us. What makes you ask?"

I slowly release the breath I was holding. *So be it.*

"No reason. Just wondering."

Just wondering what else the Three know that they aren't telling; how much deeper the lies will go.

We continue down the path. Fox makes small talk about what needs to be done over the coming weeks as we prepare for the return of winter. I'm barely listening, thinking instead about all I need to do in the next five days before we leave. We reach the quiet cluster of Groundling shelters in the charcoal light of dawn.

"Fennel," Fox says. "I know you're not the same girl now who left the caves to face the Scourge alone."

I don't answer; I won't be able to keep the bitterness I feel out of my voice.

"You've been in danger, and your life was threatened. You lost your mother, and you fell in love. Tragedy and wonder all in a brief period of time. You must be confused."

Yeah, you could say that. I remain silent.

"I hope you know that I care about you. I've always treated you like one of my own."

I nod.

"Change is not a bad thing. You're becoming a woman with a," he chuckles, "*definite* mind of your own. But I hope one thing hasn't changed. Your mother taught you to think about your duty to your community first; I hope you haven't forgotten her lesson. Because that would truly be tragic."

He takes my hand, placing something long and silky on my palm. The feather that fell from Peree's hair.

"I will inform the Three that you once again disobeyed our orders." He pauses. "We can't allow our way of life to be threatened by two young people determined to put our safety in jeopardy." I don't know what expression he saw on my face, but he touches my shoulder, and his tone softens. "It's not easy for me to take a hard line. Especially with you, Fennel. But when you're responsible for the welfare of a group of people, sometimes you have to. It's as simple— and as difficult—as that."

He leaves me standing, my heart galloping, in the murky predawn. Why haven't I learned by now that I can't conceal anything from the Three?

Kadee catches me on my way to the caves the next morning, calling softly to me from the platform in the trees. Moray hovers nearby, watching for other Groundlings. For once, having him follow me around is actually helpful. I hate to admit it, but it would have been helpful to have him as a lookout last night. I'm still kicking myself for letting Fox sneak up on me like that last night.

"Peree sent me. Are you okay? Did Fox know he was there?"

Each hour I didn't sleep last night are grains of sand lodged in my eyes. I'm tired and cross.

"He knew we'd been together. He said he would tell the Three, so I'll probably be punished. I can't meet Peree again."

"He knows; that's why I'm here. He said to tell you he's sorry, and he loves you. He'll be watching, if you need him."

I smile half-heartedly.

"Someone's coming," Moray says in an undertone. "Hurry it up."

"I have to go," I say.

"Good luck, Fennel. I'll see you in Koolkuna."

I wave to her.

"Aw, look. It's Bear. Coming to see the one that got away," Moray says.

He didn't have to tell me. I can smell Bear's particular scent—tree sap and wood smoke—as he approaches.

"Fenn, I need to talk to you. Alone," Bear says.

"I'm hurt, hero. You don't count me as someone you can tell your secrets to?" Moray says.

"I don't count you at all," Bear says.

"Stop it. Both of you. I'm not in the mood." I rub my eyes, trying to relieve the dryness, but only irritating them more. "C'mon Bear, help me move some supplies into the caves while we talk. Moray, keep watch."

"Getting pushier, aren't we?" Moray says, but he stays by the mouth to the caves as Bear and I enter.

"What's up?" I ask, as we carry the first load through the passage, his torch flickering at my side.

"I want to go."

I know exactly what he means, but I'm even less sure now that I can agree to bring anyone else to Koolkuna. "I don't know, Bear."

"What do you mean, you don't know? A group is going. You and the Lofty are leading 'em, right? Well, I'm in."

I groan. "Perfect. Where did you hear that?"

"Vole. A few kids in the gardens were talking about it when he was there fixing the plow. He's thinking about going, too. And thanks a lot for telling me, by the way." Bitterness and sarcasm seethe in his words.

I'm going to throttle Eland. Maybe I didn't make it perfectly clear that this was a secret. A *big* one. At times like this I'm reminded that he's still a child.

"I was going to ask you . . ." Whatever else I say now will only sound weak, so I don't try. "Anyway, what I meant was, I don't know if any of this is such a good idea. I'm afraid of what the Three will do if they get wind that a group wants to go. Which they're very likely to do now, thanks to my big-mouthed little brother and the way gossip spreads around here. I don't want anyone to get hurt. I don't want to be responsible for that."

"Are you saying you're *not* going?" Bear's tone is cold.

I hesitate before answering. "I'm going, but I'm not sure I want to risk starting something with the Three by taking anyone other than my big-mouthed brother." And Moray and his brothers. Now probably isn't the time to tell Bear they're going, too.

I shift the armful of food I'm carrying as I speak. He grabs me, and I almost drop it all.

"Who goes and who stays isn't really your choice, Fenn."

I scowl; he's hurting me. "Yes, it is. I don't have to take anyone anywhere."

"Why did you even come back then? Only for Eland?" He's hissing like steam building in a teakettle.

I keep my voice even. I don't want to fight with him. But I can't help saying, "Sometimes I wish I hadn't."

He releases me quickly, like I burned him with my words. I stalk off, but he catches up a moment later.

"So you don't want me to go?"

The pain he's desperately trying to conceal in his voice is too much for me. I let out a long breath. "I don't want to endanger anyone else I care about. Two of us leaving is a lot different than a group."

He doesn't say anything for a moment. "So you care about me, but you don't want me to go with you to Koolkuna."

"Of course I care about you. You're one of my best friends."

He grabs my shoulders, making me face him. "And so you think you know what's best for me, huh? Your choice of partners tells me you don't have a clue what that is." He releases me again. "Forget I said that. I *am* going. And there are others."

I shake my head, upset by his tone more than his words. "Bear—"

"Fenn, think about this. If you think you can make this choice for people, then you're no better than the Three."

We deliver the supplies to the tunnel where Peree, Petrel, and I agreed to meet in five days time. Bear does a lot of stomping, but doesn't say much. I don't know what to say to make it better between us. I'm feeling trapped.

Last night, talking with Kadee, it seemed that allowing people to make their own choices was the right thing to do. If they want to go, then who am I to deny them a chance at a better future in Koolkuna?

But Calli and Fox almost changed my mind. What if allowing people to choose gets them hurt, or worse? What if the Three retaliates? Even if we get away without incident, what if there's an accident in the caves? Or trouble with the sick ones? Or with the *anuna*? And what will happen to those who stay behind? How will I live with myself if this all goes wrong?

I suddenly understand Fox's point from the night before, about making unpopular decisions. No matter what I do, someone could be hurt, or at the very least, they'll hate me. How did I end up here, making decisions for other people?

Maybe it's time to think only of myself. But then I'd be a lot like . . . Moray. Not exactly tempting.

Bear leaves the caves without saying goodbye. Unfortunately, Moray notices.

"Trouble in paradise?" he asks as we take another load in.

I scoff. "Paradise? Hardly."

"Hey, there are girls in Koolkuna, right? It's not all men or old people or something?"

I shake my head. "Yes, Moray, there are lots of women. In fact, there's one called Frost who I think would be *perfect* for you."

"Yeah? Is she good looking?"

"How would I know?"

"Does she have big—"

"Moray!"

"Just asking."

I have to change the subject before I do something I might regret.

"What are you going to do about your mother when we leave? Will you tell her you're going?"

"Not a chance. She hates your guts. Blames you that Adder's counting worms now. I think they were, y'know . . ."

"What?"

"Getting busy. Doing the deed. Rolling in the grass. Going fishing. Rubbing bellies—"

"Okay, I got it!" My nose wrinkles. "Yuck, are you serious?"

"Completely. Think I'd make that up about my own mother?"

"Yes, actually." I shake my head, trying to shed the thought of Thistle and Adder being *together* like that. "What will you do about her, then? Leave her here without saying anything?"

"Probably." He sounds like he hadn't thought much about it.

"How do you do that?"

"Do what?"

"Not care? About other people, I mean?" I may not be able to stand Thistle any more than she can stand me, but she's his *mother*. We dump the supplies we're carrying and start heading back to the entrance.

"Easiest thing in the world. You should try it sometime. Worrying about other people is exhausting."

I cock my head. "But it's not really true that you don't care about anyone, is it? You care about your brothers. Otherwise you wouldn't have wanted to bring them to Koolkuna."

"Reinforcements. I'm not going someplace with a bunch of crazy people who think the fleshies are safe without someone to watch my back."

"And your baby?"

"That baby's a little piece of me. Of *course* I care about it." He sniggers.

I shake my head again, this time with disbelief. "I don't even know what to think about you."

"You think too much as it is. Give it a rest."

"That's the most caring thing you've ever said to me, Moray," I say sarcastically.

"Caring about you isn't part of the deal. I provide protection. That's it."

"Then how come you're helping me carry all this stuff?" I grab another armful of supplies, this time to bring to the storeroom in case anyone's checking. I have to at least pretend to do what I'm supposed to be doing in here.

"Exercise. Don't want to get flabby. All those women in Koolkuna are counting on me being in top shape."

He really is unbelievable. I locate the huge load of stuff he's already carrying and throw on another sack. "You can carry a little more then can't you, big guy? For the ladies?"

"I like the sound of that. Keep it coming."

We deliver the rest of the supplies, and I spend the remainder of the morning arranging the storeroom. Moray apparently feels his helping role stops at the entrance to the storeroom, because even when I ask him nicely to put a few things up high, he refuses. He sits and whistles that irritating tune, deliberately going off key whenever I plead with him to stop.

My stomach is snapping at me, ready for lunch. Moray and I make our way to the mouth of the cave. We're about to round the last bend in the passage when I hear footsteps and see a light where there shouldn't be one. Moray steps in front of me. I may not be able to believe a thing he says, but he does seem serious about his commitment to protect me.

"Fennel, I'd like to talk to you." It's Vole. After what Bear told me this morning, I'm pretty sure I know what he wants.

"Okay." My voice is wary. And weary. "Moray, will you give us a few minutes?"

"Sure thing, sweetheart." He leans in a little too close to whisper in my ear. He smells like this morning's breakfast of rabbit meat and porridge. Moray always smells like whatever he ate last. "Remember, all that caring could get you killed." He pauses. "Not that I care."

Not that I thought he did. I wave at Vole to follow me deeper into the caves.

Bear and Vole aren't the only ones who come to find me. People tap on the door of our shelter in the middle of the night. They follow me into the caves. Ivy and Dahlia even ambush me in the heavily wooded toileting area. I *really* didn't appreciate that.

Over the next few days, a handful of Groundling families of varying sizes tell me they want to go to Koolkuna. Their reasons are all different, but they boil down to one thing: hope.

They have hope that their lives, or the lives of their children, will be different—better—than they are here. *My* hope is that I'm telling them the truth when I assure them they will be. I think of our friends in Koolkuna. Will their lives be better, when Peree and I bring an assorted group of Groundlings and Lofties—about as close as you can get to bitter enemies—to their peaceful village?

Anxiety builds in me as the days slip and slide by. I was very worried about what the Three would do to punish me. When nothing out of the ordinary happened, I started worrying about Peree instead. I haven't heard from him at all. I don't know if Kadee left for Koolkuna or how Moon and the hatchling might be doing. What if the Three told the Covey that Peree trespassed, and *he* was punished instead? He could be hurt, or worse, and I would never know.

The pile of assorted fears is a rock grinding constantly in my stomach. So I'm not that hungry as I sit down for breakfast with Bear, Cricket, and Calli on the fifth day—the day we're due to leave. We warm ourselves at the fire and wait for our meals to be passed around from the cooking fire.

Birds chirp and chuff in the greenheart trees around us. The ground is damp with dew, and the air smells of smoke and my own unwashed hair. I need to visit the water hole for a bath sometime today. The rock in my gut shifts as I think about what might be in store over the next few days. I might as well be clean for whatever it is.

I'm feeling especially miserable because Bear still isn't really talking to me. We've taken a step back from the camaraderie I thought we'd achieved, especially the day he taught me to use a knife.

I've been practicing with Eland in our shelter at night. It makes me cringe every time to deliver the "killing" blow, but he loves pretending I skewered him, complete with gurgles, burbles, and dramatic drops to the floor. The knife hangs in my pocket all the time now.

A small group of people takes their meals nearby, murmuring to each other. Moray's voice is among them. They pass bowls from the cooking pot to Calli and Bear. I have to wait for mine.

"Yum, porridge. Again," Calli complains. We haven't had much variety in our diet since the gardens almost dried up after the long stay in the caves. The hunting parties haven't had luck, either. They need to bag a large boar or two soon, or winter will be especially thin this year. *Not that I'll have to worry about it*, I think. But I feel guilty.

When I'm finally handed a plate, I pick at my food. Apart from the awkwardness with Bear, I need to talk to Calli, to ask her if she wants to come with us to Koolkuna. I'm pretty sure she'll say no, given what she told us before, but I would feel terrible leaving without at least asking. I need to pick the right time, though. Tell her too early and the Three might get wind of it. They may have already, but if so, why haven't they taken any action to stop us?

I force myself to take a few large bites of my porridge, only paying sporadic attention to my friends' conversation. They're talking about swimming later. I chew and swallow half-heartedly as I listen. My hand slides around my stomach. It really is hurting now. I frown and hunch over.

"What is it, Fenn?" Calli asks. "You look like you ate a crampberry or something."

I put my plate down and try to keep my voice quiet. I don't want to insult whoever's cooking. "Something tastes off with my porridge."

"Tastes good to me," Bear says through a mouthful.

My guts are playing a game of catch with the rock, tossing it painfully around my insides. I swallow repeatedly, fighting the urge to vomit.

Dryness spreads through my mouth and throat, a slow burn. I swallow again to tamp down the heat, but that seems to make it worse. My eyes bulge as the feeling grows like a small but deadly wildfire, engulfing the flesh of my tongue down into my chest. I clutch my throat. My pulse pounds, and my heart hops frantically in my chest, raising a silent alarm for the rest of my body.

"Fennel? Are you okay? Are you choking?" Calli's voice seems to come from a long way off, like she's shouting, but I can barely hear her.

I shake my head, trying to clear the gathering haze. I stand, but my legs are weak and shaky; I fall back to the ground. Heat fills me, as if the flames in my throat have the power to raise the temperature throughout my body. No, I've fallen nearer the fire—too near—but I can't push myself away.

That's when I hear them. The Scourge. They're coming through the forest, their terrible howls growing every second. Why didn't the Lofties raise the alarm?

"They're coming!" I croak. "Run! They're . . ." My tongue seems to thicken like rising dough. I choke. "Run to . . . caves!" My body shakes uncontrollably. I bite my tongue and blood seeps in my mouth.

The creatures surround me, their breath rank. Their moans and shrieks pierce my ears, and I wail at them in return. The chill flesh of their hands smothers me. I kick and writhe, fighting, trying to escape, but strong arms imprison me.

Teeth sink into my skin; I scream in agony. Tears bathe my face. The creatures howl at each other like competing scavengers as they rip my flesh. Biting, tearing, groaning with hunger and longing.

Can't fight them, can't stop them, can't get away.

CHAPTER FIFTEEN

I'm ready. I want to go, to be gone from here.

The pain and the terror consume me as I wait to become one of the Scourge, like so many of my people before me.

But a voice keeps me here. A high, clear voice. The voice of a child. *Kora.* My young friend from Koolkuna slips her tiny hand into mine. I try to warn her about the creatures, to keep her away, but I have neither the words nor the strength. The creatures push and nudge to keep their ghastly hold on my body. They strip my flesh.

Cold hands cover my cheeks, forcing my mouth open. I clench my teeth and turn my head, but I'm not strong enough to fight it. A venomous liquid slides down my throat. It's scalding, yet somehow quenches the flames. How can that be? More liquid pours through me, around me, over me; I float in a deep and dark pool of pain, anguish, and fear, waiting to finally drown.

The full bloom of a waking nightmare withers only slowly.

It fades—the pain of the creature's renting, tearing bites.

It distorts—the screams and cries, into unrecognizable speech.

It dies—leaving me ripped and torn and bleeding.
I lie still, holding Kora's hand.
She sits by me.

The sun is warm on my face. I lie coiled in on myself, an abandoned snail shell. Deserted, discarded, hollowed out.

Kora still holds my hand.

No, not Kora.

This hand is bigger, rougher. Dirty. *Eland.*

Hazily I remember the last time I came to and found Eland holding my hand. I flinch away from the memory of hearing about Aloe's death.

The burn in my throat is still there, but much fainter. My tongue feels two sizes too big and there's a horrible aftertaste in my mouth. I form words, but no sound emerges. I wet my lips. This time I manage it.

"Eland?"

"He's asleep." The voice swims to me through the shallow, murky water of my consciousness. It belongs to Marj. I only catch every few words. "Rest . . . exhausted . . . frantic."

"Where are we?" I ask.

"Shelter."

"The Scourge?" I listen, but I can't hear any sounds of the creatures nearby. My hands tremble. My dress is soaked with sweat.

"Gone . . . drink." She comes closer, but I turn away. I'm afraid; the repellant liquid that nearly drowned me still squats on my swollen lips.

". . . tea. Only tea. Few sips . . . help. Take the cup. Won't force you."

Tea? I hold my hands out tentatively. The cup is warm and welcome in my cold, shaking fingers. I try a small taste and grimace. The liquid is the same bitter brew as before, but the mundane act of sipping it helps me feel more myself. I take a larger swallow. Marj moves around her shelter as I drink. I feel her watching me.

I finish my cup, spilling a little on myself with the trembling. She pours me more. Halfway through the second cup I finally feel able to ask a few questions. My lips and tongue are still uncomfortably numb and swollen, but my thoughts are a little clearer.

"What happened?"

"Drink, Fennel," Marj says soothingly. "I'll tell you, but don't stop drinking." I take another sip to oblige her.

"Fennel . . .," says Eland sleepily. "Fennel! Are you . . .?"

"I'm okay. I'm . . . here."

He grips my hand like he thinks if he lets go I might slip away again. His hand quivers as bad as mine. "What was wrong? You went mad! You were screaming, and crying, and hearing things we couldn't hear. You kept saying the fleshies were coming, but they weren't, and then you kind of collapsed and were muttering and sweating and yelling out—" He stops to take a breath. "Are you sure you're okay?"

I cover my mouth with my hand. Could it be that none of what I heard and felt was real? *Am* I going mad?

"I heard . . ." I try again. "I *thought* I heard them coming. Through the woods. They surrounded us and . . . and they were shrieking, and people . . . were shouting. One of them grabbed me—"

"No one grabbed you," Eland says. "Unless you count Moray."

"Moray?" I don't remember him being there.

"He brought you to me," Marj says.

My forehead wrinkles. "The sick ones . . . they weren't really here?"

"No, Fennel."

My hands shake harder. "Why could I hear them and feel them?" I can *still* feel their cold fingers clawing my skin. "What's wrong with me?"

Marj answers. "I think you were poisoned."

Eland sucks in a breath.

"What kind of poison?" I whisper.

"I suspect banewort. It can cause this kind of reaction. Is your mouth very dry?"

I nod.

"Stomach pain? Weakness?"

The rock still sits in my stomach. "Yes, all of those."

"What did you eat this morning?" she asks.

"Porridge. And only a few bites."

"Any berries?"

I shake my head.

"Powder form, then. Banewort roots can be dried and powered. It must have been mixed in your food. Or sprinkled on it. Don't worry, I suspected a toxin and gave you an emetic right away."

So that's the horrible taste in my mouth.

"How? Who?" I ask, but thanks to my puffy lips and tongue, the words come out sounding the same. The cook this morning was an elder, an old friend of Aloe's. I can't imagine her trying to poison me. But I can't really think. My brain feels as ponderous as my tongue.

"None . . . none of it was real?" I ask. "Why did I think the sick ones were here when they weren't?"

"You were delirious, hallucinating. Both symptoms of banewort poisoning. It takes each person differently."

"It was so real," I whisper. I have a sudden understanding of what Eland and Bear, and Jackal and Rose, and any of the other sighted who'd been exposed to the Scourge felt. I *believed* they were going to kill me, or make me one of them at the very least. I have a feeling if the sick ones had actually been around, I might not have come back to myself at all. The belief that I was dying was too overpowering. I squeeze Eland's hand, wanting to feel something warm and solid. Real. He squeezes back.

"Drink more," Marj urges.

"Is the powder you gave Eland in this tea?" I ask. "It tastes awful."

"No. You taste the antidote to banewort."

"It saved your life," Eland says.

I nod, and take several more sips. "Thank you, Marj."

The fire dwindles in my throat, but the fear remains. I'm not sure the remedy for that will be as simple as throwing up the poison and drinking tea. I know what it's like now to believe I'm being consumed.

It's not something I'm likely to forget soon. There's a knock on the door, and it cracks open.

"Marj, how is she?" Bear sounds rattled. I'm happy to hear his voice.

"Come in," Marj tells him. "But only for a short time, mind."

"Are you all right?" he asks me. "You were so . . . I mean, you were raving."

"I know," I can't suppress a shudder. Eland fills Bear in on Marj's suspicion. He's as shocked to hear her conclusions as we were.

"Who was there? Around the kitchen fire?" I smile weakly. "Anyone who particularly wants me dead?"

Bear growls. "Moray."

My cup hovers midway to my mouth. Moray? I thought we'd made progress since the day he attacked me. I wouldn't call him a friend by any stretch, but I don't think he would try to kill me now, either. He's spent so much time protecting me, and he wants to go to Koolkuna; he won't get there without me.

"Why didn't he find a way to get rid of me in the caves?" He could have killed me six different ways on any of the days we were alone together in there.

"Wouldn't leave much doubt who was to blame if he did it then. He's smarter than that—marginally," Bear says.

"Why did he bring her here, to Marj, if he wanted her to die?" Eland asks.

"Covering his tracks," Bear says. "I think I really might kill him this time."

I'm still not convinced Moray was responsible. But I can't be sure.

Panic rises in me. Could this have been a delayed punishment by the Council of Three? Would they try to *murder* me? Or was my poisoner the same person who nailed the dead animals to the wall and started the fires? I rub my temples. My head is aching, and all the tea is making me need to relieve myself.

"Does Peree know what happened?" I'm afraid of what he'll do, how he'll react.

"He knows. It's okay. We've got it covered."

I cock my head. What does *that* mean?

"Marj," Bear says with the warm tone he uses when he turns up the charm. "I have a favor to ask."

"What is it this time, little Bear?" She sounds suspicious, but also affectionate. She has no children of her own, and it's no secret that Bear's one of her favorites. She patched him up enough times when he was a child.

"Can Fennel stay here with you for the rest of the day?"

"Of course. I'd like to keep an eye on her anyway. That's not a big fav . . . Wait, what else do you want me to do?"

"Don't tell anyone she's doing better. Tell them she's the same. Or better yet, tell them she's worse."

"Bear," Marj chides. "You're asking me to lie to everyone? About a patient?"

"Yes. Including the Three."

"Lie to the . . . Bear, what in stars are you talking about? I will not lie to the Council of Three!"

Bear starts to wheedle. I suppress a smile; he can be pretty persuasive when he wants to be.

"Marj . . . Moray tried to kill Fenn—probably by order of the Three. If they find out she's recovering, they'll try again. We need time to figure out what to do, how to protect her."

"The Three wouldn't . . . they wouldn't do that." I hear the note of uncertainty in her voice.

"Are you sure about that? Sure enough to risk her life?" Bear says.

"Even if it is true, which I highly doubt, what can you do?"

"Leave that to me. Keep her here and keep her safe. Eland, too. I'll be back for them at nightfall."

I sit up, wishing someone would stop hammering the inside of my head. "Bear, what are you—?"

He stops me. "For once, Fennel, please do what you're told. Rest."

I hold my hands up in surrender and lie back.

"That's more like it," he says. "Now remember, Marj, no one gets in or out of here until I come back. Okay?"

"You're lucky you've collected so many plants and herbs for me," Marj says. "I don't think the Three—"

"Humor me?" Bear asks. I hear him kiss her cheek. "Thank you. Eland, stay out of sight. Fennel, try to look completely deranged if anyone comes to check on you. Shouldn't be hard after this morning, eh?" He kisses my cheek, too.

The door rasps open, and Bear leaves.

"What in the world is going on, Fennel?" Marj asks. "Why would the Three want to kill you?"

Did she completely miss the news about the dead animals and the fire or the rumor that our small group is leaving? I'm not all that surprised. Marj's head is usually either in the clouds or buried in her work. She wouldn't be the first one to listen to gossip. I hesitate, hoping I can trust her. She's taking a risk for me by lying to the Three; I don't mind taking one for her.

"I'll explain, I promise. But first, do you have a bedpan or something?" I wave my empty mug around by way of explanation. "*Please?*"

I wash up as best I can and rest. In other words, I do what I'm told.

Eland helps Marj with small tasks around her shelter. He's supposed to be dusting, but I think he's actually sweeping dirt straight up into my face, given how much my eyes and nose are running. I still have a headache and my tongue slouches in my mouth, but I improve with each passing hour. I've been drinking Marj's tea nonstop. The bedpan and I have become close friends.

Marj is surprisingly unperturbed about the news that a group is leaving for Koolkuna. I try to entice her to come with us by telling her about Nerang and his marvelous healing powers. I describe his little room full of intriguing tinctures and powders and his powerful healing incense. But that isn't what fascinates her the most. She wants to hear more about the sick ones and how the *anuna* almost care for them.

"They *feed* them?" she asks wonderingly.

"They feed them, because the sick ones *need* feeding. They can't always find food on their own, especially the sickest among them. The *anuna* care for them for the same reason they invited us to live with them. We need a safe home and a new beginning. They're sharing what they have with us."

She thinks about what I said. "And how does the Scourge react to being fed?"

I think back to the first time I heard one of the sick ones speak. It was absolutely unforgettable. "They say thank you."

I tell her more, as I did with others who were curious the last few days. I describe the Feast of Deliverance, the building full of books Kadee showed me, and I describe the warm waters of the Myuna. I'm sure I have her convinced to come with us by the time I finish. So when I finally press her to come, she surprises me by declining.

"Why won't you come?" Eland asks. "You don't have a family."

"Their community already has an herbalist—a wonderful one, by the sound of it. They don't need two. You and your sister are young; life is still full of possibilities for you. But I am old. This is my home, and these people are my family. The elders are my elders, and the young people are my children. Those who remain here will need me. I can't abandon them."

Her voice is gentle, but I feel ashamed all the same. I'm not that self-sacrificing. Marj must see the shame contorting my face, because she says, "Fennel, your path is different. It always has been. You must do what's best for you and Eland even if that isn't what's best for others."

Her words are so similar to Aloe's, it's almost like she's here. I blink tears away, but more push in behind them. All the tears I've yet to shed for my mother. Thousands of tears. One for each day of my life that I won't spend with her.

"She was always fiercely proud of you and Eland. That would never have changed, no matter what you did," Marj says, patting my back a little awkwardly. "You may not have been a child of her body, but you were always a child of her heart."

I can't stop the tears then. They come unbidden, unabashed.

Eland's arms wrap around me while I cry. Marj fusses over us, bringing ever more tea and nibbles she keeps stashed for hurt children in her care.

Like Aloe, Marj never cries. I guess she can't afford to. With as much loss as she's endured all these years of taking care of our people, if she allowed the tears to come, they would never stop falling.

People stop by to check on me over the course of the afternoon. Eland hides, and I lie on the pallet Marj uses for her patients, doing my best to look unhinged like Bear commanded—or at least asleep. Marj shoos them all away, saying I'm not well enough for visitors. The Three never make an appearance, though, which I think is strange. And suspicious.

I try to rest as much as I can, but I'm still mentally and physically drained. I feel like I've been sitting on pine needles for most of the day. When darkness falls, we wait for Bear to come for us. He didn't exactly say we were leaving tonight, but I have to assume we are. I hope we have enough supplies stored away for our trek through the caves.

In my mind I run through everything we pilfered over the last week: food; multiple sacks of water; extra clothes and blankets; torches. It's easier to focus on the prosaic-yet-necessary preparations, rather than thinking about the enormity of what we're about to do.

My thoughts stray often to Peree. If all goes as planned—I won't let myself think about the countless ways it may not—we won't be apart anymore. If there's an ointment to soothe my aching conscience, it's that thought, and the knowledge that I can provide a peaceful future to my brother and a few other families. That has to be worth it, doesn't it?

Eland chatters incessantly about the shelter in the trees he plans to build in Koolkuna. It will stretch between two trees, maybe three, and have at least four rooms: one for him, and one for the big cat he plans to tame and bring to live with us. I don't have the heart to tell him I don't think I can live in the trees thanks to my tree-sickness. Not to mention that I highly doubt any predator like a big cat can be trapped and tamed as a pet.

The door finally, finally opens, and Bear asks, "You two ready?" He has the tone he uses when he's about to go hunting. Serious, focused. But not apprehensive, which was how he sounded every time I went out to face the Scourge as the Water Bearer.

Marj hands me a lumpy pouch. "Medicine. And more of the tea leaves for you, Fennel. I put an extra large portion in, just in case."

We all three embrace her, and she holds Bear for an extra-long moment. Then, to my surprise, she pulls me aside before we walk out.

"Fennel . . ." She sounds uncomfortable, which is unlike Marj. "Tell your intended something for me."

I wait for her to continue, curious.

"Tell him . . .tell . . . Peree . . . I wish I had not had to give him up in the Exchange. It is the biggest regret of my life."

I freeze. "He's your natural son?"

"I named him Wolf . . . but Peregrine suits him much better."

"He'll be glad to know." I find her shoulder. "Marj, are you sure you don't want to come with us? You would have the rest of your life to get to know him."

"It's too late now." She sniffles, causing the lump in my own throat to swell. "But please take care of him, Fennel, as I didn't have the chance to do. I'm very glad you two found each other."

I promise her that I will. And I mean every word.

CHAPTER SIXTEEN

It's full dark and unusually quiet as Bear leads us away from Marj's shelter on the outskirts of the clearing. I inhale the familiar scents of my home: wood smoke, fresh sawdust, a hint of mustiness from the water hole, and the penetrating aroma of the greenheart trees. I won't be here to sample this particular combination of fragrances again, not anytime soon. The thought fills me with both anticipation and sadness.

"Where is everyone?" I ask Bear.

"Water hole. The Three called a meeting. I'm supposed to be checking on you to report back to them. We don't have much time."

"What about Peree?"

"The Lofties are meeting us at the caves."

"I need to stop by our shelter for a few things," I whisper. I planned to pack earlier, not knowing I would spend the day hiding out, pretending to be insane.

He changes course silently. We inch the door open and file inside. Eland stops so suddenly, my mouth and chin hit the back of his head.

"Were you going to leave without saying goodbye?"

"Cal, what are you doing here?" Bear keeps his voice pitched low.

"I wanted to see you before you left." Calli's natural good humor, the byproduct of being Fox's daughter, is nowhere to be heard. She sounds deflated. "I went to Marj's shelter to check on you, but she wouldn't let me in, so I came here to wait instead."

I can't help it; I have to ask. "Does your father know we're leaving tonight?"

"It wasn't that hard for me to figure out tonight was the night. The Three may know, too."

Bear swears under his breath. "Wish you'd told me that earlier."

"Would it have changed your minds?"

I let out a long breath, trying to control my spiking heart rate. It doesn't help the slow throb in my head. "Probably not."

"So you are going then."

"Yeah, we're going," Eland says. He sounds determined, steady. It gives me courage.

"Come with us," I plead.

"I can't."

It feels like an impassable trench yawns between Calli and me. We shared everything as children. Every adventure, every bit of mischief, every terror, every hope—until the day I became the Water Bearer. Then it all seemed to change.

My childhood is a lump of wet sand in my fist—rough and a little misshapen, but easy to grasp. Becoming the Water Bearer was like thrusting that fist underwater. All the individual grains of sand that made up my life slipped, slid, separated, and washed away, until what was left was only the hope of a new life somewhere else. A life I can mold and shape myself.

"I understand." If Eland had insisted on staying, then I wouldn't be going either. "We'll try to come back. If things have changed, maybe you can come back with us then. To Koolkuna. Maybe you can all come."

"Maybe."

"We have to get to the caves now," Bear says.

"I'll walk with you," she responds.

I move around our shelter as quickly as I can, gathering the few items I can't leave behind. Extra clothes for Eland and me go into a pack, and an old doll of mine, sadly neglected, for Kora. Now her doll, Bega, will have a friend to gossip with. I add the rabbit's foot Bear gave me for luck my first day as the Water Bearer and the scrap of fabric I stitched a bear on for him. I have Peree's knife in my pocket, as always. Eland gathers his arsenal: his still-uninitiated hunting knife and the bow he made with Peree. They never had the chance to make arrows for it, but there will be plenty of time for that in Koolkuna.

Finally, I grab Aloe's walking stick where she always left it at night, propped in the corner by her sleeping pallet. I've never wanted to use a stick—I have too much stupid pride. But it was so much a part of her that I can't bear to leave it behind. Leather strips twine over and around the top of the stick. I wish, as always, that the hands that wore them smooth with use were here to guide us now.

"I'll take it," Eland says somberly. I hand him her stick.

Shouldering our bag, I pull him to me. We whisper our goodbyes to the home we shared with our mother. Her strong spirit and the fading ghosts of our childhoods draw close, making us shiver.

We follow Bear through the woods to the mouth of the caves, avoiding the path in case a guard is watching. We keep to the shadows. I hold Calli's hand, determined to maintain the connection between us for as long as I can. The night is cooler than it's been in many moons. The birds are silent in the trees, but I hear muted voices as we approach the cave mouth.

When I pick out Peree's musical voice, I run to him and he catches me. He gathers my tangled, wild hair behind me and covers my mouth with kisses. I wish we had a little more time and a little less of an audience.

The rest of the Lofty group is here, too. Frost's voice mingles quietly with the others. I wonder what she'll do when she finds out Moray and his brothers are no longer invited to come along. At least Koolkuna will be a safe place to raise her child, and she's definitely better off without him.

"Fennel, finally," a rapid-fire female voice whispers—Moon. She sounds relieved. "We were a little worried you weren't well enough, although Bear promised us he'd get you here."

I blink. *He did?* Since when were Bear and the Lofties even on speaking terms?

Moon's still talking. "Peree was starting to pace and get that ferocious look he gets. That's never a good sign, is it, Petrel? How are you, Eland? Thrush is here, ready to compare bows and knives and arrows and whatever other weapons he could find. Thrush! Put that down!"

I'm a little breathless just listening to her. "How are you feeling, Moon?"

"Huge. Ready to have this hatchling." She hugs me, and I jump as the baby kicks us both, probably annoyed at being squashed. Moon groans. "If he kicks me in the spine one more time, I think it's entirely possible he'll break me in half."

Petrel touches my back. "Glad to see you, Fennel." He sounds tense.

"We'd better get moving," Bear says. "Too many people here. Too loud."

"Agreed," Peree says.

I grope behind me, searching for Calli. I can smell her peculiar scent, like the water hole after it rains. Earthy,

I take Calli's hand and put it in Peree's. "Peree, this is Calli. I really wanted you to meet her before we left."

She says hello, sounding embarrassed, probably remembering all the times she avoided Peree when he was on the ground. I try to forget that now. I want to leave the bad memories behind as much as I can.

"I wish you were coming with us," Peree says. "Fenn will miss you."

"And I wish she'd stay," Calli says. "But she'd miss *you* more, and I'd rather she be happy."

I find the familiar features of her face. Her smile wobbles and threatens to fall.

"I love you," I tell her. "You'll always be with me, wherever that may be." She kisses my cheek, and we hold each other. For the second time in the last few hours, I cry.

"No hugs or tears for us, boys. As usual."

My hands curl into fists when I hear Moray's voice. Peree and Bear make almost identical sounds of wrath. It would be funny if I weren't so angry myself. Even Calli bristles. She and Eland step closer to me. My friends create a physical barrier around me.

"What do you think you're doing here?" My voice is as sharp as the blade of Peree's knife in my pocket. The knife I fully intend to *really* use on Moray if he comes any closer.

"Going to Koolkuna. I'm hurt you didn't let me know the plan for meeting, Fenn. I had to send Cuda and Conda to stake out the caves."

"I thought after almost killing me you'd sort of get it through your thick skull that you and your brothers aren't welcome!"

"What are you going on about? I didn't give you enough poison to kill you, only enough to make you—you know—go a little out of your head for awhile. Now look at you with all your people around. It's touching." He sounds as genuinely contemptuous as always, but no more sinister.

"So it *was* you that poisoned her," Bear hisses. He calls Moray a string of names, most of which I agree with.

"Had to," Moray says. "Thistle was on to me. If I hadn't poisoned Fennel, she would've stuck to me and the boys like tree sap all day. Couldn't have that when I was trying to get the last of the supplies pulled together. I thought I was doing you a favor. Did your work for you while you had a nice rest up in Marj's shelter."

"A favor?" I hiss. "I was out of my mind for hours!"

"Better than dead." He pauses. "And dead is what Thistle and her friends had in mind for you, if I hadn't slipped you the banewort."

Her friends?

"Marj was right," Eland whispered behind me. "About the banewort."

"Stay behind us," I mutter to him.

"Face it, sweetheart," Moray says. "If I hadn't tried to kill you, you'd be dead right now."

I try to wrap my mind around that bit of Moray-esque logic. I'm not terribly surprised he was responsible for the poison, or that Thistle hated me enough to try to kill me . . . but who was Thistle in cahoots with?

Calli stiffens at my side.

"What is it?" I ask. Then I hear approaching footsteps.

"What's going on here?" a voice calls out. It's Fox, and he's not alone.

~

"Calli?" Acacia shouts anxiously.

"I'm just . . . I'm . . ." Calli's voice has a desperate edge to it. She probably doesn't want to give us away to her parents.

"Calli's only here to say goodbye," I tell them. "We're leaving. Please don't try to stop us." Peree takes my hand, supporting me. My chin lifts a notch.

"We have to try to stop you, Fennel," Pinion says. "Of course we do."

I curse to myself. I thought it was only Fox and Acacia, but the Three must all be here. And there are other Groundlings with them. I hear their voices and footfalls now.

"Calli, come here," Acacia pleads.

"Let her be, Cacia. She's not going anywhere. Groundlings, listen to us," Fox says. "You don't know exactly how to get where you're going. You don't know what you might encounter along the way. And with apologies to Fennel and Peree, you don't know what kind of reception you'll get when—if—you arrive."

I snort. That pretty much describes every day of my life.

Bream speaks. His voice finds its usual monotonous rhythm, as if settling in for a long, hard march. Or maybe that's just how it feels to listen to him. "There are many accounts of Groundlings who tried to find a way to the source of the Hidden Waters, only to never be seen again. The last time a group of this size went to find a new place to call home, it left the community in shambles. Three generations were required to build back up to the numbers they had before the group left. The people who left were reportedly consumed by the flesh-eaters. Furthermore, history tells us—"

Pinion interrupts him. "What Bream is trying to say . . . I think . . . is that this community may not survive the loss of your departure. Vole and Bear, who will take over the repairs of our structures and the creation of new shelters if you go? Ivy, who will watch over the little ones? Fennel, who will collect the water when the Scourge comes? Have you thought of that?"

Of course I've thought of that. "No one has to stay here. We wanted you *all* to come with us. You made the choice to stay. And you don't need me—the creatures are sick, not dangerous." I wish I didn't sound so defensive.

"So you say." Pinion says. "But if you really believe that, why were you so terrified when you believed the flesh eaters had come today?"

I nibble on my lip. She's right. If I'm really honest with myself, a large part of me still believes the Scourge *is* dangerous. I wish I didn't, but there it is.

Pinion presses her point with the group. "You're following two young people on the basis of some tall tales—stories they clearly have trouble believing themselves. Are you sure you want to risk your lives, and the lives of your children, in this way?"

"Between the Scourge and the Lofties," Vole says, "we risk our lives every day staying here in the forest! What's the difference?"

"Are you comparing us to the fleshies?" a Lofty retorts. "That's rich. We could say the same of you."

A few people in our group shout at each other. My stomach clenches; the feeling in the clearing is so similar to the morning of the Reckoning. Peree lets go of my hand and pulls his bow off his back. I lay a cautioning hand on his arm.

Fox speaks up. "We received explicit warning, passed from Councils before us, not to leave our part of the forest. They said there are things—people—beyond our borders that are worse than the Scourge. It's why our ancestors settled here, so far from the City where the Scourge originated. Our lives here might not be perfect, but we have persisted and found ways to survive. If we leave, that may no longer be true. Aloe herself cautioned me about this, Fennel."

I frown. What did the past Councils know that we don't? What did Aloe know that she'd never be able to tell me?

The scent of rosemary—Aloe's scent—drifts to me on the cool evening breeze. And with it, a moment of relief and confidence, like pushing through unfamiliar vegetation in the forest and finding I was on the right path after all. I can almost feel her touch me now, telling me she's with me. Telling me to trust myself.

"I think if my mother was still alive, and she heard about what we experienced in Koolkuna, she would have changed her mind. Aloe believed we should all do our duties to the best of our abilities. But I think she also understood that sometimes the right path is the one you're told not to take."

Peree speaks. "The people gathered here have chosen to leave. What does it say about life in our community if this many people are willing to follow us into the unknown?" He raises his voice. "Lofties and Groundlings, Fennel and I will take you to Koolkuna. We know the way. But anyone who's changed their mind is free to stay." He pauses. A few people mutter and shuffle, but no one speaks out. "Groundling Council of Three, our group intends to leave. Will you let us go?"

"I'll tell you what we won't do," Fox says.

I wait, my body tingling, all of my muscles tensed. I'm torn by the conflicting desires to run and to stand my ground and fight for what I believe to be the right choice for my family and me.

"Adder and the last Council chose the path of violence," Fox says. "I have many faults, but the inability to learn from mistakes—my own and others'—isn't one of them."

I release the breath I was holding. Based on the exclamations around me, I wasn't the only one relieved by Fox's words.

"We came," he continues, "hoping to change your minds. We wanted to convince you to reconsider your decision. But we won't force you to stay."

Calli runs to her father. From the grunt I hear, she must have practically knocked him off his feet.

"Thank you, Fox." My voice wavers. "We didn't want to sneak away like this. But talking didn't seem to be getting us anywhere. And it was becoming too dangerous to stay."

"I know," he says. "What happened today convinced me that the path we were on was wrong for many reasons. But are you all positive that leaving is what you want to do?"

Quietly at first, then with more assurance, the Lofties and Groundlings huddled in the cave mouth behind me agree.

Fox speaks again, his voice resigned now. "Then know that so long as I remain on the Council, you will always be welcomed here; it is your home."

I find my way to Fox and Acacia and throw my arms around them. Eland follows.

"Be safe, Fennel, Eland. Take care of each other." Tears muddle Acacia's words.

"Fox. Always the peacemaker." Thistle's voice is harsh with derision. "I knew you didn't have the strength of will to make the difficult decisions for the Council. Now my boys will leave me, and the rest of us will die here, because the Three are too weak to lead."

"It didn't have to be like this." I recognize Osprey's cold voice in the treetops. "The Groundling girl led you astray, Peree. She's tearing us apart. And you—you broke your grandmother's heart."

"I can speak for myself," a woman says. I don't know the voice, but it's timeworn and proud. "Peree, you are a disappointment to me and to your people. Your father would be ashamed if he were—" she falters, but recovers quickly, her voice strong again. "You chose a Groundling over the well-being of your own."

"I told you before, Shrike trusted me." Peree's voice is soft and sad, regretful. "He would believe in me now if he were still here. Your loss has twisted your heart, Grandmother."

Breeze?

"And love has blinded yours." Her bitter words burn my ears. It suddenly feels too exposed out here. I hunch protectively over Eland as I herd him back toward our group.

"Oh, no. You won't get away again, girl," Osprey says. "Not this time." If tongues could slice through flesh, his would flay me.

Words will never hurt you, I remember Aloe telling me once, after another child teased me about being Sightless. Arrows, on the other hand, will.

Shouts and cries of alarm as an arrow whistles toward us from the trees. Peree yells at me to run. I reach out to propel Eland toward the cave mouth, but before I can get a good grip on him, someone pushes me, hard, in a different direction. I hear Eland fall. I scramble back to him and find his body, trying to haul him up by his arm. He screams.

"Eland? Eland! Get to the caves!" I yell.

My hands grope across his back. It's wet. I don't understand. How did Eland get wet? I rub my fingers together; they're sticky and slick. There's a rusty smell that I know well, but don't want to identify. I rub my palms on my dress and try again to get Eland to his feet. He moans.

An arrow skims by my ear, and an exceptionally heavy body crushes me into the ground. The breath rushes from my lungs. Eland's hand slips out of mine. I gasp for air and cry out for him. *Why won't he answer? What's wrong with him?*

Thistle shrieks. Arrows *thunk* all around me. I thrash my arms and legs, trying to free myself from the person pinning me, wanting to reach Eland.

"Stay down," Moray says in my ear, his voice unusually serious. "Unless you want to be dead, too."

I still at his last words. *No.*

"Cuda, Conda, get going!" he yells. The heavy footsteps of his brothers thump toward the caves. He shakes my shoulder roughly and moves his bulk off of me. "When I say go, you run. Got it?"

I croak, "Who's dead, Moray?"

"Go now," he says.

I don't move.

"Go!"

I try, but I can't.

"Have it your way." Moray scoops me up and runs, moving easily for a man his size. Arrows buzz around us.

He's hit. He stumbles and grunts and almost falls. Someone cries his name from the caves. Frost, I think. I writhe in his arms, begging him to put me down, screaming for Eland.

A cold sensation builds inside me, as if the comforting fire that usually heats and lights my body has been doused. I pant like an animal in a trap. I can't breathe, can't think.

Moray keeps moving, a little slower now, but fast enough. The darkness of the caves finally covers us. Other footsteps echo beside us, around us. Ragged breathing. Someone's lit a torch; the light dips and slides in front of us.

I want to shout, ask who was hit. But I'm afraid, so afraid, to hear who will answer. And who won't ever answer again.

CHAPTER SEVENTEEN

"I 've got her," Peree says from nearby. *He's alive.*

Moray slows and transfers me to him without a word. We push forward again.

"Where's Eland?" I whisper to Peree. There's no answer, only his breathing. "Peree? Talk to me!" He crushes me against his chest. I start to shake. My hands are freezing; sticky. "Where *is* he, Peree?"

"Osprey was aiming for you, Fennel, not him." His voice breaks. "They were aiming for you."

A scream tears through my head. The sound drowns out every other thought I might have had. I go rigid in Peree's arms, solid and unmoving, a living cave formation.

He sets me down when we reach the cache of supplies. I think that's where we are. I can't be sure.

Peree squats next to me and puts his hands on either side of my face. "Fennel, listen." He pauses, swallowing. "How can I tell you this?" His voice wavers like it might splinter any moment. That's how I feel, too. Like I will break apart. A tiny, weak rock under the foot of some terrible creature with the power to shatter me.

"Don't tell me. I don't want to hear it," I whisper, rolling onto my side. I can't listen to him say the words. The words are the terrible creature. If I hear them, they'll destroy me.

His lips brush my hair. "Okay."

This can't be happening. I scramble up to sitting. "Where is he now?"

"I couldn't get to him. I tried—"

I start to rise. "I have to go back! He might be injured! I can't leave him there, I have to—"

Peree holds me firmly. "He's gone, Fennel. He couldn't have"—he swallows hard again—"survived that." His words come faster now. They spill out of him like blood from a fatal wound. I rub my hands over and over on my dress. "Osprey and the others were aiming at you. Moray pushed you out of the way, and the arrows hit Eland instead. I didn't know they were planning that. Of course I didn't know. And Breeze . . . I can't believe she would . . . She didn't want to come. Wouldn't even discuss it. She tried to talk me out of going. But I didn't realize . . . she must have blamed you for everything. I didn't know." He says more, but his voice fades until I can no longer hear him.

I feel the rock under my hands, rolling the small bits of gravel under my fingers. I want to curl up and go to sleep. Maybe if I sleep none of this will have happened. But I can't sleep. I have to move. We all have to move. It's time to go.

Someone places a pack on my shoulders. It must be mine. I register the additional weight, but it doesn't feel real. Nothing does. I'm floating somewhere above and beyond this moment, listening.

That's not me down there, retching in the black passageway as Peree tries to comfort me. That's not Eland outside—dying alone. That's not us.

The girl below me starts walking, putting one foot in front of the other. I listen to her short, dull responses as people speak to her, horror and sympathy in their voices. Words with no meaning that offer no relief.

They talk and talk and talk.

We walk. And rest. And walk again. I smell the trail of crampberries. I hear the echoes. There's hard rock beneath my feet and cold rock against my fingers and tears that refuse to fall from my eyes. The scream builds inside me, over and over, only to perish on my lips.

Then I don't hear or smell or feel anything. I walk until I'm lost in an unending labyrinth, silent and dark. I wander from passage to dead-end to passage again.

I don't really care to find my way out again.

Young one.

Go away, Nerang, I whisper. *I don't want you.*

Perhaps, young one, but you need me.

No, I don't. Needing people means you care about them. The people I care about die. And I don't want to lose you, too.

He doesn't speak.

It hurts so much, Nerang.

I know, young one. I know.

I wait for some other pearl of wisdom. *That's it? You know?*

Yes, I know. It does hurt. There's nothing I can say that will make that not true.

At least Nerang won't go on about how time will make it better. That I have to carry on. That Eland would want me to. How does anyone know what Eland would want? *I* don't even know what he would want.

I force myself to think the words: Eland is dead.

The shrieking starts up again, like a thousand fleshies crowding inside my head.

I can't have lost Eland, too.

If he's not with me, all of this will have been for nothing.

I keep putting one foot in front of the other. But I don't let myself think anymore. And I definitely don't let myself feel. Feeling is deadly.

We spend the first night in a cavern.

I can't eat, and I barely drink. The few sips of water Peree cajoles me into taking taste stale and make me sick. I can almost smell his concern, like the breath of a sick person. If he smells sick, I must smell dead.

I don't speak to him or anyone else. I curl up, my back to the group, before the fire even goes out. Peree lays a blanket over me.

But I can't sleep.

Before I became the Water Bearer, things weren't perfect. Not by a long shot. But I had Eland and Aloe. Calli and Bear and Fox and Acacia. I had people I cared about and people who cared about me. Now, I have only Peree.

And what does Eland have? An eternity of nothing.

My breath halts its tortured march in and out of my lungs and my heart convulses. I was wrong before, when I thought I was being selfish; I wasn't going to Koolkuna only for myself. I didn't even realize how much I was doing this for Eland. What's the point without him? Why go on?

Don't go down that dark path, young one. There is always a reason to go on.

I ignore Nerang's gentle, insistent voice, listening instead to the fire mutter and hiss.

Moray curses. "Leave me alone, woman."

"Let me help you," a female voice says. Frost. "We need to change the bandages."

"I'm fine. You just focus on growing my baby."

"Is that all you care about?" Her voice is glum.

"Yeah, pretty much," Moray says.

"She's only trying to help," a quiet male voice says. It sounds familiar, but I can't place it.

"Butt out, Conda," Moray growls. That's why I don't quite recognize the voice. It belongs to the brother I can't ever remember.

"She's not a receptacle for your child, Moray. She's a person," Conda hisses, almost whispering. *Whispering . . .*

"I said shut it, brother." Moray's voice is a knife at his throat.

I bolt up. Peree touches my back.

"It was you. You set the fire." I'm accusing Moray's brother of trying to kill me, but my voice is anything but indignant. It's frayed and worn, like fabric beyond its useful life.

"I wouldn't have hurt you," Conda says. He actually manages to sound remorseful.

"Why did you do it?" I ask.

"My mother and Frost's father, Osprey, planned it. He set the fire in the trees to confuse things and agitate their people, and we did the same in the caves," Conda says. "They blamed you for the Reckoning. And they didn't like the idea of us all mixing. It was the one thing they agreed on."

"Osprey is Frost's father?" I'm too worn out to be shocked.

"He found out about Moray and the baby," Frost says. "He was furious."

So Thistle and Osprey formed an alliance. Osprey set the fire in the trees, then blamed me for it, while Conda set the fire in the caves. Moray, or one of his brothers, must have killed those poor animals, too. And of course he poisoned me.

But I don't hate Moray for any of that. I hate him for keeping his word and saving my life.

My fingers unfurl one by one. It doesn't matter now. Nothing matters now. I lie back down.

Peree rubs my back. "You okay?"

"I didn't know Osprey was Frost's father."

"I didn't think it was important," he says, regret strong in his voice. "He always hated Groundlings, and she didn't tell me he knew she was pregnant. I'm sorry."

I shrug.

"Why do we have to sleep in the caves?" An older-sounding man —a Lofty—complains. "It's bitter in here. And I don't want to sleep with a bunch of stinking Groundlings."

"Get used to it," Peree says in the voice he uses when he's frustrated. Maybe I missed something between them. That wouldn't be a stretch. I don't remember much about the day.

"You don't smell that great yourself, bird man," Cuda says.

"Okay, okay, none of us smell good," Bear says, his voice coming from the other side of the fire. *He's alive, too.* The thought drifts away as soon as it enters my mind. *Doesn't matter.* "Now the lot of you shut up and go to sleep."

"Hear, hear," Vole says, sounding thoroughly annoyed.

"When we get to the new place, will we have to sleep with the Lofties?" Dahlia asks her mother loudly. Ivy shushes her.

I tune out their voices, but sleep won't come.

I never imagined my life in Koolkuna without Eland. Never. He was always there, in my dreams of what it would be like. Peree and I would have built a little house for us and for Eland. On the ground, or in the trees, if I could've overcome my tree sickness. Nerang might have taken an interest in him. Eland would have had a whole group of people to show him how to be strong, compassionate, kind, generous.

Peree is my Keeper. He watched over me, tended me. After we lost Aloe, I wanted to be that for Eland, until he became a man. But our people, Peree's and mine, took that chance from both of us.

And we were all complicit. For generations, we carefully nurtured our feelings of superiority, protected our obsolete traditions, and held close our conviction that the Scourge was evil.

We've all been the Keepers of hate, of prejudice, of violence. We've all been the Keepers of the dead.

I clutch myself as the rising tide of darkness builds again, a great destroyer wave. I want to release it. But if I do, I might split apart, leaving only a terrible, gaping hole.

I gasp. The pressure is too much. I can't hold it in. I can't breathe; I'm drowning in sorrow.

I don't know when the tears come, but I feel Peree's arms wrap securely around me as they do. He anchors my body against his, holding me in place as the grief rushes out of the bloody gash in my chest where my heart used to be.

∾

We get moving early the next morning. My body feels heavy and sluggish, like I've jumped into the water hole wearing all my winter clothes. I'm sinking, but I don't have the will to fight to the surface.

I can't eat, even when Peree begs me to take a few bites. I know he's worried, but if I didn't care much last night, I care even less this morning.

Nightmares punctured my sleep. I woke well before the others, sick to my stomach and sweating despite the frosty air in the caves.

Eland sat beside me. I smelled his scent: sweet like a boy and sharp like a man. I almost cried out with joy as I reached for him.

"Eland," I said. "Eland, I love you. I'm sorry."

He didn't speak. *He's angry with me*, I thought. There was no sound. None except the slow trickle of blood from his wounds.

I didn't sleep after that. I don't ever want to sleep again.

We pack up and plod on through the endless passages. Peree leads the group, following the cramberries. I stay in the back with Moon, Petrel, and Thrush. They try to draw me into their conversation with little questions about Koolkuna, but they give up when I don't respond. I know they mean well, but all the talking exacerbates my aching head and sick heart.

We take a short rest in one of the many smaller caves we will pass through. I collapse on the ground, not bothering to take off my pack. Petrel and Moon sit nearby. Thrush talks, but I'm not listening.

He tugs on my dress. "Fennel?"

I lift my head a little.

"I said I'm sorry."

"For what?" I ask.

"It was my fault." He stops.

"Go on, Thrush," Moon says. "Tell her."

"I told her . . . Breeze. I told her I saw you and Eland in the trees that night. She thought you set the fire. I'm sorry I told her. I didn't mean to get you in trouble."

I want to be angry, but what's the point? He's a child. Anger and accusations won't bring Eland back. I take a deep breath. "It's okay, Thrush."

He doesn't say anything for a moment. "I wish he wasn't dead."

My throat closes, the swell of sadness washing over and through me once more.

I keep moving along with the others. I'm shaky and dizzy from not eating or drinking. My chafed fingers bleed through the cloth Peree wrapped around them. I press them together now, taking a grim comfort from the stinging pain. At least I can feel something.

I hold myself together as long as I can, but Thrush's boyish conversation is too heartbreakingly familiar. I scramble backward a few feet before my stomach empties.

Moon follows me. She pats my back, making soothing sounds.

She'll make a good mother, I think fuzzily.

And then I faint.

CHAPTER EIGHTEEN

I come to slowly, groaning as I grip my pounding head. A flame flickers near where I lie on the freezing rock, and someone shifts their weight nearby. I don't hear much else. The rest of the group must have moved on. Good.

"Drink," Bear says. He puts what feels like a sack of water to my lips, but I let the water dribble over my mouth. "C'mon, now. You have to drink."

I turn my face away from his voice.

"I know you're hurting, Fenn. Believe me. But you need to eat and drink and keep walking. That's the minimum."

His words bounce around us before they fade out to silence. I hear them without understanding their meaning, like listening to birds calling to each other from one tree branch to another.

"What do you want me to do here?" Bear asks. "Force you to drink? Because I will."

I tuck my arms against my chest. The poisonous moat inside me has filled up again. "Leave me alone."

"Well, now, that's the one thing I can't do."

"Why not?" I whisper.

"Because I care about you."

"You shouldn't."

"Yeah, tell me about it. Now drink. I mean it, Fenn. I want to see you swallow." He puts the sack to my lips again. I fight him, but his other hand is on the back of my neck, and it's not taking no for an answer.

"That's it. Drink some more . . . good girl." He releases my head and settles back. "You're probably wondering why I'm here instead of your Lofty."

Actually, I wasn't, but I don't say it. I can't seem to find the energy to care.

"We needed him to guide. The Lofties aren't about to follow a Groundling, of course, and since he's the only one who's been this far into the caves before . . . the only functioning one, I mean . . ."

Something flashes to life inside me. "Sorry I can't *function* for everyone right now," I hiss.

He pats my arm. "That's my girl. Fight. Fight it."

I slump back down, already exhausted from the short fit of anger. "Tired of fighting. Doesn't do any good."

He puffs out a breath. I can almost feel it, warm against the frigid air in the caves. It billows away. "I don't like seeing you like this, Fenn. You've never been one to give in to self-pity. You're a fighter. Don't give up now."

I may have been a fighter, but that's only because I always had someone to fight for. Now I don't.

He makes me drink again. I've only taken in a few swallows of water, but I feel more focused already. I hate it. Oblivion is better; safer.

"You remember when my parents died in the fever?" he says after a while.

I do. Bear was a mess. He was either fighting or stewing in silence. Calli and I did our best, but we weren't sure how to help. He mostly bit our heads off. We ended up tiptoeing around him or avoiding him all together.

He goes on. "Aloe talked to me one day. Gave me a piece of her mind. I bet I didn't tell you that, did I?" He doesn't wait for me to answer, but he's right. He didn't tell me. "She found me hacking a downed tree trunk into tiny pieces. I was supposed to be chopping it for firewood, but I got carried away. She was probably glad it wasn't a person, all things considered. Anyway, she sat there for a while with a little frown on her face, listening to me maul that tree. Totally calm, like always. I ignored her. When the trees was practically in chips I finally collapsed, and she still didn't say anything. After a while I asked her what she wanted. 'I want you to stop feeling sorry for yourself,' she said.

"Aloe wasn't one for the touchy-feely stuff, was she?" Bear asks me.

My lips twitch. "No."

"'You have a responsibility, now, Bear,' she said. I asked her what that might be—and not very politely. 'To live,' she said. 'What? For *them*?' I asked. I'd heard that one a few times already. 'No,' she said. 'For us. The community. We need you.'

"I think I laughed at her and said something rude, so she grabbed my arm. Damn, that woman had a strong grip; I had finger-shaped bruises for a week. But who could blame her? I was being an ass. Anyway, she said, 'It's a gift that you're still alive, Bear. A gift your family wasn't given. Don't squander it.'"

He pauses, probably hoping his story is sinking in. And to my dismay, it is—a little. I can hear Aloe's steely voice and feel her even steelier grip. The whole story is so *her*: the insistence that the community is more important than any of us as individuals; that we must accept what happens, and make the best of it.

"I can't say her words made me turn the corner," Bear says, "but I haven't forgotten them, either. I thought you'd want to hear what she told me."

Tears drip down the bridge of my nose, across my cheek, into my hair.

Bear scoots under me, holding my head in his lap. "Is this too weird?"

I shake my head.

"I'll miss Eland, too," he says. "Him and Aloe. I guess I always sort of thought they'd be my family eventually." He clears his throat as my tears flow faster. He fishes something from his pocket to mop my face with. "I'm glad I can still be your friend. I wasn't sure there for a while. Peree—he's not a bad guy. Now that I've been around him more, I . . . I see what you see in him. Not literally see in him, of course, but . . . I mean I might actually like him. Eventually. Like in five or ten years."

I cry harder.

Bear holds me closer, almost strangling me in his anxiety. "C'mon, don't cry, Fenn. I'm sorry, you know I'm not great with this stuff—"

I squeeze his arms and try to control my watery voice. "I love you, Bear."

He snorts. "About time."

And I smile again. Just a little.

Peree is my future. I know that; I feel it in every part of me, despite my suffering. But if Bear weren't here, I would have almost no connection to my past, to my life with Eland and Aloe. And I definitely can't face that.

My old friend cradles me as I cry for my family and for the people and places I'm leaving behind. Crying for them doesn't take the pain away; it only dilutes it for a little while. But that's something.

Bear gets me on my feet sometime later, after I take a little more water and a few bites of dried meat. My stomach wants to reject the nourishment, but I keep at it until the food stays down.

The labyrinth still surrounds me, refusing to let me go. I wish I could stay here and sleep. Or drink some of the plum wine we had at the Feast of Deliverance in Koolkuna. A few cups of that would do the job.

I lean on Bear as we make our way through the passages. I don't usually let myself do that, but I can't seem to walk straight without help. The stink of the crampberries is overpowering in my nose. I can almost taste them, which doesn't help me fight my gag reflex.

"Did he . . . do you think he . . . suffered?" I can't help asking, as much as it hurts. I need to know, but I hope Bear lies to me if the answer is yes.

He puts his arm around me. "The arrow hit Eland pretty square on. It was quick."

I can't get enough air to speak. I grasp my stomach. I've washed my hands, but they still feel slicked with his blood.

"Don't run away from the pain, Fenn. Feel it, respect it, and move on, like Aloe told me to do. Burying it only makes you sick inside. Trust me."

I swipe at the tears that flow silently again. I didn't know I had so many tears. I never used to cry often, but it seems like that's all I've done lately. We start moving again, and I ask him another question to distract myself.

"Why did you want to come, Bear?" I know I'm part of the answer, but I'd gotten the sense from things he said that I'm not the entire answer.

"After my parents died, the one thing I really wanted to do was run away. I thought seriously about it. I've seen parts of the forest other people haven't, thanks to the hunting trips. Signs of life before the Fall—ruins of shelters, plots of land that looked like they could've been gardens, stuff like that. Never anything that made me believe anyone else was still out there, but still."

I frown. "You never told us that."

"The Three always . . . encouraged . . . us to keep it to ourselves. Didn't want to give people ideas, I think." He shifted the pack on his back. "When you came home saying you'd found another community, it didn't surprise me that much. What did surprise me was how much I wanted to see it for myself."

"I think you'll like it," I say. "And they'll be lucky to have you."

"Sure. Another strong back never hurts."

"That's not what I meant. You're smart, you're an amazing friend, and you care about people. Plus, you'll make some girl in Koolkuna really, really happy."

He coughs. "Hey, I think we're getting close. I can hear them squabbling from here. Good thing the fleshies don't come in the caves. We'd be dead with all the noise they're making. What's the plan for getting us from the caves to Koolkuna?"

"Kadee is supposed to meet us at a cave exit. From there, I guess we'll have to walk."

Which assumes she made it back to Koolkuna to let them know we were coming. She was able to walk there through the forest thanks to her resistance to the poison, or whatever it is that allows her to see the sick ones the way they really are.

"How much longer until we get to the exit?"

"A few hours, maybe? I'm not sure."

I'm not sure about much. It's taking all my strength to put one foot in front of the other. The voices are close now; we've caught up to the group.

If my internal map is correct, they've stopped at the side of the enormous cavern that Peree and I traversed, only to have to retrace our steps an hour later when we couldn't find an exit. I recall the utter silence when he left me to explore a passage. I panicked, until I remembered I could follow the foul scent of the crampberries back home.

Being here again is like having the same dream twice. I can still follow my nose, but this time there's only one direction I can go: toward Koolkuna. Going home is no longer an option. It's not even home anymore.

Two separate small fires sparkle in the hovering dark. I hear some quiet conversations, but mostly I feel a strained silence. If I had to guess, the Groundlings are sitting around one fire and the Lofties around the other. Stupid, but not surprising. The fact that our group isn't exactly getting along concerns me, but in a distant sort of way, like hearing an elder tell a story about it.

I smell Peree's honey-tinged scent before he reaches us. I expect him to take my hand or hug me, but he doesn't.

"I'll . . . go find something to eat," Bear says. His arm pulls away from my waist, where it had been resting.

I reach for his hand before it disappears, holding it in both of mine, trying to communicate all my emotions with that one simple touch. Gratitude, regret, friendship, guilt, loyalty. I hope he can feel all of it. Then I turn to Peree.

"How are you doing?" His voice is inscrutable.

I wrap my arms around him and rest my cheek against his chest. His muscles are tight at first, but he slowly relaxes and pulls me against him.

"I wanted to stay with you," Peree says. "But someone had to lead the group."

"I know. Bear explained."

"Oh . . . I didn't think he . . . well, good."

We're quiet for a minute.

"I wish we were alone in here again, the way we were before," he says.

I think of his savaged thigh. "Before you were hurt."

He lays his palm gently over my heart. "We both have new scars."

I place my own hand, blemished from a lifetime of struggling to find my way in the dark, on his, and we hold each other in the all-consuming blackness.

Petrel finds us there, entwined like tree roots, a few minutes later. He doesn't tease us this time. Maybe he understands we needed a little time together to reconnect in some tangible way.

"I offered to lead the group—it's not like I can't follow that nasty smell myself by now—but some of the Groundlings seemed to think I'd take them into some kind of trap. Whole damn place is a trap, if you ask me. Anyway . . . you said Koolkuna has a good herbalist, right?"

I nod. "Nerang is the best."

"That's good," he says mildly.

"Why?" Peree sounds alarmed. He must have heard something in Petrel's mellow voice I didn't yet recognize.

"Moon's been having some pains."

Peree's hand grips mine. "Pains? You mean, the baby?"

"Probably from all the walking. Being on her feet all this time. But you know, it's close to her time."

Peree swears.

"How much longer do we have to go, do you remember?" I ask him, thinking about Bear's question.

"A few hours, at least. But I'm not positive. We took a wrong turn after we left this cavern, and ended up where we spent the second night, remember?"

I'd forgotten about that. The crampberry trail has helped us move much faster than the first time Peree and I stumbled through the caves, but there's still a lot that could go awry with our plan to get to Koolkuna. And now we have the possibility of Moon giving birth early to worry about. I try to shift the cloud of gloom around me so I can focus on getting our people through this in one piece. But it's not easy.

I hurry with Petrel and Peree to Moon's side.

"Oh, Petrel, I told you not to tell them. They have enough to worry about." She must see the concern on our faces. "Peree, I'll be fine. I've been having a chat with the hatchling. I let him know he can't come yet. He needs to nest in there a little longer. You get us to that village, and he'll stay put in the meantime. He's a good boy; he'll listen. Fennel, are you okay? Do you need anything? I mean, anything we can get you?"

I shake my head, ashamed that she's thinking about me when she must be dreadfully worried about her baby. I forgot all about Moon's condition, and how uncomfortable she must be, since we came in the caves. I make a promise to myself to remember I'm not the only one with problems.

"Go," I tell Peree. "Get the group moving. I'll stay in the back with them."

He touches my necklace, his fingers lingering longer than usual on my collarbone, then he starts barking orders at both groups to extinguish the fires and pack up to leave. Someone grabs my elbow— Bear. He hands me something. It feels like a burning ember from the fire against my frozen digits, but it's only a cup of strong tea. I take an appreciative sip.

We start walking, and it isn't long before Moray and the Lofty man get into it again.

"You better watch your back when we get there," the man says.

"Yeah, watch your back, Moray. The bird man might peck you to death," Cuda snickers.

"All those muscles aren't good for much when it comes to an arrow, Groundlings. Except giving me more of a target."

"Yeah, if you don't die from old age while you're working up the courage to try," Moray says.

"Moray, please stop antagonizing him," Frost pleads.

"Whatever you say, love," Moray says. Which could have been sweet, if he said it with any kind of affection in his voice. I wonder if she has a good idea now who she's gotten herself involved with. I feel bad for her.

"You're being an ass, brother," Conda says. He might have threatened me, but I like this one better and better the more I hear from him.

"It's best to ignore Moray, Frost. That's what we do," I say.

"Welcome back, Fennel! Thought we'd lost you to the living dead," Moray says. "Relax. Cuda and I are only having a little fun."

"Clearly they aren't enjoying it." My voice is sharp. Something unstable—dangerous—bubbles in my gut. "You're not helping the situation."

"Never said I'd help anything," he responds. "I made a deal to protect you so I could come to Koolkuna. Bargain worked out well, didn't it?"

The rage that's been simmering inside me since Moray poisoned me, and probably well before that, explodes to furious life. My hands shake so bad the hot tea spills all over them. I throw the mug at the ground, pulverizing it, and stalk toward him. "Our *bargain* killed my brother! It's because of you he's *dead*!"

"And it's because of me you're alive," Moray says coldly. "Not that I'll get any thanks for it."

"Thanks for nothing!" I scream at him. I thrust my hand in my pocket, gripping Peree's knife. I've never had the desire to use it as much as I do right now. Bear's lessons hurtle through my mind: where I'll aim to strike, the angle I'll use, the necessary strength it will take to pierce anything vital on a man as big as Moray. Which only serves to remind me of my practice sessions with Eland. Fresh gusts of despair blow through me.

I slash at Moray. To my surprise, the knife meets flesh. I almost drop my weapon.

"Good one," Bear says with satisfaction.

Moray grabs my wrist; I struggle against him.

"That's the only one you'll get, sweetheart." His voice is strained from pain, giving me more pleasure than it probably should. "Put the knife away before you start something you can't finish."

I shake with fury. "You should've let the arrow hit me!"

"Next time I will," he says. And he sounds like he means it.

"Right, that's enough," Peree says. Wrapping me up, he almost carries me away from Moray and puts me down a safe distance away. I start to pace.

"What can I do?" he asks me.

"Nothing. There's nothing you can do. Nothing anyone can do. I've lost him. It's my fault."

I keep pacing until the group starts moving. Pocketing my knife, I stay near the back with Petrel and Moon as Peree reluctantly leaves me to go to the front of the group. They ask if I'm all right, but I don't do a very good job convincing them that I will be. Not a big surprise. I can't convince myself.

CHAPTER NINETEEN

My head pounds and I feel off-kilter after my outburst. I think I shocked the group into silence. Even Moray and Cuda keep their verbal jabs to themselves for once, which is a welcome change.

My head swirls in a confusing cloud of justification for feeling angry and remorse for letting my anger get the better of me. I don't recognize myself. I don't know how long it will be until I do again.

We move as swiftly as possible through the bleak caves, making our way toward the fork in the tunnel where Peree and I originally took the wrong turn, then had to backtrack. When we reach it, the stench of the crampberries slaps us from both directions, but Peree leads us into the right-hand passage without hesitation. It will take us to the exit where we'll hopefully meet Kadee.

We planned our supplies pretty well, I note to myself, more out of habit than pride. There's been at least one torch lit the entire time we've been in the caves, and I haven't heard any mention of not having enough blankets, water, or food. There's been plenty of belly-aching about the bitter cold, the near darkness, and of course the constant stink of the crampberries, but that was to be expected. And it's tempered by the Lofties' grudging admiration of the miraculous formations posed throughout the caverns and caves. They seem as awed by the frozen majesty of the place as Peree was when we were searching for the Hidden Waters.

Moon moves increasingly slower the longer we walk. She takes frequent breaks now. Either Petrel or I hang back with her to rest, catching up with the rest of the group as they stop. One of us has to stay with Thrush, to keep him out of trouble. I volunteered to be with him all the time so Petrel could remain with Moon, but frankly, Thrush listens only to Petrel. And not all the time. He's already earned several yelps and one angry reprimand for stepping on people's heels or plowing into them while prancing around the back of the moving group. Not to mention he almost set himself on fire playing with a torch during a rest stop. I don't know how the Lofties survived raising him in the trees.

As challenging as Thrush can be, he allows me to focus on something other than my own misery. His boyish exuberance reminds me of Eland a few years ago, although he was never that mischievous, thank the stars. The distraction doesn't make my sorrow easier to bear, but I can shift the burden of it from one arm to the other once in a while.

When I'm with Moon, I take her arm to give her the support she needs, and she guides us. She doesn't complain; she quit trying to talk a while ago. Her shoulders are bowed and she sucks in her breath often. I pretend the baby is only kicking her again, but I know it's her labor pains. I can feel her focus turned deep within her body.

"Are any of your people experienced with hatching . . . birthing?" she pants after one particularly nasty "kick." Her voice is slow and scratchy, remarkably different from her usually chipper speech.

I run through the small group of Groundlings who came with us in my head. "I'm not sure . . . Ivy, maybe. Should I go get her? And Petrel?"

"Not yet." Her teeth clench, and she clamps down on my arm as another pain seizes her. I try to pick up our pace after it releases her, but she stops again a few steps later. She sways, and I hold her close to me.

"Fennel, I think my water broke."

I push my hair out of my face and shove down the anxiety prickling over my skin. "Okay, what should I do? Do you want to lie down?"

"Not here. Need supplies the group has . . ." Moon can't contain a short scream the next time the pain comes. She leans heavily on me as we hobble along the passage together.

Luckily the others aren't far ahead, resting in what is probably only a wide spot in the passage. I call to Petrel; the frantic tone of my voice brings him to my side in an instant. Peree arrives a moment later, and they lower Moon carefully to the ground. Petrel speaks to his partner in a quiet, comforting, voice, but I hear the fear in it.

"How much farther to the exit?" I ask Peree.

"Not sure." He sounds almost as uneasy as Petrel. "We've been heading uphill for a while, so I think we're close."

"Should we send someone ahead to see if Kadee is there?"

"I already sent Bear. I figured I could trust him to keep his head if he saw the sick ones outside, like we did."

Moon moans, and Peree and I kneel beside her. I feel her forehead. She's sweating like she's inside a baking oven instead of on the frigid, rocky ground of the caves.

"Ivy?" I call out. "Can you help?" Footsteps move near and stop a few feet away. "Do you have any birthing experience?"

"Yes," she says, but she sounds tentative.

"So what should we do?" I fight to keep the impatience out of my voice as Moon pants on the ground by my knees.

"I've only ever helped with *Groundling* births," Ivy whispers loudly. Like the Lofties all around us won't hear. I grit my teeth at the absurd ignorance behind her words.

"I doubt a Lofty baby comes out a different way," I snap. I wish Marj or Calli was here. They wouldn't hesitate to help a laboring mother, Lofty or otherwise. *I think.* "I don't care if you've only birthed rabbits before, you're all we've got. Please, tell us what to do."

"We need some warm water," Ivy says after a moment's hesitation, "and a few blankets."

I'm pleased when Frost brings over her extra blanket and offers to watch Dahlia while Ivy is helping us. But I'm especially gratified when I hear Conda say he'll start the fire to warm the water. Within minutes it flickers to life on the ground a few feet away from us. Moon howls with pain.

"I'm going to see what's keeping Bear," Peree says. He sounds like he'd rather be doing anything else other than sitting here watching his cousin give birth.

"Maybe you should take everyone with you." I doubt Moon and Petrel want an audience, either. "Leave the fire lit for us."

He gets the crowd moving through the next passage in no time. Thrush wants to stay with Moon, but Peree and Petrel refuse him with equal firmness. Peree hustles him out with the others, squeezing my shoulder as he leaves.

Petrel, Ivy, and I stay behind with Moon. For her part, Moon seems like she could care less who's there so long as the baby comes as quickly as possible.

When she's not issuing spine-splitting screams, she mutters to herself or to the baby. Or she curses Petrel. He ignores that, instead whispering to her about how wonderful their life will be in Koolkuna with the hatchling. Moon has always referred to the baby as a boy, but Petrel keeps saying "her" and "she." I guess we'll find out who's right soon enough. Assuming everything goes well. But we're in a frozen cave passage far from any real healer. Anything could happen, and in my experience, it usually does.

I hold a water sack for Moon to take sips from between the pains. I've heard lots of babies being born—that's hard to avoid in the close quarters we all live in—but this is the first birth I've been a part of. My heart beats unevenly, and the sweat rises on my forehead. Ivy busies herself down below. To her credit, she stays focused on her patient, talking to her and telling her what to do.

The pains seem to go on and on, striking faster each time. Moon writhes and bucks, riding each shockwave that crashes into her body. It's horrible. Gasping, punctured by the shrieks and groans, is all she's able to manage now. Petrel keeps up his quiet murmuring by her ear.

Ivy takes me aside during a quieter moment. "Something's wrong. The baby should be here by now. Unless a Lofty birth is different."

"They *aren't* different," I say. "Moon's a woman exactly like us. What can you do?"

"I don't know *what* to do," Ivy says. She sounds panicked. It's understandable; she's not a healer, and she's not much older than I am. I put my arm around her.

"It's okay, Ivy. Just . . . keep doing the best you can."

I'm glad Moon is too far-gone to pay attention to us. I'm sweating myself, and my stomach twists. *Not another death,* I plead to whoever might be listening. *Please, not another. Another will break me.*

I grasp at straws. "Any idea what Marj would do in this situation?"

Ivy straightens up. "There is something."

"Try it, whatever it is," I urge her.

"I need something to put under her hips," Ivy says, her voice high and strained.

"Like what?" I ask.

"A pack maybe? It needs to be firm enough not to flatten."

"Here's mine," Petrel says. He sounds on the edge of desperation. I know how he feels.

Ivy busies herself with the pack. "Moon, you'll have to do kind of a back bend. It . . . it won't be easy." Moon grunts her understanding.

"What will this do?" I ask.

"It helps the baby get unstuck." She pauses. "I only saw Marj do it once. I hope I have the pack in the right place," she mutters to herself.

Moon screams as the next pain hits her.

"What do we do now?" Petrel asks frantically.

"We wait," Ivy says. "Through three pains. I remember that. Three."

The waiting is agony. Moon shakes with the suspended pain of the awkward position she has to lie in now. I hold her hand, and I start to sing. Aloe sang to Eland and me when we were hurt or scared, and I can't think of anything else to do that might help.

I sing a lullaby, imagining myself singing to the baby, calling to it to come out. I sing as the second pain wracks Moon. She lies still, exhausted. I keep singing while the third pain hits her, although I want to hold my breath, waiting to find out if Ivy's idea worked.

"What now?" I ask her in an undertone after the third pain comes and goes.

"I don't know. It should have happened by now." She speaks quietly, defeated.

"Moon, you can do this," Petrel says. His voice cracks; tears spring to my eyes. "Don't leave me. Please . . . find the strength." A grim hush falls over us.

Moon cries out. Her scream is longer and louder than any so far.

She gives a lusty, satisfied grunt. A wet, sloshing sound follows, and an angry wail echoes against the walls of the caves. The baby has surprisingly powerful lungs. I grip Petrel's shoulder; he's shaking with sobs of relief.

"I need something to wrap the hatchling up," Ivy tells us. "She'll freeze in these forsaken caves. And a knife to cut the cord."

At least I can help there. While Petrel scrambles to locate a clean blanket, I yank Peree's knife out of my pocket and present it to Ivy. I'd much rather it be used for this purpose than for any new acts of violence. I need to remember that the next time rage threatens to take me somewhere so dark and dangerous.

"Do we have anything to tie the cord with?" Ivy asks.

We all fumble around, until I remember my necklace. I untie it and hand the leather strip to her, slipping the wooden bird into my pocket. Ivy hands me my knife back and holds the mewling baby, cooing to her.

"A girl," Petrel says, emotion suffusing his voice. "Told you, Moonbeam." I wonder what bizarre Lofty girl name they'll give her.

Moon asks for her child. Her voice is weak and watery, but around the tears I hear a blazing happiness so intense and intimate, I have to stand up and move away. It feels intrusive to be so close. I fight back tears of gratitude, or sadness—maybe a few of both—as I hear the new parents cuddle and murmur to their baby, and the first sounds of suckling.

Ivy joins me. I squeeze her hand. "Well done. You could have a career as an herbalist before you." She seems pleased by my praise.

Then I kneel to congratulate Moon.

"Would you like to hold her?" She sounds terribly tired, but triumphant, too.

I take the baby in my arms. She's as light as a loaf of bread. My fingers skim her damp curls, tiny, squashed nose, and squeezed-shut eyes. I wonder if she bears any family resemblance to Peree. I hold her closer, breathing in her scent. She smells like . . . possibility.

As soon as Moon is able to get to her feet, we light a torch, douse the fire, and make our way slowly through the passageway, on to the exit from the caves. I help Petrel support Moon; Ivy carries the baby. I can't believe Moon got to her feet so quickly after her ordeal, but she's determined to get the hatchling someplace warmer.

It seems to take forever. Eventually Petrel spots firelight ahead of us. Then we hear the arguing.

"What now?" I mutter. I'm so very tired; I can't imagine how Moon must be feeling.

Petrel curses and Moon stiffens. I'm about to ask what they see, when the smell hits me. The sick ones are outside. I hear their savage cries now.

We approach the cave mouth cautiously. Our group is huddled in the cave mouth, based on the sound of their troubled voices. It's the textured sound of a thunderstorm: the rumbling thunder of fear from our people is punctuated by the lightning shrieks of the sick ones. There's no light from outside the cave; it's nighttime. An entire day, or more, has slipped away since my brother was killed.

There's a momentary silence as we enter the space. Dahlia bursts into tears and calls for her mother. She must be frightened. Peree reaches us first; his fingers dig into my arm.

"The hatchling?" he asks.

"Is fine," I tell him. "A baby girl. See for yourself." I gesture behind me at Ivy. His breath rushes out of him.

Thrush is right on Peree's heels. "A *girl*?" He makes a gagging sound.

"She's your niece," Peree reminds him.

"Yeah. A *girl* niece," he reiterates. "She *promised* to have a boy."

Peree speaks quietly to Petrel and Moon, congratulating them and admiring the baby. As he does, the arguing starts up again.

"What are we going to do now?" a man is saying. I think it's a Lofty. "How can we get to Koolkuna with *them* out there?"

"What's going on?" I ask Peree when he returns to my side.

"Kadee's not here yet. Everyone's jumpy, especially my people. They aren't used to being on the ground, much less this close to the sick ones."

"What can we do?" I ask him.

"I've been trying to keep everyone calm, but—"

Sure enough, I hear the sounds of a scuffle. Peree darts away to break it up.

I move to stand in front of the cave mouth and wave my arms. "Listen to me, please. If you can be patient, Kadee will be here soon." *I hope.*

"What then?" Vole asks. "How can we get to Koolkuna with the fleshies out there?"

I flounder. I have no answer for that.

"Was this some kind of plot, Peree?" the Lofty man who'd been arguing with Moray asks. "Bring us here so the fleshies can get rid of us?"

"Of course not. Why would we do that?" I ask. I gesture around the group. "We've come so far." *And lost so much.* "Please stick together for a little longer."

"I can't do this." The man sounds like he's scrambling to his feet. "I can't stand this anymore."

"Shut *up*, bird man," Cuda says.

A fist connects with a jaw or some other body part. And then it's like the storm I imagined earlier breaks open. Shouts, screams, and more sickening crunches, amplified by the rock around us. The sick ones shriek mournfully.

Peree and Bear demand the fighters to stop. I yell, too, but it's impossible to be heard. I thrust my hands into my hair. Did we come all this way only to have our thrown together group tear each other apart a mere stroll away from Koolkuna?

One voice thunders above the rest. Unbelievably, Moray orders his brother to back off. The fighting comes to an abrupt halt.

"I'm going to knock flat the next person—that goes for you, too, Cuda—that raises their voice above a whisper," Moray says. His voice is calm as dawn, but no one seems to doubt that he means what he said. Silence. "That's better. Now—listen to Fennel. She got us this far, and fleshies or no fleshies, I'm sure as hell not going back. Continue, sweetheart," he says to me.

I'm more than shocked that he intervened; I cast a grateful smile in his direction. But now everyone seems to be waiting for me to speak.

I want to say something profound that allays their fears. But all I have is the truth, as I know it.

"I don't know how we're going to get to Koolkuna."

There are a few murmurs; a grunt from Moray shuts them up. Peree comes to my side and takes my hand.

"This is what I do know: Kadee will be here," I say, "because she said she would be, and I trust her. And I know that even if we have to wait out the fleshies, we'll get to Koolkuna. And I know that life there is better than the life we left." I pause. "Isn't that worth being patient for?"

A few moments later a voice breaks the silence. Only it comes from the cloud of sick ones at my back.

CHAPTER TWENTY

"Well said, young one. Well said."

I whirl. "Nerang! You came!"

He embraces me.

"You got here in the nick of time," I mutter near his ear. He smells strongly of clove from the pipe he favors.

"So it would seem. And how are you, Myall?" he asks Peree, using the nickname he was given while we stayed in Koolkuna. It means "Wild Boy" and was by no means an insult, at least to the smitten girls of the village.

"A hell of a lot better now," Peree says as he greets Nerang.

Kadee joins us. I throw my arms around them both.

Her voice is warm as she says hello. "But where's Eland?"

My chest spasms with sadness. Peree pulls her aside to explain what happened in a low voice. She squeezes my hands.

"I'm so sorry, Fennel." She sounds genuinely sad, which I appreciate. She barely knew him.

"I am sorry for your loss as well, young one," Nerang says.

I rub away the moisture that seeped into my eyes. "I wanted so badly for Eland to meet you."

Nerang pats my cheek. "One day I will, perhaps. As I hope to meet Yindi again."

Hearing him speak of his partner who died of an illness years ago offers me some hope. If Nerang can talk about her so easily, maybe I'll be able to say Eland's name someday without despair. For now, I have to stay focused on the tasks before us. If I give in to the grief that fills me, I won't make it.

"How are we going to get to Koolkuna?" someone shouts. Moray snarls at them.

"I will tell you," Nerang answers. "But first we will have tea. May we borrow your fire to boil the water?"

He asks the question like we're sitting around after a cozy dinner on a quiet evening in Koolkuna. As if there weren't a bunch of bleating sick ones outside the caves and explosive, terrified humans inside them.

I'm confused but willing to go along with it. "Sure, help yourself."

"Ah, I see there is already hot water ready for brewing. Excellent. Kadee, if you will?"

"Tea?" the older Lofty man says. "We don't need tea. We need a way out of here!" He yelps as Moray thumps him. At least, I think that's what happened.

"Yes," Nerang says placidly.

"How long have the sick ones been here?" I whisper to him. "Do they look like they'll leave soon?"

His laugh echoes around the cave mouth. It's the easy, gentle peal —like song—that I remembered. How can he stay so calm in the midst of a crisis? And why can't I?

"I have spent a great deal of time studying the *runa*,"—what the *anuna* call the sick ones—"but I cannot yet predict their comings and goings. They come when they must and leave when they will."

I shake my head. "You don't know our people, Nerang. Patience isn't one of their virtues."

"Kadee said you and Myall did your best to persuade all of your people to come to Koolkuna, but they would not discuss it."

"We did. We tried. They . . . were afraid, I think." I can't find the words to describe the depth and breadth of my failure, especially when it came to Eland.

"Yet some listened. That is remarkable in itself. Those who are here took two young people at their word and followed them into the Dark Places. Most astonishing. You should be proud of yourselves."

I don't feel proud, not after all that's happened. But his words salve my raw emotions a bit. He's so generous with his compliments, unlike Aloe. Somehow he makes me want to try harder right when I'm ready to give up.

"A lesser person would have stayed in Koolkuna when given the chance. You didn't. You went back for your people. You offered them an opportunity for a better life. Sometimes that is all we can do."

I think of Eland. *And sometimes we can't even do that.*

Kadee begins to pour out the tea. I help her pass it around.

"There are more fleshies out there than birds in the trees," I hear Petrel mutter as I go by, "and their solution is *tea*?"

Peree squeezes my hand as I pass him a mug.

As I go by, Nerang touches my shoulder. He says in a low voice, "Do not drink it."

I turn to him. "What? Why?"

He doesn't answer.

"Let us enjoy a warm drink together," he says to the group. "Then I will tell you how we will make the last part of your journey to Koolkuna."

I hand a mug to Bear, my thoughts spinning. "Tea?" he mutters. "What's going on, Fenn?" I shrug. I have absolutely no idea. "But you trust him?"

Despite Nerang's strange warning, I don't hesitate. "Yes, absolutely."

I can trust Nerang. Of course I can. Like I found I could trust Fox after all. My instincts aren't that badly off, are they?

"I don't like tea," Dahlia proclaims in a voice that's half whine, half warning. If I had to guess, I'd say a tantrum is imminent.

"If you drink it," Nerang says, "you may have a treat. A special sweet. I make them myself."

"They're good," I tell her, thinking of the snack of pressed fruit he gave me when I left Koolkuna.

"Can I have one, too?" Thrush asks.

"Of course," Nerang answers. "If you drink your tea."

A few people continue to grumble, Moray and Cuda in particular, but it's surprisingly easy to persuade them to drink. Maybe it's the tea itself, which smells rich and inviting. The heat is welcome. We're all chilled to the bone.

Peree joins Bear, Nerang, and me at the edge of the group. I hold my mug in my hands.

"Have some. It's delicious," Peree says. He must have noticed I'm not drinking.

I raise the mug to my lips and pretend to swallow, then force a smile. Why can Peree drink it, but not me? What on earth is Nerang up to?

The sick ones rage outside the caves as everyone sips their tea inside. It's a strange juxtaposition. But the drink does seem to have a calming effect. The tense, whispered conversations around the room begin to die down. Within a few minutes, there's barely any sound at all.

I only realize things are not at all right when Peree slumps over on me, knocking my tea into my lap. I drop my cup and try to hold him up, but he's too heavy; he slips to the ground. Bear slurs a word and falls over on my other side. I shake them, calling their names, but there's no response. Not from them. Not from anyone.

I scramble to my feet. "Nerang? Kadee? What's going on?"

A new sound catches my attention—an army of footsteps approaching from outside the caves.

CHAPTER TWENTY ONE

The sick ones' cries are as furious as ever. Whoever is coming toward me from outside doesn't stop.

I hover near Peree and Bear, unsure what to do. "Nerang!"

I shake Peree's still body again. Could they have . . . is it possible that Fox was right, and the *anuna* have betrayed us somehow? This can't be happening.

"Nerang! What have you done?" I almost scream.

Someone moves to my side. I flinch away.

"Be calm," Kadee says. She must have Moon's baby in her arms. I can smell the infant; she's already absorbed Moon's particularly floral scent. "The *anuna* are here."

The *anuna*? Sure enough, the people of Koolkuna flow into the cave mouth, smelling of cool night air and the greenheart forest they passed through to get here. People touch my hands and welcome me back. I greet each one in a daze.

A small body slams into me, almost knocking me over. "Fenn! You're back! *Finally*. Bega has *so* much to tell you!" Kora's spindly arms grip my hips in a fierce embrace. I smooth her coarse curls, and she presses her doll into my hands. "Bega wants a hug, too."

I snuggle the lump of cloth. It smells like their water hole; Kora must have taken her swimming recently. "I missed you, Kora. And you too, Bega, of course."

"Welcome, Fennel," a soft, feminine voice says. It's Kora's mother, Arika. I greet her, but I'm just going through the motions. This feels like a bizarre dream.

"Which one of the bodies is my friend Myall?" a man asks, sounding amused. It's Konol, Nerang's son. I point down at my feet.

"What's wrong with them?" I ask no one in particular.

The baby starts to cry. I reach for her without thinking, and Kadee places her in my arms. I rock her gently, and she calms again after a moment.

"Nothing at all. They are merely sleeping, in a manner of speaking," Nerang says.

Understanding hits me way too slowly. "The tea ... you spiked it."

"An herbal mixture. I use it to coax my patients to sleep, including you, not so long ago. It helped you rest and heal."

"Nerang ... I'm not so sure—"

"Not now, young one. We must go."

The *anuna* are moving all around me. They speak to each other in the first language, their native tongue, so I can't understand them, but they sound focused and like they're in a hurry.

"What will we do with them?" I wave around the cave mouth with one arm, and hold my tiny, warm bundle with the other. I'm thoroughly bewildered.

"We're taking them to Koolkuna!" Kora fizzes with excitement beside me. "Almost all of the *anuna* came! We brought lots and lots of blankets and we're going to carry your people back to the village!"

"*Carry* them?" I repeat.

"If your people cannot see or hear the *runa*, they will not be afraid," Nerang says. "They will sleep peacefully, and wake up safely in Koolkuna. Clever Kora presented the idea."

"I thought of it after reading a story," she says proudly, "about a princess, a girl who would lead her people one day. A bad woman cursed her. She said if the girl pricked her finger she would die. So she was magically put into a deep sleep to protect her." She giggles, probably at my dumfounded expression.

"Nerang . . . this is mad," I say.

"I suppose it is," he agrees. "If you have another idea, we would be happy to consider it."

It *is* a mad idea. But it could also work. If the group stays asleep, they *should* be safe. I guess this is where my belief in everything we learned in Koolkuna is put to the test.

"Why did you tell me not to drink the tea?" I ask.

"One less body to carry," Konol explains as he walks by.

I shake my head at Nerang. He *drugged* everyone, including Peree, without explaining what he was doing. I understand why, but I can't say I agree with his methods.

"I wish you would have been honest with us."

"Would your people have drunk the tea?"

I sigh. "No, probably not."

"Well, then." He sounds like that settles it. "We must be going. The effects of the tea can be unpredictable. If they wake surrounded by the *runa* . . ." He makes a clucking sound.

The hatchling stirs in my arms. "What about Moon's baby? Will she be okay?"

"The *guru* will be perfectly safe. Perhaps you would like to carry her to be sure?"

"Bega and I will guide you," Kora offers, her voice suffused with confidence. "We're very good with *gurus*."

The *anuna* grunt with effort as they lift and carry our unconscious people out of the cave. I don't envy whoever is carrying Moray and his brothers. Or Bear, for that matter.

I freeze, waiting for the sounds of a struggle with the *runa*. The creatures still scream, but as far as I can tell, they don't interfere. I step to the edge of the cave mouth, trembling, my arms cocooning the baby. Even now, after everything, I can't quite believe it's safe. The Scourge is out there.

"Step outside, Fennel," Kadee says from beside me. "You are safe. We all are. We always have been."

Taking that first step into the darkness with a newborn clutched in my arms and little Kora by my side, surrounded by a throng of howling flesh eaters, the stench of their bodies assaulting my nose and my ears ringing with their cries, is incredibly difficult.

But they were right. They were always right. We're perfectly safe.

Kora is true to her word, conscientiously escorting me around obstacles as we follow a path that snakes around groves of greenheart trees. I step cautiously at first, afraid I might stumble, or trip and drop the baby. My friend is more quiet than usual as we make our way. I ask her what's wrong.

"They keep asking for help, and their faces are so sad. I don't know what they want. I wish I did."

I forgot the *anuna*, including Kora, could hear the *runa* speak. It will take days before the clean water from the Myuna works its magic and I'm able to hear their words, too. In the meantime I only hear the rabid groans. I cuddle the baby closer, lifting her up to my ear to hear her steady breathing.

The *anuna* begin singing as they carry the bodies of our people through the greenheart trees on blankets. Kora, the baby, and I follow in the gentle moonlight. We must make a truly strange procession.

Bega fills me in on all the gossip I missed. Her father, Derain, almost severed his finger carving a new toy for her brother, Darel. Wirrim, the *anunas'* story-keeper, has been ill; he's one of the few who did not come tonight.

"Where's Kaiya?" I ask. I haven't heard Peree's admirer's voice.

"Helping to carry Myall," Kora says.

Of course she is.

Koolkuna turns out to be ridiculously close to the cave mouth. I'm able to get my bearings when we cross the stream by the clearing where Peree and I spent the night after the Feast of Deliverance. The same stream I was wading in alone when I was surprised and frightened to hear one of the *runa*. Memories of my time in the village flood through me, not all of them pleasant. Yet being back here feels unexpectedly like coming home. It seems wrong to be this happy without Eland and Aloe.

A few minutes later we file into the *allawah,* the large shelter where the *anuna* hold their gatherings. *The anuna* spread out around the space, laying people on pallets they prepared for us that morning.

"I will take the baby now," Arika says as I stand around, unsure what to do. "You need to rest."

I hate to give up my sweet-smelling bundle, but she's probably going to need to nurse soon and I'm definitely no help there. I pass her to Arika, who pats my arm.

"Sleep. Your people are safe. You've done well, Mirii."

I give her a wobbly smile, wondering why she called me *merry.* I'm too worn out to ask. I collapse on the nearest unoccupied cot, wondering hazily where Peree is. Sleep creeps around me like a swift-moving fog. I curl into it gratefully.

CHAPTER TWENTY TWO

I wake slowly. At first I'm only aware of conflicting, confusing perceptions—the musty odor of the water hole and the appealing smell of a sizzling breakfast. Light floods the *allawah*. At least I think I'm still here.

I smell another scent, almost as familiar as my own. "Peree?"

"Morning." His lips brush mine. "I didn't know you slept with a doll." He plucks something soft and stuffed out of my hands that I didn't realize I was holding.

"Bega?" I guess with a sleepy smile. That would explain the mildew smell. Kora must have tucked her in with me when I fell asleep.

People stir all around us. They sound grumpy and disoriented, but at least they aren't panicking.

"What's going on?" I ask.

"No idea. I've only been awake for a little while myself. I didn't want you to wake up alone, but now that you are . . . I need to go find Nerang and wring his skinny, hairless neck for drugging us."

I grab at his arm. "Peree, don't be angry. I don't agree with what he did either, but he only did it to get us here safely. And we *are* safe. In Koolkuna. Together."

"True." He pulls me into his arms and kisses me again, with more focus. "Still going to kill him."

"Kill who?" someone says.

"Your father," Peree answers, getting to his feet. "Where is he?"

"Where's my knife you borrowed?" Konol demands. His voice has the same quality of suppressed laughter as his father's.

"Right here. Come and get it."

They wrestle for a minute, laughing.

"What do we have to do to get some food around here?" Moray shouts from somewhere across the room. I cringe and wonder if the *anuna* banish people for being obnoxious. If so, he won't last long. The thought gives me comfort.

More people are awake now. Dahlia starts to cry, and Moon and Petrel's baby joins her wailing chorus. Peree and Konol flop down next to me, panting.

"How's the hatchling?" I ask Peree.

"She's fine. Arika's helping them out. I think you and Ivy might be Moon's favorite people now. Watch out—as soon as she's on her feet she'll be cooking nonstop for you . . . Speaking of cooking, breakfast is here. That'll improve people's moods."

The *anuna* begin to wind around the *allawah*, serving plates of food. Konol sits with us as we eat thick porridge topped with sweet berries. He tells us what we missed while we were away. I already know most of it from Bega, but it's fascinating to hear about the *anunas'* preparations for our arrival, including agreeing to Kora's idea to put everyone to sleep.

"So that's your father's evil plan?" Peree asks. "Sedate us whenever we get out of line?"

Konol only laughs.

"Where is everyone going to stay?" I ask him. Surely we won't all sleep in here for long. We'll kill each other.

"We began building new homes for the *lorinya* after you left Koolkuna—some on the ground, some in the trees." *Lorinya* means *stranger* in the first language. I heard it everywhere I went when I first visited Koolkuna.

"Really? You did that for us?" I wish, for the hundredth time, that my brother could be here to experience their generosity.

"We saved your home for you, Myall," Konol goes on. "Thought you would want it back."

Peree squeezes my shoulders. "What do you say, Fenn? It's on the ground."

"But you like to be in the trees." I'm fighting the pain that ripples through me whenever I think about Eland.

"Maybe we'll build one up there later, when you feel better about it. For now, I'm happy wherever you are." His voice is quiet.

"People of the forest, welcome. We extend the peace of Koolkuna to you." Wirrim's fragile yet authoritative voice rises over the din of breakfast. "We have a tradition of welcoming *lorinya* with a story. The story I will tell you was passed down to us through the generations of our people. Now we offer it to you."

He coughs. It's the bleak sound of the winter wind. He sounds weaker when he speaks again. I've only heard Wirrim tell a few tales, and each time was unforgettable in its own way. Given how he sounds now, I can't help wondering if this is the last time I'll hear him speak.

He shares the story of hearty trees that refuse to offer an ailing bird shelter, until the lowliest of the group—Pine—agrees. That selflessness is why Pine alone was granted the great honor of keeping its green needles throughout the cold season.

Everyone is silent, even the children, as Wirrim finishes. He draws in a deep, rasping breath.

"We offer you a life sheltered among our branches, people of the forest. And in offering you this, we rest easy in the knowledge that the Creator will bless us all and give us peace."

We spend the next few hours showing our people around, reassuring them and answering their questions with Kadee and Konol's help. Being knocked out and finding themselves somewhere other than the last place they remember wasn't exactly the best way to start off with the *anuna*, but most people seem more preoccupied with the present, and their immediate needs.

Where will they live? What will they eat? This person needs new shoes, that one Nerang's healing attentions. It's not easy to meet everyone's demands, but we do the best we can. I welcome the distraction. Staying busy keeps my mind out of the past. I dread when I have to slow down long enough to try to sleep.

By lunchtime, we're slowly getting organized. There aren't enough homes to go around yet, so some of the *anuna* offer to take people in, like Kadee did when I was a *lorinya*. Petrel and Moon will have one of the new homes, and I'm happy to hear that Arika and Derain invited Bear to stay with them until his home is ready.

The *anuna* stop us often to say hello, usually calling Peree by his name in the first language, Myall. One of the first to speak to us, a girl I worked with in the gardens when I was here before, calls me *merry* again. I ask her why.

She giggles. "Not merry, *Mirii*."

Peree elbows me. "Fenn got a nickname, too? What does it mean?"

"Star," the girl answers. "Wherever she goes, people follow."

"Like you, Myall," Konol teases.

"I'm not ashamed to admit it." Peree slips his arm around my waist.

I don't feel much like a guiding light. From what I know about stars, they seem very sure of their role and position in the night sky, while I question every decision I make. Then again, maybe that's what stars do at first, too, and the confidence comes later.

"What do you think of your new name?" Peree asks me.

"I hope I can live up to it," I say.

"You already have. You got us here."

Not all of us, I can't help thinking. Anyway, he's being generous. *He* got us here, while I was mostly comatose in the caves. Some star.

A little later we help Moon, Petrel, Thrush, and the baby settle into their home. It's in the trees. They thought about a home on the ground, but decided they were still more comfortable up in the air.

The choice was set in stone, so to speak, when Thrush discovered the ropes-and-rock way down that sends you heedlessly crashing to the ground. He rides it down at least ten times. Moon's convinced he's going to be crushed by the counterweights, the heavy boulders, but Petrel and Peree insist it's all in good fun. I'm inclined to agree with Moon.

Their new shelter isn't as large or elaborate as their old home, and they only have a few pallets on the floor for furniture so far, but they don't seem to mind. Arika lent them a cradle for the hatchling that Kora and Darel outgrew years ago. I sit and rock her as we talk, leaning in every so often to inhale her scent: a blend of Moon's bouquet and her own fresh aroma, like spring grass.

Petrel and Peree finish arranging the pallets where Moon wants them, between the two windows so they can catch the evening breezes. We can hear Thrush hollering and pelting up and down the walkway outside with another boy. How is it that children make friends with strangers so easily? If only adults did, too.

"I wasn't so sure when we woke up with a tea hangover this morning," Petrel jokes, "but I'm starting to think we made the right decision in coming."

"Thank you, cousins," Moon says. "I'm so grateful to you both, and to Ivy for delivering our hatchling." I can tell she's exhausted—she's actually speaking at a normal rate—but she also sounds supremely happy. "Oh! Did Petrel tell you? We decided on a name for her."

Peree pounds Petrel on the back. "Good news. What did you decide to go with?"

I plaster a smile on my face and brace myself, preparing to gush over the Lofty name no matter how preposterous it sounds to my Groundling ears.

"Yani," Moon says.

"Yani? That's . . . beautiful." And I actually mean it. They laugh, probably at the surprised tone in my voice. "Is it like a . . . type of cloud or something?" Lofty women are usually named for something in their environment.

Petrel answers. "We figured we're starting a new life here, so maybe it's time for a new tradition. We asked the locals what the word for *hope* is in their language. Turns out it's *yani.*"

"We thought it was perfect," Moon says.

I nuzzle little Yani, who sleeps contentedly in her cradle. *Hope.* "It *is* perfect. I love it."

"Now, can you tell me something?" Moon says. "What does *lorinya* mean? Everyone keeps calling us that."

And it's my turn to laugh.

Peree and I leave soon after, agreeing to take the new family to the water hole the next day for a swim. The cooling air is crisp as apples. We stroll along the walkway heading for the descending platform, stopping to chat with people along the way. I refuse to use the ropes-and-rocks method unless I absolutely have to.

"Care to come home with me?" Peree asks, a teasing note in his voice. It's been a while since we've been alone together.

"Shouldn't we do a little more to help people get settled in?" I ask, waving my hand around.

"It can wait. We promised to get them here. Mission accomplished. We can sneak away for an evening, don't you think?"

I don't answer right away; the silence grows between us. He unexpectedly pulls me off course, leading me across a wide platform. My stomach rolls in protest at the abrupt movement.

"There's a nice view from here; let's sit for a while."

He guides me to the edge and seats us with our backs against a supporting tree. I hear people above and below us, laughing and talking, but for the moment we're alone. The diving sun offers us a soft blanket of warmth, and birds serenade us from the surrounding branches. It's peaceful, exactly what Koolkuna is supposed to be.

But the moment I think about letting myself relax, thoughts of Eland steal in. It's impossible to sweep away the burning embers of regret in my chest. I didn't think I could miss someone more than Aloe, but I do.

I can tell Peree's going to ask me how I'm doing, and the last thing I want to do is cry again. So I preemptively change the subject.

"I have something to tell you," I say. "Something I learned right before we left." He waits. I take his hand, stroking his rough fingers. "Your natural mother—it was Marjoram."

"Your herbalist?" he asks.

"She told me she hated that she had to give you up, that it was the biggest regret of her life." After being with Moon as she gave birth, and losing Eland, I have a better understanding of exactly how awful the Exchange really was.

"I'm glad to know," Peree says. "I never put much thought into who my natural parents were, but of course I was curious."

"She was a good person," I say. "And she obviously loved you."

He winds his fingers around mine. "I'm glad we won't have to go through that, if we have children."

I nod.

"Fenn . . . you said before, in the caves, that you didn't want children because of the Exchange. Do you still feel that way?" He sounds cautious.

I shrug. I haven't had time to process everything that's happened, much less to think about the future. We don't speak for a few minutes, listening to the drifting chatter of the *anuna* around us. Thrush runs down the walkway behind us every so often, howling excitedly. It pierces me through each time I hear him.

"Have you ever heard the story of the coyote?"

A story would be nice. Maybe it will put off thoughts of Eland for a few minutes. "What kind of animal is a coyote?"

"Kind of like a dog. Do you know what that is?"

I nod. Kora told me a story about dogs. Supposedly they were animal companions for humans before the Fall. I'm not quite sure I believe that. It seems like an incredible luxury to live with a good-sized animal and not eventually have to eat it.

"Coyotes used to roam all over," Peree continues. "They ate small animals, like rabbits, and were very adaptable."

"What's a rabbit?" It's my weak attempt at a joke. If any animal thrived after the Fall, it's the rabbits. They're everywhere.

"Ha, ha. Coyotes were solitary animals. They only came together to make little coyotes."

He slides his hands around my waist. I drop my head back against his chest, bone tired, and allow his words to take me away from my misery for a little while.

"In the time before time," Peree says, "Coyote and his mate lived together, raising their family. They lived in the low mountains, hunting across the hills and through the wide-open spaces under the blue sky and bright sun. They never separated. When they had litters of young, they both tended them, taking turns to hunt. In the summer, food was plentiful. In the winter, they shared what they had to survive. They relied on one another, happy to be together.

"One winter the snows came early. Storm after storm fell over the coyotes' mountain home, and the sun never came to melt the snow. The small animals burrowed and hid from the weather, so the coyotes began to starve. Worse than that, their young starved, too. The pair watched their children wasting away, one small life at a time, taken by the unforgiving frost and snow. By the time spring peeked through the smothering blanket of winter again, their young were all gone."

I stiffen, thinking of Eland, and Peree kisses the top of my head in apology.

"Coyote was terribly sad. His mate was inconsolable. She had wasted to the point of death, refusing to eat when he brought her food. Coyote didn't know what to do. One day, the warmest yet after the harsh winter, he found her sitting in a high place, looking out over the valley below. The mountains were still shedding the whites and grays of winter and wrapping themselves in the soft colors of spring.

"Coyote watched his mate, hoping the hint of light he saw in her golden eyes meant she was starting to recover from their loss. Maybe she was ready to begin again, start a new family, he thought. But his hopes were crushed when she spoke.

"'I'm leaving,' she said, her voice as desolate and broken as the higher ground above them, still clutched in winter's deadly grip. 'Then I will go with you,' Coyote said. His mate shook her beautiful, dappled grey head. 'No. I will go alone.' He realized then that the light he'd seen in her eyes had been the last bit of hope going out. It burned bright, but only for a moment, before extinguishing. He wanted to plead with her not to go, but he could see it would do no good. She would not recover from losing their young. Her heart was broken, the remnants washed away, never to be whole again. And he understood. For the last untouched part of his heart—the part that held and protected his love for her—was breaking, too."

Tears slip out of the corners of my eyes. Peree clears his voice before going on.

"The next morning she was gone, and from that day on Coyote lived alone. He still hunted under the blue sky and the bright sun, but he was never again happy. He rarely saw his mate. Yet sometimes, in the lonely darkness of night, they called to each other across the wind-swept mountains, sharing plaintive howls of sorrow and loss. And all that heard them prayed to be spared from such sorrow themselves."

Peree falls silent. I can't speak at all.

"I love you with all that I am," he finally says. "If I could, I would give my heart to you. But I'm afraid that even giving you my whole heart won't be enough to heal the damage done to yours."

I feel the compassion in his words, and the fear. I'm afraid, too. So afraid of losing someone else I love. I've been wondering if loving people is really worth it.

Because I know now—with painful, absolute certainty—that to truly love someone means risking everything; safety, security, contentment. Maybe forever.

"You're all I want." His hands tighten around my waist. "If it were up to me, I would partner with you as soon as possible. Tomorrow. Today. Right now. But I can wait until you're ready. I can wait until your heart is healed."

That's the problem. I don't know if my heart will *ever* heal. If I'll ever be truly carefree and happy again. I love Peree with every fiber of my body, but why do I deserve to be happy when Eland and so many others will never have that chance? What would they think of my selfishness?

Peree's arms stay frozen around me, like time has stopped, as he waits for my response. How can I tell him I can't partner with him, after everything he's done for me, for us? He's lost at least as much as I have. He *does* deserve to be happy.

And that's when it hits me: my broken heart is irrelevant. How Eland or Aloe would feel doesn't matter much, either. It's far too late to worry about that. But I can make Peree happy. I can do that.

Isn't that what love really is, after all? Setting aside your own problems to be there for the other person when they need you? It's what Peree's always done for me.

I put my hand in my pocket and pull out the bird carving, holding it up. "Do me a favor? Make a new cord for my necklace. I want to wear it for the ceremony. That's part of the Lofty tradition, right?"

He traps the bird tightly with his hand, as if he's worried it might fly away like the cassowary woman did. His voice is tight with emotion when he speaks. "Are you sure? I don't want you to agree only for me."

"For who then? After the Feast of Deliverance you asked me to be your future. That's what I want, too. A future with you. Today, tomorrow, and every day after."

He turns me around and kisses every part of my face that he can reach. His whispered words of love and devotion help curb the bleeding of my heart. I take his face between my hands and kiss him desperately, passionately, matching every contour of his mouth with my own.

My heart may never be hardy and whole again, but I don't want to be like Coyote's mate, living alone with my grief. Instead I will pour myself into Peree, and accept him in return, hoping that by sharing our sadness, somehow it might be easier to bear.

CHAPTER TWENTY THREE

W e set the date.

Kadee insists on organizing a feast for us for the day of our partnering ceremony. She suggests using a blend of our traditions to mark the moment, an idea that Peree and I love. We'll exchange bonding bands—leather bands that we'll wear around our arms to symbolize our partnership—as Groundlings do.

I'll wear my bird necklace, and I'll remove the feathers from Peree's hair during the ceremony, as Lofties do. Apparently the action symbolizes that he no longer needs to attract a mate. I have to laugh at that, which sort of offends him. Which ends in me apologizing. And us kissing. Then again, everything we do ends in us kissing these days.

Peree and I will also share the story of how we fell in love, and we'll give an offering to the *runa* as the *anuna* do. We'll have to prepare our people for that. It will be the first time they see the sick ones after a few weeks of drinking from the Myuna.

Fortunately for my raw nerves, I don't have much time to dwell on the impending ceremony. Peree and I are needed all over the village, helping out as our people learn the ways of Koolkuna. It's odd to be the experts now, when we were *lorinya* here ourselves not long ago.

For the most part the *anuna* seem to accept the intrusion of so many people into their village with good graces, but it's hard to approve of the likes of Moray and his brothers. I hear the *anuna* grumbling about their rudeness by dinner on our first day.

Most of the Groundlings choose homes on the ground, while the Lofties decide to stay in the trees. Old habits die hard, I guess. But Moray and Cuda select a house in the trees. They seem as fascinated by the ascending platform, the intricate walkways, and the homes perched in the branches as any Lofty. Conda, on the other hand, decides to stay with Konol for a while, on the ground. I would think it was an interesting choice, if I had much time to think about it.

Moray insists that Frost stay in the trees near him, even though it means another family has to give up their home for her. I wish I could say it was out of love, or true concern for her well-being, but he's only interested in keeping her pregnancy viable. He could care less about her, so long as she's growing his child properly. It's disgusting.

Maybe I'll forgive Moray at some point for saving my life. But not yet.

Bear decided to build his own house on the ground. The site he chose is about as far away from Peree and me as possible. I understand. At least he's here in Koolkuna.

It will take him a few weeks to finish building, so he is staying with Kora's family for the time being. Her four-year-old brother, Darel, is now permanently attached to Bear's leg as he moves around the village.

I meet up with him to gather water together at the water hole, about a week or so after we arrived. We're alone—if you don't count Kora, Bega, and Darel.

Bega takes careful notes on what we're saying so she can report the exact details of our conversation to anyone who will listen. At least I imagine that's what she's doing, given the gossip she's shared with me about what the *anuna* think about the Groundlings and Lofties we brought with us. I have to assume the information flow goes both ways. Darel runs around and around us, alternately jabbering in the first language and repeating Bear's name.

We fill large clay jugs and water sacks to carry back to the village. Kora and I can only manage one unwieldy container between us, so I'm grateful Bear and his broad back are there. He lifts a jug easily out of the water and sets it on the ground next to us.

"If you knock this over, you're getting the next one," he warns Darel.

"What do you think of Koolkuna?" I ask him as we fill a sack together. I asked Peree almost the same question once.

Bear thinks about it. "It's nothing like what I imagined. And yet, in a way, everything I hoped for." He hoists the sack up. "I didn't expect it to feel so . . . safe, I guess. At home I was always on alert—watching for the flesh-eaters, calculating how far it was to the caves and how long it would take for me to get there. I hunted, fearing the Scourge would catch up to us. I repaired people's shelters, wondering how long they'd get to live in them before the fleshies came again. It was like my life, almost every minute of it, was focused on the Scourge in some way. Here, nothing is. The *anuna* don't even carry weapons. It's strange. Everyone has a job, but they don't work all that hard. They take time to enjoy themselves. I can't figure out if that's just how they are, or if maybe not being afraid all the time makes them that way. But either way, I like it."

He picks up a filled jug. The next moment it crashes down between us, shattering and splashing water all over my legs. I jump away.

"Are you okay?" I ask.

Bear steps in front of me, yelling for Darel to come to him. I reach out to Kora, automatically pulling her into my side.

She slides out of my reach. "You don't need your spear, silly Bear. The *runa* is only thirsty."

I hear the sick one now. Not a howl or a moan, but words. It's asking for water, the voice as ruined as the water jug at our feet. I put my hand on Bear's arm, hoping to calm him.

"Kora, Darel . . . don't get near it!" Bear says. The muscles and tendons of his arm are rigid under my hand as the children apparently approach the *runa* together. I hear the sick one drink thirstily. "I can't believe this," he says, wonder in his voice. "Is this real?"

I slide my hand into his, and we stand side by side in the cool air by the water hole as all that he believed to be true splinters and reforms into an unfamiliar new shape. I know the feeling.

"It's real," I tell him.

"What is this place?" he murmurs.

"Home," I answer. "The way it always should have been."

A few days later I go with Kadee to the gardens to help with the late-summer harvest. It's a novelty to be able to work out in the sun and the fresh air every day after years of working in the caves. And I feel closer to the memories of Aloe and Eland as I dig in the earth. Maybe it's the scent of rosemary and freshly turned soil, but it's the only place I find real peace.

As I walk home from the gardens, covered in dirt, I hear a familiar voice. Kai. I haven't spoken to her since we returned to Koolkuna. Bega told me she was upset by the news that Peree and I are partnering. I'm not surprised; I knew she developed feelings for him the last time we were here. I also can't say I feel all that bad about disappointing her. She'll have to get used to the idea that he's officially going to be mine soon.

So I try—really try—not to feel jealous when I hear the voice of the man who's going to be officially mine in the next moment.

"That's it. Pull the arrow right to your chin . . . and release. Good. Let's try another."

Okay, they're practicing archery together. Big deal. Peree and Konol have been practicing with everything from knives to spears almost every day, getting ready for a hunt.

Peree calls to me. I wrench my lips into a smile and wave at them, but I keep walking. I can be mature about this, can't I? I can, until the arrow whizzes by my head. I hit the dirt.

"Watch it, Kai!" Peree yells.

"Oops," she says.

Peree jogs over and helps me up. "You okay?"

Blood boils into my face, but I dig deep and nod. "No harm done."

"That's enough for today, Kai. See you around." He guides me away, keeping a tight arm around my waist. He's probably worried I'll explode like I did with Moray.

"Fennel," Kai calls. I turn back toward her. "Congratulations. You're lucky." Her words are nice. Her tone? Not so much.

I smile again. It comes more naturally this time, because I know she's right. "Thanks."

A moment later an arrow slams solidly into its target nearby, making me jump. "But if anything happens to you, he's mine."

My smile vanishes. We walk on, and Peree sort of stutters. I think he's speechless.

My laugh is hollow. "Well, at least I know where I stand."

The day of our partnering ceremony arrives. Kadee is busy pulling the feast together, so Arika helps me bathe and dress. Moon came by earlier to wish me luck, but she went home to take a nap. Yani is delightful, but a good sleeper she is not.

I was at a loss for what to wear until Konol brought me the dress that his mother, Yindi, wore when she partnered with Nerang.

"We thought it might fit you," he said gruffly.

And it does. The dress is elaborate by our standards, made from some sort of soft, supple hide adorned with patches of thick fur and feathers here and there. I feel a little self-conscious, but I want to look the best I can for Peree. I haven't spoken to him since he slipped out of our home this morning with a kiss and a promise to see me later.

Arika uses some unfamiliar dyes on my face to "heighten my beauty," and she arranges my long hair artfully in a style full of braids, twists, and knots—a physical reflection of how my insides are starting to feel. Kora and Darel are so excited about the festivities that they're whirling around the shelter like dirt devils. Arika, normally sweet and soft-spoken, finally loses her temper.

"Come you two! We must collect the wild flowers for Fennel and Myall."

She marches them out of the shelter. I shake my head, imagining Aloe ordering me out to pick flowers when *she* was upset. I wish Aloe was here now, temper and all. Kadee has been wonderful, but it's not quite the same. I miss my mother; and my brother; and my best friend.

Calli would have loved all of this. She'd be talking nonstop, nervous for me. She wouldn't have left my side. But this day wouldn't have been possible at home; it wouldn't have been allowed. Everything that's happened—good and bad—seems unavoidable now, like it couldn't have gone any other way.

I finish fiddling with my hair and sit carefully on the edge of a pallet, afraid to mess up Yindi's beautiful dress. I have nothing to do except think. My head buzzes and my stomach rolls. My hands grow cold; I blow on them to warm them. Just when I think I might burst open like a boiled berry, spewing sizzling anxiety, there's a soft knock on the door.

"Fennel? Are you ready?"

Hearing Peree's voice makes the overwhelming emotions floating around inside me snap back into perspective. The doubt, the sadness, the guilt—they don't exactly go away, but they fade to the background where they should be. I wish my family were here. But the only one I *need* with me now is him.

"I'm ready." I take a calming breath and step out the door.

"Wow. You look . . . I don't think there are words." His voice is sort of awed. He takes my hand gingerly, like I'm something of value that might break with a rough touch. So I have no choice but to plaster myself against him and kiss him.

"Thanks," I whisper. "Wish I could say the same about you." He groans at my bad joke.

I skim my hands over his shoulders and chest. He has a new shirt on—a kind I've never felt before—soft leather with intricate stitching all over it. His exquisite honeysuckle scent is strong; it always is after he bathes.

"Kai was right," I say. "I'm *incredibly* lucky."

He kisses the hollow at the base of my throat, then reaches around to tie my bird necklace into place. "I'm the lucky one. Lucky to be able to spend the rest of my life with you. I love you."

I touch his face, running my fingers along the smooth ridge of his jaw, and tracing his lips. "I love you, too. I wish so many things had been different, but not that. Never that."

Our mouths meet again . . . and someone clears their throat. We both jump back like guilty children.

"The *anuna* are gathered. If you two can find the time to join us for the ceremony?" Nerang asks, the quiet laughter in his voice. "Ah . . . you look beautiful, young one. Yindi would be pleased."

"Thank you, Nerang," I say. "And not only for her wonderful dress. For everything you've done for us."

We make our way to the water hole, where the ceremony and the feast will be held. I can already smell roasting meat and the scent of toasty bread. It reminds me of the Feast of Deliverance—a very good memory. The sun beams down at us as we walk along the path, and the birds sing in the trees like groups of small, flighty choristers. It's an absolutely gorgeous day.

Peree and I link arms, following Nerang to the front of the gathered crowd. Moon and Petrel embrace us along the way, Yani in their arms. Bear hugs me, too, whispering that he's happy for me. His voice carries only a touch of sadness. Several of the *anuna* press my free hand as I pass, and offer me their blessings, as do many of the other Groundlings and the Lofties. I wish Eland and Aloe and Calli were among them.

The last few weeks have been the most challenging of my life. And that's saying something. But no one ever said that doing the right thing would be easy, or that it wouldn't involve sacrifice. No one said everything would work out for the best. It hasn't. I've hurt people with my decisions, even when I was determined not to.

Yet, at this moment, I'm proud that Peree and I honored our

promise to those of our people who wanted to listen, like Moon and Petrel, Ivy and Dahlia. Even Frost and Moray. Groundlings and Lofties alike. We brought them here, to safety. Now they can put down roots together in the fertile soil of Koolkuna and shelter and sustain each other as I'd always hoped.

And Peree and I? We've earned our chance to be happy. I'm determined to make the most of it.

THE END

His loyalty was to his people. Until he met her.
Get Peree's side of the story in The Keeper, available now for FREE

Brilliant Darkness 3: Fennel and Peree are finally together and safe from the Scourge in the protected village of Koolkuna. Except, on the day of their partnering ceremony the children of the village are stolen away—Fenn's loyal companion, Kora, among them.
Read The Fire Sisters (Brilliant Darkness #3) now!

READ NEXT

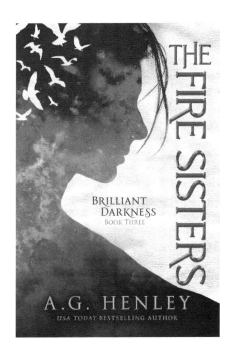

The Fire Sisters: Brilliant Darkness #3

Chapter One

I grip Peree's hand as we stand beside the fire lit for our partnering ceremony. My palm is slick with nervous perspiration, but I'm prepared to speak the words that will bind our lives and souls together. Among our friends and family in the peaceful village of Koolkuna, I'm ready to intertwine my life with his.

Nerang chats with others in the first language of the *anuna,* the people of Koolkuna. I have no idea what the talented healer is saying, but it doesn't matter. The warm tone of his voice tells me he's happy to be part of our celebration. We're only waiting for our friend, Arika, and her children, Kora and Darel, to arrive. I won't start without them.

I can't see the group gathering nearby—Groundlings, Lofties, and the *anuna*—but I still hear echoes of their well wishes as we entered the clearing to stand beside the water hole. I smell the musky scent of the heather burning over greenheart wood in the fire, a combination I was told would encourage love and longevity for our union. I feel Peree's warm, bow-callused hand clasping mine now. And I taste his last kiss on my lips, a sweet drizzle of honeysuckle.

Everything is perfect—a validation of all we worked so hard to accomplish, a small recompense for what we lost as we led our people to safety in Koolkuna.

My thoughts are splintered by the sudden noise of a woman's shrill screams and shouts, coming from the path to the village.

"Help! Help me!"

Peree pulls me close, and fear punctures my heart.

"What's going on?" I ask.

"I don't know."

The woman reaches the clearing, her feet slapping unevenly against the dry ground, as if she stumbles as she runs.

"It's Arika. Her head is bleeding." Peree's normally musical voice is low and rough.

What? Is she all right? Did she fall and hit her head or something?

Nerang ministers to her, speaking softly. I tug Peree forward to hear what they're saying.

"Tell us what happened," the healer asks.

"They took the *guru*," Arika cries. "The children are gone!"

Gone? My body tingles.

"What do you mean?" a man says.

"Took them?" a woman asks, her voice rising. "Which of the *guru*?"

"Let her speak." Nerang's firm words are lined with distress.

"Frost and I... led a small group of *guru* into the forest to gather wildflowers for the ceremony." Arika chokes on her tears. "We were on our way here, when we... we were attacked. They were all taken!"

"Thrush was with Frost!" Moon gasps.

"He was there. Kora and Darel were with us," Arika says with fresh sobs, "and four others. I'm sorry... I'm so sorry. They are gone."

Horror rushes through me. "I don't understand... who took them?"

"What did they look like?"

"Which way did they go?"

People shout over each other, their voices loud, harsh, and frightened. I can't tell anyone apart. The clamor hurts my ears and makes me dizzy. Peree puts a steadying arm around me; I clutch his waist to ground myself.

"Quiet!" Nerang says. "*Who* took the *guru*, Arika?"

"I don't know." She pants. "They came suddenly... out of the trees. They wore strange clothes, and their hair was painted... they carried weapons, and... and they were all women. I tried to keep hold of Kora and Darel, but one of the women put a blade to my throat. She struck me with the butt and took them away." Her voice breaks.

Peree hisses out a breath. I feel faint.

"There were no men?" Kaiya asks sharply.

"No, no. Only those terrible women."

"Were there colorful feathers at their waists, like the one in Myall's hair?" Kai says.

"Yes!"

Peree's feather?

"We must follow them," a man yells. Others shout, agreeing.

"It won't do any good." Kai sounds shaken. "Those feathers are their mark."

"Whose mark?"

"The women who took me away when I was a child. The Fire Sisters."

Arika moans. I put a hand on my friend's shoulder.

"*Why* did they take the children, Kai?" Peree asks.

"The Sisters live without men." Her voice is bleak. "They gather girls from other groups to survive."

We erupt with fresh cries.

"We will catch them!" Derain, Arika's partner, says. "Can you lead us to where they attacked you?"

She says she can. Running feet pound out of the clearing.

"Kadee's here," Peree says to me. He places my hands in a smaller, softer pair, and his lips brush the top of my head. "I'm going ahead."

"Peree—!" I don't have time to tell him to be careful. He's gone with the others.

Kadee, my natural mother, holds my arm as we run after the group, following footfalls and the sounds of parents calling their children's names. We reach the path to the village, but rather than turning that way, we enter the forest ahead, pushing through the grasping arms of trees and bushes.

We stop in a clearing—the light brightens and I'm no longer surrounded by vegetation. Frightened voices flutter around me, birds flushed from their nests by a predator.

"Do you see anything?" I ask Kadee.

"Only the trees and our own people." Her hand is icy on my arm.

A poisonous brew of dread and helplessness oozes through my body. I close my eyes and listen for any sound of the children.

"Which way did they go?" someone yells.

"Here," a woman shouts in a quivery voice. "The bushes are crushed!"

Kadee pulls me in that direction. We crash into the woods again as people fall in behind us. Branches and brambles claw at me again, drawing stinging trails along my face and arms.

We move this way and that, following those in front. I'm jostled and jerked, but I can only think of Kora and the other children.

A battle cry pierces the air over our heads as if the trees themselves scream out. The voices are feminine and fierce. They aren't the wails of the sick ones, the Scourge, but the same prickling feeling crawls along my scalp.

Those ahead of us shout warnings as what sounds like spears whistle past, hammering into the trunks of trees all around us. I freeze, my heart rocketing in my chest, waiting for the agonized screams of the injured.

"Back! Go back!" a man yells.

We all turn and run the way we came. People push and shove into Kadee and me, and in the confusion, I lose her and stumble. Another, larger hand grabs my arm, righting me.

"I've got you."

Peree. I gasp, relieved to hear his voice. He puts my hand back in Kadee's and positions himself behind us, probably to shield us, as we charge away with the rest. When we reach the clearing again, people begin to shout.

"Does anyone have a weapon?" Peree yells. "A bow? A knife? Anything?"

"No!" a man says. "Why would we be armed at a partnering ceremony?"

Why indeed? Few dangers lurk in Koolkuna. Because of the Myuna, the village's pure, underground water source that supplies its water hole, we aren't even exposed to the poison that creates the monstrous illusion of the Scourge.

"The armory!" A group of people sprint noisily from the clearing, heading toward the village to collect weapons.

"There were knives for the feast back at the Myuna. I'll get them." It's Bear, my old Groundling friend. His voice is grim.

Peree touches my hand. "I'm going for my bow." He tears away again.

Nerang's voice rings out. He sounds as upset as I've ever heard him. "Amarina, Derain, Konol, track the *guru*. Stay far enough behind to be safe."

Branches crack and leaves rip as bodies push into the trees, moving slower—more cautiously—this time.

"The rest of you remain here," Nerang says. "Do not approach these intruders again. Their spears were warnings only. If they had wanted to kill us, they could have."

"I am not standing around while my daughter is taken from under my nose by *lorinyas*!" a man shouts.

The forest swallows the sound of his running footsteps a moment later. *Lorinyas*. Strangers. That's what *we* were to the *anuna* until recently.

"We cannot wait, Nerang," a woman says. "We should go after the *guru*!"

"Of course we will. But we must have weapons to defend ourselves. You cannot help your *guru* if you are dead. Now, which of the children are missing besides Kora and Darel?"

Arika whimpers at the sound of her children's names. My heart contracts with fear for Kora, my first companion in Koolkuna. I can feel her small hand as she led me around the village, gossiping about her people through the observations of her doll, Bega. Darel, her younger brother, is only four years old. They *can't* be gone.

"My brother, Thrush." Moon, the partner of Peree's cousin, Petrel, sounds destroyed. Her newborn, Yani, howls. The baby's name means *hope* in the *anuna's* language. Hope feels far away now.

Exuberant and pesky Thrush reminded me so much of my own brother, Eland, when he was younger. Pain rips through me as I think of them, our brothers who only met once. One is dead. One is now missing.

The parents and guardians of the children say the names of their beloved. Seven in all were taken, five girls and two boys.

"And Frost." I recognize Conda's voice, one of the younger brothers of my Groundling tormentor—and protector—Moray. "But I don't understand why they took her and not Arika."

"Frost is still young enough to be trained in the Sisters' ways," Kai says, "and she's pregnant. Her baby is even more valuable to them. If she has a girl, they can raise her as their own."

"*My* baby?" Moray says. "I don't think so."

I wish I could say he was worried for Frost, too, the Lofty girl of about fifteen or sixteen who somehow got mixed up with him back home, but he's only ever been concerned about their child. *His* baby. While Moray's not my favorite, he doesn't deserve this. No one does.

I hear Bear passing blades around. Others clatter into the clearing soon after, hopefully with more weapons. Peree and Petrel's voices are among them.

"We're going after them," Peree says, touching my arm.

"I am, too," Moray says.

Which means his brothers, Cuda and Conda, will follow. They seem to follow him everywhere. Right now, I'm glad. The group jogs off in the direction the Sisters took the children, and I send a silent prayer of protection after them.

Kadee and I stand with the rest of the villagers. Some cry softly, others wail. Still others argue, their voices crashing together like the waterfall meeting the Myuna. I find Moon and put my arms around her and Yani as they both sob. What else can I do? I'm desperate to look for Kora and the missing children, but I can't move as fast as Peree and the others. I'd only hold them back. I don't know the first tree or bush in this forest.

Kora, where are you?

"These Fire Sisters," someone asks, "where do they come from?"

"Their home is called the Cloister." Kai's voice is hard, her words clipped.

"Where is it?" I ask.

"Many days' walk through dangerous territory." Her voice grows even colder and sharper when she speaks to me. "Along the River Restless."

River? A stream runs out of Koolkuna from the Myuna, but I had no idea there was a river somewhere.

"We must find them before they get that far!" someone says.

"You won't catch the Sisters if they don't want to be caught." Kai's voice dips. Is she upset about the children, or are her memories painful? Both? It's hard to tell with her. "And you'll have no chance of getting them back if they reach the Cloister. Flames that never die protect the Sisters' compound. High walls are guarded day and night. No one gets in or out unless they allow it." She pauses. "They... they aren't like the *anuna*. You can't reason with them or talk them around. They'll kill you if you try to take the *guru* back."

I bite my lip, drawing blood, as people cry out.

"What of the boys?" Moon's voice quavers. "You said they gather girls and have no men. What do they do with the boys they take?"

I hold her closer and rest a hand on Yani's plump, velvety thigh, reassuring myself she's safe. My pulse slows a bit in response.

"I don't know. I didn't see any boys in the Cloister," Kai says. "Only girls and women."

If Eland had survived, if he'd come to Koolkuna with us, he might have been taken with Thrush. I would have lost him anyway. Our world is so precarious. Why do I try to pretend otherwise? I sway on the edge of the dark well of guilt and grief I've often fallen into since my brother's death.

People begin to shout at Nerang and at each other. My eyes fill with tears. Although we've only been in Koolkuna a short time, I've come to care deeply for the community—the people who live here and the place Peree and I hoped to call home.

"What can we do, Nerang?" The woman's voice thrums with sorrow.

"Calm yourselves. Perhaps the others are already bringing the *guru* back to us. In the meantime, look around. We might find something of importance."

Nerang's probably buying time, giving us something to do, but standing here talking about the awfulness of the Sisters isn't helping anyone. With a gentle squeeze, I let go of Moon. I may not be able to *look* for clues, but that doesn't mean I can't find any.

Dropping to one knee, I feel the ground, trampled under our feet. All I feel are the crushed remains of grass and flowers, their petals still soft but already wilting. If there's anything else down here, it's been smashed flat. I listen to the agitated voices of the *anuna* as they search... the breeze rattling leaves in the branches of trees around us... the song of one intrepid bird not driven off by the commotion. Breathing slow and deep, I sift the air as I might a handful of grain.

And there *is* something else.

One scent stands out. It's like the smoke from a fire, only more abrasive, as if it were created by something other than burning wood. I realize it's been needling my nose and throat; I just wasn't paying attention.

"I smell something—" I start to say, but someone interrupts.

"Is this one of their feathers?" a man asks. The group goes silent.

"Yes," Kai says.

"Arika." Kadee speaks from a few paces away, regret in her voice. "I found Bega."

Kora and Darel's mother breaks down again. Kora would never willingly leave Bega behind. How much more can the poor woman take?

I reach out for the doll. Soft wood shavings escape into my palm from her lumpy body. I hold her to my nose. She smells dirty and mildewed, but under that, I detect the familiar scents of my young friend. Tears leak from my eyes.

When I hugged her, Kora's thick, curly hair hinted of the spices of Arika's cooking pot, the grassy meadows where she played with the other children, the water hole where she swam, the smoky *allawah* where she learned the stories of her people from Wirrim and Kadee, and her own cozy bed. All the sunny settings of her young life.

I bring Bega to Arika and hold her as she shakes with sobs. Rage courses through me. How can these women *do* this to us? Are they completely heartless?

"Nothing like this ever happened before the *lorinyas* came, Nerang," the man who found the feather says. His voice sounds menacing. "*They* brought this ill luck to us."

"We should never have taken them in," a woman says.

I stiffen, and a shiver runs down my back. They mean *us*: Peree, me, the other Lofties and Groundlings.

"We didn't cause this." My voice stays even.

"How do we know that?" the man says. "Myall wears the same kind of feather."

I clutch my hands together to keep them from shaking. "We found it in the woods back home. We didn't know where it came from."

"Maybe the Fire Sisters were there, watching you. Maybe they followed you here." The woman's words pulse with accusation.

"Through the caves?" Kadee asks. "The Sisters couldn't have followed them that way without being seen."

"Well, we had no trouble before the *lorinyas* arrived," another man says. "It's their fault!"

"Enough," Nerang says. "We will not treat our new friends like criminals; it will not help bring the *guru* back."

The shouts die down to grumbling, but the damage is done. I already feel sick about the children. Now I wonder if it could be our fault. My best friend Calli found that feather in the woods around our home; she gave it to me to give to Peree. *Did* the Sisters somehow follow us? Did we bring this terrible fate on Koolkuna?

People begin to pace as we wait, their feet swishing the grass, back and forth, back and forth. I sit with Arika, Moon, and Yani, gnawing my thumbnail, wracked with worry for Kora, Darel, Thrush, Frost, and the rest of the children. Wracked with guilt that we might be responsible. Wracked with a desire to *do something*.

"Kadee," I murmur. "Didn't the *anuna* already know about the Fire Sisters if they took Kai when she was young?"

"This is the first I've heard of them," she says. "Kaiya wouldn't speak of what happened to her. We knew she disappeared from the Myuna, and her father never came back from trying to find her. She was with the *runa* when she was discovered, and Nerang nursed her back to health. That's all we know."

Kadee told me before that Kai was one of the few people to

survive living among the sick ones. What did it do to her? And what happened when she was with the Sisters?

I catch the sounds of people moving through the trees toward the clearing, and I jump to my feet. I allow myself a flash of hope, but from their slow steps and the silence of the *anuna* around me, I can tell they don't have the children. Desperate for some kind of comfort, I clasp the wooden bird that glides at my throat, the pendant Peree carved for me as a sign of his devotion.

It's a relief when he finally hugs me to him, smelling of salt and bitter sadness. He takes my hands in his, rubbing gently to warm them. I shouldn't be this cold. It's late in the summer, nearly fall, but the temperature is still mild in the afternoon. It's the shock. The clearing feels weighted down with it.

"We lost them." Derain's voice buckles with grief. "They left one woman behind to fend us off with her arrows, and then she slipped away in the shadows of the branches, moving like the wind. We searched, but we couldn't find them again."

"Then we have no time to lose," Nerang says. "A search party will leave as soon as possible. Who will go?"

There are a few declarations from the group. I hear Derain, and a woman's high voice, like birdsong, that I think belongs to Amarina. I worked with her in the gardens. She sounds as breakable as a thin stalk of the maidengrass that grew around our water hole at home, but Kadee told me she's a skilled tracker and woodswoman who can coax fire out of little more than a handful of damp kindling.

"My brothers and me are going for sure," Moray growls. I don't trust them much, but they're tough and cunning. We need whoever can help bring Frost and the children home.

"I'll go." My voice is strong, decided. I feel better for saying the words.

Peree squeezes my shoulders. "I will, too."

I'm afraid to enter an unfamiliar forest, chasing after a group of kidnapping warrior women. I'm no fighter.

But I want to go for Kora and her family. They were the first to befriend Peree and me when we washed up in Koolkuna, helpless as babies.

I want to go for Thrush, Moon, and Petrel. I know all too well how it feels to lose a brother.

I want to go for Frost. Pregnant and afraid, she risked her father, Osprey's, rage to free Eland and me when we were trapped in the Lofty trees.

I want to go for Nerang, who saved our lives, and for the *anuna,* who took us in, even if some might unfairly blame us for this tragedy now.

And... I want to go for Eland. I couldn't save him. I can still save these children.

Everyone has done so much for us. How can I sit here, enjoying the protection and comforts they secured for us, hoping someone else will help?

I can't.

I'll go, and I'll do whatever it takes to find Kora and the others and bring them home.

Read The Fire Sisters (Brilliant Darkness 3) now!

AFTERWORD

Thank you for reading *The Defiance*. Reviews and word of mouth recommendations are so important. If you enjoyed this book, would you please help me spread the word about the Brilliant Darkness series? You can help in two ways:

1) Leave a review.

2) Join my reader tribe. Receive two free ebooks and be the first to get new book alerts.

Thanks again,

Aimee (AG) Henley

ALSO BY A. G. HENLEY

Nicole Rossi Thrillers (Young Adult)

Double Black Diamond

The Brilliant Darkness Series (Young Adult Fantasy)

The Scourge

The Keeper: A Brilliant Darkness Novella

The Defiance

The Gatherer: A Brilliant Darkness Novella

The Fire Sisters

The Brilliant Darkness Boxed Set

The Love & Pets Series (Sweet Romantic Comedy)

Love, Pugs, and Other Problems: A Love & Pets Prequel Story

The Problem with Pugs

The Trouble with Tabbies

The Downside of Dachshunds

The Lessons of Labradors

The Predicament of Persians

The Conundrum of Collies

The Pandemonium of Pets: A Love & Pets Christmas

The Love & Pets Series: Books 1 - 3

~

Novellas (Young Adult Fantasy)

Untimely

Featured in *Tick Tock: Seven Tales of Time*

Basil and Jade

Featured in *Off Beat: Nine Spins on Song*

The Escape Room

Featured in *Dead Night: Four Fits of Fear*

ACKNOWLEDGMENTS

Thank you to ...

Ryan for twenty years of love and partnership. You make writing about strong, supportive men effortless.

Mom, Dad, and Ginger for always being there for me.

Hilary, Jenny, and Kim for your steady friendship and enthusiasm. You guys keep me sane. And Hilary for gifting me the title.

Lindsey Alexander for her solid editorial work.

Caryn Wiseman, my agent, for watching out for my interests.

Steve Lamar without whom I'd have no online presence. Or at least not one I'm proud of.

Authors Sandhya Menon, Katie French, and Kristi Helvig for your friendship above all and for reading critically and helping me improve my work.

H.G. Wells, for his amazing story, "The Country of the Blind," which Peree tells to Fenn. The story Wirrim offers is adapted from a Cherokee legend. Coyote's story and that of the bird whose feather becomes a spear are my own.

And thank you to my readers for reading. Without you there would be little point.

ABOUT THE AUTHOR

A.G. Henley is a *USA Today* bestselling author of novels and stories in multiple genres including thrillers, romantic comedies, and fantasy romances. The first book in her young adult Brilliant Darkness series, *The Scourge*, was a Library Journal Self-e Selection and a Next Generation Indie Book Award finalist. She's also a clinical psychologist, but she promises not to analyze you . . . much.

Find her at:
aghenley.com
Email Aimee

Made in the USA
Monee, IL
21 August 2023

41396886R00139